FIGHT ME DADDY

Skyler Snow

Fight Me Daddy © Copyrighted Skyler Snow 2022

This is a work of fiction and is for mature audiences only. Names, characters, businesses, places, events, and incidents are either the products of the author's imagination or used in a fictitious manner. Any resemblance to actual persons, living or dead, or actual events is purely coincidental.

No part of this publication may be reproduced, stored in a retrieval system, or transmitted in any form or by any means, including electronically or mechanical, without the prior written permission of the copyright holder.

All products and brand names mentioned are registered trademarks of their respective holder and or company. I do not own the rights to these, nor do I claim to."

Cover Artist: Charli Childs

Formatter: Brea Alepou

Dedication

*For Brea Alepou for convincing me to be my dark, twisted self.
And to all of the readers who are loving it. Thank you!*

Warning and Triggers

Triggers: Fight Me Daddy includes scenes of violence, torture, implied trafficking, watersports, and dubcon.

Go to Skylersnow.com for more in-depth trigger warnings including which chapters can be skipped.

Prologue

Calix

My mother's picture was the only thing that brought me comfort.

I stared into the golden locket and took in the sight of her bouncy, brunette curls and her big, red-painted smile. She held me in her arms, beaming with pride at the camera. I was seven, laughing as my father kissed her cheek.

Happier times. Better memories.

I closed the locket and laid my head on the cool wood of the desk. In my left hand was the letter that my father had left behind. My fist closed, crinkling it up as I sucked in a shuddering breath and willed my burning eyes not to produce tears. I moved my head enough so that I could glance down at the letter through my blurry vision.

Calix,

I know you're probably pissed and I'm sorry. Believe me, I wanted to stick around but I owe the Bianchi's too much money. I won't tell you where I went cuz I don't want them knowin' you know. But with me gone they'll go after me and not you.

I couldn't keep putting you in danger.

I'm sorry.

Dad

I shot up and balled up the letter before I threw it into the trash. "How delusional are you? Are you really that goddamn naive!"

Did my father really think he was going to disappear and the Bianchi's wouldn't kill me? Or torture me to find out where he was? Even though I had no clue, that wasn't going to stop those assholes from tearing me apart to get to him.

I paced back and forth, wracking my brain for some way out of the mess my father had gotten me into. There had to be a way out. Walking over to the safe, I turned the dial and yanked it open. The semi-empty space held a few documents and a small amount of cash for bills. But there was nothing else there. No sudden stack of money to hand over to Gabriele Bianchi when he inevitably showed up with Niccolo and demanded this month's payment.

I reached into the safe and counted out the bills. Six hundred dollars, it wasn't nearly enough. I sat the money on the desk and closed the safe before I began pacing once more. The gym would be open soon, people would be coming in to train, take their classes or practice. And I still had to pay the people that worked with me; Sam and Tallia.

Maybe I should run too. I can get out of here. There's a little money left in the bank.

I thought about it for only a split second because the truth was that I only had about a grand in there as well. Running the gym, paying rent, my own bills, putting gas in my car; I didn't have enough money to do it all.

At this rate, I'll be broke before the week is out.

If I ran, I would have to survive off of pennies with nowhere to go. And I would ruin the progress I had made in the ring. MMA was the only thing I had left and the only thing that could cover my bills. Besides, the gym wasn't just my father's dream. It was my grandfather's and it had become my dream to own it one day as well. I couldn't abandon it.

My phone rang and I stopped staring out into space. I snatched it off of the desk, my heart racing as I stared at the number. *Right, Tallia.* I pressed the answer button and pushed it to my ear.

"Tal?"

"I'm outside," she said and I heard her knocking. "What's going on? Are we closed or something?"

I sighed. "No, we're not closed. Shit, here I come."

"Are you okay?" she asked.

I walked out of the office and Tallia waved on the other side of the glass. She looked concerned however and I knew she was going to have a thousand questions that I didn't want to answer. Hanging up, I walked to the door and unlocked it as Sam walked up as well.

"What's wrong?" Tallia asked as she stepped inside, her gym bag slung over her shoulder. "You look pale."

I wiped a hand over my face, my beard scratching against my palm. "It's a long story." I looked between the two of them and I was tempted to hide the truth, but they needed to know. This was their job and they had the right to know what was going on. "There's something I need to tell both of you."

"Spit it out," Sam said with a nod. "Come on, we can take it."

Could they? Neither of them had any idea what I was about to say.

Sam had a fiancee and a daughter at home. Losing out on this job would be devastating for him, and Tallia was moving into her girlfriend's house soon. She would need every dime to help renovate the place the way they wanted.

God, I don't want to tell them.

Tallia touched my hand. "We're here for you, Calix. Tell us."

I blew out a breath. "There's been some...issues as you're both aware." When they nodded, I kept going, trying to push down the ball of anxiety that had lodged itself in my throat. "My father took off."

Tallia gasped. "No! He wouldn't," she said, her face scrunching up in anger. "That no good-"

I waved a hand. "It's not his fault. He got in too deep with his debts and I think he's scared." I shrugged. "Either way, it's not like any of that makes a difference. He's gone and he's not coming back."

Why would he? He had to know that if he returned he was going to have a huge target on his back.

Sam slapped a hand onto my shoulder and squeezed. "I'm sorry, Calix."

"It's..."

The lie almost fell from my lips that it was fine, but it wasn't. I had never been so lost in my goddamn life. But I couldn't show that weakness, not now. Especially since Sam and Tallia were about to be affected by what I said next.

"There's one more thing," I started slowly.

I needed to tell them how little money was left. How we were teetering on the brink of nothing. But the concerned looks on their faces and the worry in their eyes made me swallow the words down. *I can't let them down. I'll fix this. They deserve that much.*

"I'm taking over ownership of the gym," I said finally, cursing myself in my head for not being able to tell them the truth. "Everything's going to be fine."

I saw movement out of the corner of my eye. When I glanced in that direction there Niccolo was. "Mr. Gonzalez. Where's your father?" Niccolo asked as he shoved into the gym and looked around. "Back office?"

"Shit," I swore under my breath, a shiver racing up my spine. before I looked at Tallia and Sam. "We'll talk about this later."

They both nodded, but Tallia leaned forward. "Be careful, Calix."

I snorted. "Don't think that's going to make much of a difference in this situation." My eyes flickered up as Gabriele stepped inside after Niccolo and my throat tightened. His gaze trained on me and I swallowed hard trying to go back to acting normal. "I need to go handle this," I said, tearing my eyes away from the man. "Be back."

My palms grew slick and I wiped them off on my shorts trying to calm down. You couldn't let men like this see you sweat. They were bullies and bullies always wanted to prey on the weakest one in the room. I wouldn't give them that satisfaction.

Chapter One

Calix

"Yo, Calix. You deaf or something?" Niccolo grinned, but there was a flicker of danger behind his eyes. "Where's Daddy?"

"We should talk in the office," I said as people started coming into the gym. "Tallia and Sam, just go about things as usual."

"You got it," Tallia said, glaring at Gabriele and Niccolo. "If you need anything, holler."

Niccolo chuckled. "Calm down, princess. I'm not going to bite your boyfriend."

I saw the way Tallia's fist tightened and shook my head. Sure, we might be able to get in a few good hits on the Bianchi men, but at the end of the day, they were mobsters. A few punches now would result in a couple of bullet holes in our bodies later. My father always said to be civil and calm with them.

And I had already broken that rule.

Gabriele Bianchi had run into me when I first met my friend Six's crazy asshole boyfriend. Only Six would be dragged into mafia nonsense, but then again, he was impulsive as hell. I shook my head. Ever since that day, Gabriele's been hanging around, staring at me, making me feel like I'm constantly under a magnifying glass and about to get burned like an ant on the sidewalk.

I walked into the back office and closed the door after them, my heart pounding in my chest. There was no way out of my situation. I knew that once I was alone, one of them could kill me if they didn't get the answers they wanted.

I don't want to die.

Niccolo leaned against the wall while Gabriele stood in front of the door, his hazel eyes staring me down. If I made one wrong move, I'd end up as a bloodstain on the office floor. I pulled out the chair to the desk and sat down before I looked up between the two of them.

"So?" Niccolo asked. "Where's Daddy?"

"Gone," I said. "He left me a letter and took off." I bent down and picked up the balled-up note before I held it out to him. "I only found out this morning."

Gabriele took it from my hand and read over it. He tossed it aside when he was done as if it was trash before he stepped closer to me.

"Do you really want us to believe you don't know where your father is? Try again."

I stared up at him. "I don't know. When I came in this morning I found that note and a little bit of cash in the safe. He ran off with the rest of it."

Niccolo chuckled. "Gabriele, I think he's trying to fuck us over. How much do you want to bet he's hiding his dear old dad somewhere?"

"Hundred bucks?" Gabriele asked, glancing at the other man.

Niccolo hummed. "See, I don't know if he'd be that stupid. He hasn't pissed his pants yet so maybe he really doesn't know anything."

"That's what you're going by to see if he's telling the truth or not? If he's pissed himself?"

Nic shrugged. "I'm telling you it always happens." He grinned before his eyes flickered over to me. "Spit it out, Gonzalez. The faster you give him up, the sooner we can go break his ankles instead of yours."

I swallowed thickly and forced down my temper. No matter what my father had done, even if I knew where he was, I would never tell these bastards. I wouldn't be the reason he got hurt. Or killed. I couldn't handle having that on my conscience.

"I don't know," I said evenly. "Like I said I came in this morning and that letter was on the desk. He left early in the morning, but I figured he was coming down to practice; he does that sometimes when he's stressed out, just to relive his fighting days. But he wasn't here. Just the note."

"You've said that," Gabriele said, closing the space between us. He shoved my chair back against the wall and moved between my knees. When he leaned down I felt the warmth of his breath and suppressed a shudder. "Now, try the fucking truth."

I narrowed my eyes at him. "That is the fucking truth," I spat. "It's not my fault you don't believe me. What? You think I want to be left here with no money and stuck in the middle of you and him? I don't. I want to go on living my life, make my money, and mind my business."

"The money needs to be paid back," Niccolo said from where he leaned up against the wall, the smile now gone from his face. "Or we can take the gym. Pick."

The gym. Gonzalez and sons had been in my family for three generations. My grandfather died making it what it was and when my uncle passed shortly after, it was all I and my father had. It was still small, but it was a living and I wanted to bring it back the way it had been in its heyday.

If I gave it to the Bianchi's, they'd just tear it down or use it for illegal bullshit. Besides, Sam, Tal, and even Six rely on this place. I can't give it up.

My fists tightened. All I could see was myself repeating the mistakes my father had made, keeping something that had dragged him to the depths of hell. But I couldn't give up on this place, not when I had people relying on me.

"I want to keep it," I said, the words tumbling out of my mouth as a shiver worked its way up my spine. "How much is the debt?"

Nic shrugged. "Take that up with Gabriele. I'm just the extra muscle around here." He grinned. "If you want to keep the place, he's the one in charge of this stuff," he said as he jerked his thumb toward Gabriele.

Shit. You've got to be kidding me.

I stared up at Gabriele and his hazel eyes bore into mine. Everything about the man screamed don't fuck with me, and I was going to be smart and do just that for the rest of my life. But now? My fate rested in the hands of this psychopath. I couldn't stand him and he would be the one banging on my door and collecting the cash.

Thanks a lot, Dad.

"How much does he owe?" I asked after swallowing the lump in my throat.

"Thee-hundred eighty-five thousand, four hundred and seven dollars," Gabriele said. "And fifty-seven cents. With forty percent interest."

I stared at him as my jaw dropped. What the shit? I knew my father was in debt, but that number was ridiculous. There was no way in hell I could do it.

"I can't pay that back!" I snapped. "The interest alone would wipe me out. Come on, there has to be something else."

Gabriele's hand shot out, and I blocked it on instinct alone, my hand wrapping around his wrist. He raised a brow before he glared. *Shit*. I quickly let him go and he gripped the front of my shirt and yanked me closer.

"Good choice," he growled when my face was mere inches from his. "But if you touch me like that again, I'll punish you."

I stared at him and couldn't even form a sentence. Even though he made me nervous as hell, his choice of words did weird things to my body. Heat swept through me and I grumbled at myself and blamed my three-year-long dry spell.

Not to mention the fact that Gabriele Bianchi was a bastard, but he wasn't ugly. His black hair was long enough to brush the collar of his shirt and his hazel eyes were dark and mesmerizing. His short, neat beard, sharp nose, and plump lips were attractive and if I didn't know what he did for a living I would assume he was any other white-collar worker with an office job.

But he was a demon.

"It was instinct," I said, forcing the tremble out of my voice. "When someone goes for me, my first reaction is to deflect."

"Then I suggest you get a better hold on your instincts," he snapped and yanked me closer. "Do you understand me?"

I nodded. "Yes. Understood."

Gabriele released my shirt and straightened up. "You can either pay the money back or we can resort to more extreme measures," he said, his eyes roaming up and down my body before his gaze met mine once more. "We're not in the habit of letting our money just walk away and disappear. Your friend Six should have taught you that already."

My lips pressed into a straight line. Six had bitten off more than he could chew and ended up being Amadeo's personal little plaything. They were a happy couple now, but he'd told me how they started.

I wasn't about to be some mafia asshole's chew toy.

"I'll get the money," I said tightly.

Gabriele grinned and my heart flip-flopped. "As a courtesy, I won't charge you a dime this time, but next month..." He trailed off, the threat hanging in the air without him even having to say it. "Or find your father and I can talk to him."

I gritted my teeth. *No way I'm doing that shit.* My father wasn't going to die because of me. Yes, he'd stuck me with his bullshit, but I couldn't let him get killed.

"I said I'd pay it."

"Watch your tone," Gabriele growled. "Or I'll take back my generous offer and we can take things in an entirely different direction," he said. "You should count yourself lucky I'm in a good mood."

Are you?

I wanted to ask the question, but I liked not having broken bones more. It seemed like none of the Bianchi men were ever in a good mood. Except for Nic, they were all growly words and threatening stares. It wasn't a surprise that everyone was scared of them.

But I wasn't going to let them run over me. I would pay back the money, somehow. And once it was over and done with, I would put all of the Bianchi's behind me. It didn't matter what disaster came my way, I wouldn't be stupid enough to take out a loan I couldn't afford like my father.

I watched Nic and Gabriele head for the door. Gabriele stopped, glanced back at me, and it felt like his eyes were looking right through me. In another lifetime, a man like him would have caught my attention. Would have made me daydream about him or settle for one hot, wild night before I returned to focusing on my ambitions.

But I would rather die than touch Gabriele Bianchi.

Chapter Two

Gabriele

My thoughts lingered on Calix. The way he looked at me, the fire in his eyes, made me want to grab him and choke some sense into him. He might say the right things, but his face was what betrayed him. The anger, the uncertainty, the tightness of his jaw as he tried to fight back. Every part of it was visible to me.

I leaned against the plush seat of my car as it slipped through traffic. While my driver took the helm, I opened up my tablet and started searching through it. Focusing on Calix Gonzalez was not my problem right now. I had a plethora of shit to take care of. Meetings, checking on businesses, tracking down the assholes who had tried to kill Amadeo and Six. It was a never-ending list. But my job was to be Amadeo's second in command, to make sure things were running smoothly behind the scenes.

My phone buzzed and I checked it. Amadeo. Of course.

Ama: You're late.

Gabriele: It's been a long night, but I'm five minutes away.

Ama: Hurry up.

I stared at my phone and rolled my eyes. Amadeo was a pain in my ass, but he was my brother. And he wasn't as cold as he seemed, not to his family. Or to the young boy toy he had stashed in his house now.

Lucky bastard.

Not that I wanted someone like Six around day and night. He was fun, but he was also stubborn, brash, and a little crazy. But who didn't want someone by their side who would stick with them through the good and the fucked up?

"We're here, Mr. Bianchi."

I glanced up and noticed we'd stopped in front of the casino. *How long had I been in my own thoughts?* I gathered my things and slipped out of the car.

"I'll be back shortly. Stay right in front."

"Yes, sir."

I turned on my heels and stepped through the large, golden framed doors. Music filled the place along with the smell of smoke both cigars and cigarettes. I strolled through feeling eyes on me. It wasn't so odd. Whenever people saw a Bianchi, they tended to stare, but as soon as I made sure they were not a threat, I kept going until I reached Darla's desk.

"Good afternoon, Mr. Bianchi," she said with a bright smile. "Everyone's already inside so you can go right in." She pushed forward a paper coffee cup. "I put this aside for you. I figured you would be thirsty. And if you're hungry I have an extra muffin."

I smiled at Darla. She reminded me so much of my mother, always fussing and worrying over us. But like every Italian woman I knew, she was just as strict and straight-forward. I admired that.

"I'll take a muffin," I said with a nod. "What you got?"

"Blueberry," she said, sliding open her desk drawer before she placed a wrapped muffin in front of me. "You never eat lunch so I figured I would grab one for you just in case."

"You're a lifesaver, Darla," I sighed as I picked up the treat and coffee, balancing my tablet and phone. "Thank you."

"Have a good meeting, Mr. Bianchi."

"Just Gabriele," I reminded her for the hundredth time.

Darla smiled at me, but she didn't correct herself. She stood up and opened the door to the office, letting me in before she closed the door after me. The office itself was empty, so I walked through to the conference room and there were my brothers and cousins.

"Yo!" Niccolo called, a grin on his lips. "Where the fuck have you been?"

"I've been working," I said as I sat my things down and shrugged off my jacket. The weather was quickly changing in Atlanta making the coldness disappear into muggy heat in the afternoon. "Something you don't do."

Nic laughed. "I do a lot and you know it," he said as he leaned forward and tapped his cigarette against a crystal ashtray. "Don't be cranky."

"Shut up." I plopped down in my seat and tore open the muffin wrapper. "And you can stop glaring at me, Ama. I'm here."

My older brother had laced his fingers and his chin sat perched on top of them. His eyes narrowed even more at me and I groaned under my breath.

"What's going on is serious, Gabriele."

"I know," I shot back at him. "Who do you think has been chasing down leads and taking every spare moment to get things in order? I'm doing my best."

Ama's eyes focused on mine and I ground my teeth together. Ever since Six had been kidnapped, he was more on edge than ever. I understood it, but I also wasn't a miracle worker. I couldn't try to find out who was against him, work the jobs I needed to work, and get to meetings on time when I was barely sleeping anymore. I snatched up the cup of coffee and took a sip, surprised that it was still so hot.

Darla to the rescue.

"Anyone find anything about the tattoos?" Amadeo asked, his eyes flicking between each of us. "We need to find something out sooner rather than later. Whoever is behind this shit isn't playing. I'm still having problems with warehouses and businesses being robbed, fires starting, and now people are going missing. We can't have this shit."

"I know," I said with a nod. "I've been tracking down every lead and as far as I can find no one knows that tattoo. That's all we have to go on right now and I'm hitting dead ends. Anyone else got anything?"

"Nope," Riccardo offered, as silent as ever.

"I haven't found anything as well," Dario said with a shake of his head. "I've been trying to help you out, Gabe, and put out feelers, but nothing so far."

We all looked at Nic. "I have shit," he said with a shrug before he saw the glare Amadeo leveled at him. "Chill. It's not like I'm not trying, but I'm guns, remember? No one I work with has an issue with us or they wouldn't have any guns."

Amadeo pinched the bridge of his nose. "This is a matter of life and death. Six is with me now. I can't take these things lightly. We either figure out what's going on or we end up like those assholes that tried to take us out. Which would you prefer?"

Anger rolled off of Amadeo in waves. If there was even a hint of inattentiveness or anyone being laid back before, it was gone now. Each of us understood what it was to be in danger and to get our shit together so we could smooth things out.

"We're on it," I said, trying to calm him down instead of riling him up. "Just give me a little more time and I'll shake something loose."

He grunted. "Yeah. Hurry up." Amadeo leaned back in his seat and waved a hand. "What's going on with the accounts? We have to keep a closer eye on everything now. I want exact figures."

Dario pulled out his tablet. "I have our accounts, but I'm sure Gabriele, Nic, and Riccardo have their own as well. Let's get started."

My cousin was all business as he rattled off numbers to Amado. I did my best to follow, fighting the exhaustion that kept trying to grip me as I wrote things down on my tablet. *Damn, I'm tired.* My body craved a hot shower and a good, long nap. This shit was killing me.

As I listened, my thoughts drifted back to Calix and his gym. His father had really taken off and left everything in his lap. I've seen it before, but it still took me by surprise. He seemed as if he was there to make things right and keep his son safe, and yet he had left him with his massive debt.

What was he thinking?

I drummed up the image of Calix's face when he saw me and Nic. There was fear there, but something else as well. Anger, determination, resolve? I wanted to find out exactly what it was and then I wanted to make Calix break and bend for me. He was a game, a challenge. And I was stuck on him.

"Gabriele," Amadeo called. "Your turn."

I cleared my throat and tried to drag my thoughts back to what we were doing. Amadeo's expectant eyes lingered on me along with everyone else's. I put any and all feelings aside and focused on getting words out of my mouth instead of clamming up and saying fuck off and let me go back to sleep.

As I rattled off the number of debts that had been collected on and those left delinquent, Amadeo and Dario nodded the most, marking down the figures, Dario on his tablet and Amadeo on a sheet of paper.

"The last thing I have is Gonzalez and Sons gym. I doubt Calix can come up with the money, so we need to take over it. He seems like he'll sign without problem and we can have it by-"

"No," Amadeo said, shaking his head. "That's the gym Six uses to train and he likes Calix. I won't take over or get rid of it."

I blinked at Amadeo. "Are you fucking joking?"

"Do I look like I'm joking?" he asked, raising a brow. "Six loves it there and I'm not going to take it away from him. We both know it's not easy to please him." Amadeo shrugged. "Find another solution."

"Like what?" I scoffed, heat sweeping over my body as I gripped my tablet so hard I thought it would break. "This is the way we always do things."

"Not this time," Ama shot back before he began to smirk. "Like I said, figure something out."

I stared at my brother like he had lost his mind. *Figure something out?* How was I supposed to do that when we had been following the same protocols for decades? My jaw ticked and I narrowed my eyes at him.

"Amadeo, this is the way we work. We're going to-"

"No," he said with a shake of his head. "My boy likes what he likes and I won't take it away from him."

I groaned so hard my throat hurt. His boy. When I first heard the two of them talking that way, calling each other Daddy and boy, I didn't know what to make of it. After looking into it, I understood their dynamic more.

But that didn't mean I wanted their shit interfering with my business.

"So what the hell am I supposed to do?" I snapped at Amadeo, irritation crawling up my back. "If I let one person get away with not paying their debts, then no one will pay."

The smirk on Amadeo's face never wavered. I shifted in my seat. *Nothing good ever comes out of that goddamn stare.*

"Weren't you the one that showed Six where my expensive ties were?" he asked. "I'm still restocking my collection after he cut them."

My mouth gaped. Shit, I had definitely helped him with that. "Ama," I growled. "Seriously?"

Laughter erupted around the table and I glared at my family. *Assholes.*

"Shut up," I grumbled. "Are you all children?"

Nic snickered. "You're just mad because we're laughing at you for once," he said as he pushed his chair back.

I flipped him off before Amadeo cleared his throat.

"That's what I thought," he said as he winked at me. "Figure it out. Calix needs to pay us our money, but you can't take the gym. Find a balance. And let's figure out who these assholes are that want us dead." Amadeo stood up and looked at each of us. "Dismissed."

"Ama," I started.

"Dismissed," he said more pointedly. "I have things to do today. You do your job and I'll go do mine."

I'm going to kill them. Each and every last one of those bastards.

I gathered my stuff and stormed out of there. My brothers and cousins were happy to watch me drown, but I still had a problem to solve. Calix Gonzalez.

Wonder where he is right now?

As I slipped into my car I tried to let the irritation roll off of my back. I should be used to my family screwing with each other. But this time I had to find a way around collecting what we were owed without upsetting Ama's precious boyfriend.

Wonderful. At least I get to see Calix again.

I paused at my own thoughts and frowned. *Why the hell would I want to see Calix?* He had been on my mind constantly since the night we met ringside and I still couldn't figure out why. At most, he was a distraction.

And I needed to get rid of him.

Chapter Three

Calix

"Oh, Calix you don't have to do that."

I smiled at Sofia Lopez and carried her groceries up the steps. She was easily in her seventies and walked with a cane, but she always insisted she didn't need my help. Even when I could see the relief on her face when she didn't have to go up and down the stairs with heavy bags.

"It's no problem. I told you before, it's more exercise for me. And I need it."

Sofia rolled her eyes. "You're a charmer just like your father, you know that, son?" Chuckling, she held the door open for me and I stepped past her. "You can set them on the counter."

"Yes, before I put them away," I said as I went back to her kitchen and put the loaded bags down. "And then I'll get out of your hair."

"Stubborn like your father too."

I smiled, but it was forced. The last thing I wanted to hear about was my father. He'd put me in such a screwed-up predicament and I still didn't have the money for the Bianchi family. Soon, they would be coming for me and I had no idea what was going to happen.

Probably something involving a pair of pliers and a baseball bat.

My imagination replayed every last mafia movie I'd ever seen as a kid while I trudged back and forth for groceries. Back then, I used to think mobsters were so cool. Now I knew better. They were vicious monsters without morals or ethics.

"Would you like a glass of water, dear?" Sofia called.

"No, I'm okay," I said, shaking my head as I loaded up her pantry with dry goods. "Besides, I'm almost done." I closed the pantry and moved to the fridge. "You can always call me when you're on your way home. I'm usually here when you come back from the store."

She waved a hand. "I know, I know. But I don't like to bother you," she sighed.

I shook my head. "You're not bothering me at all." After I finished up I stood and closed the fridge door. "Is that everything?"

"It should be," she said with a nod before a frown overtook her pink-painted lips. "Calix, here," she said, pulling down a jar and reaching inside. Her hand came back full of bills. "I know your father was going through some things and money was tight. Please, take this. It'll be payback for all the times you've looked out for me."

Holding up my hands, I shook my head at her. *No way. I can't take money from anyone let alone Mrs. Lopez.* She was a widower who was living off of a pension. I wasn't going to take money out of her pockets for my own troubles no matter how badly I needed it.

"Thank you, but no thanks. I'm alright." When she looked at me wearily, I smiled, trying to reassure her. "Really, I mean it. I appreciate it, but things are under control." After she sighed and stuffed the cash away, she walked me outside. "But if you need anything else let me know."

"Now, why can you help me but I can't help you. Hmm?"

I chuckled. "You help me when you make that killer pork pozole and bring me a giant Tupperware of it," I said, rubbing my stomach as my mouth salivated just thinking about it. "With those homemade tortillas," I added wistfully.

Mrs. Lopez laughed. "Fine, fine I'll whip up a batch for you tomorrow night. How does that sound?"

"Like heaven," I said honestly. "Thank you."

She waved a hand. "It's no problem. Tell your dad I'll make some dessert too."

I smiled, but I didn't have the heart to tell her I had no idea where he was. Or if he was even alive. Instead, I swallowed thickly and nodded.

"Sounds like a plan."

A car horn blared and I jumped. Stepping out of his car in a dark suit and deep blue tie was Gabriele Bianchi. He smoothed his hand down the front of his clothes and strolled around the car, not even looking out for traffic, as if it would all just stop. For him.

Shit. Shit. Shit.

I'd always known that they were aware of where we lived. But knowing that and seeing a Bianchi in my space were two very different things. As he swaggered up to the sidewalk, Sofia scoffed beside me.

"Never liked gangsters," she muttered, crossing herself quickly. "You can see them coming a mile away. I wonder where he's going."

"Gonzalez. We need to have a chat," Gabriele said, stopping on the sidewalk in front of Mrs. Lopez's porch. "Let's go."

"He's here for me," I muttered as I glanced over at her.

Sofia stared him down, a frown tugging on her lips. "Are you going to be okay hijo?"

I nodded and laid a hand on her shoulder, giving it a soft squeeze. No one else needed to get mixed up in the insanity that was my life.

"Why don't you go back inside and get some rest," I suggested to her. "I know you've been on your feet all day and that's not good for your circulation. Why don't I check on you tomorrow?" I smiled. "And I can pick up that pozole. I can't wait."

She chuckled and smiled up at me, her warm brown eyes reminding me of my mother's. "I'm happy to do it for you, Calix. Goodnight."

"Goodnight," I said with a nod before I turned and faced Gabriele and was met with his impatient face. "Let's go inside my place."

His eyes lingered on Sofia's and I cleared my throat. She walked inside and I led Gabriele next door to my home. As I trudged up the stairs, I felt his eyes boring into me, but I refused to turn around and look at him.

A shiver licked up my spine as I opened the door and stepped inside. Gabriele slid in, his eyes on me the whole time as if I was going to attack him. Maybe he thought I would. In his line of work, I doubted he could afford to be lax about watching his back. Once I closed the door and threw the lock, I turned to face him.

"Cup of coffee?" I asked on instinct.

"Sure, why not."

I nodded and moved around him. The floorboards creaked as we walked over them and I couldn't stop picturing him shoving a gun up against my spine and firing. My heart raced with every step, but I refused to just lie down and let the Bianchi's kill me. Even if I was going to die, I would fight every step of the way.

"You can sit down if you want," I said, waving a hand at the small table in the kitchen.

"I'll stand," he said, reaching into his pocket and pulling out a pack of cigarettes. "Do you care if I smoke?"

"Nope." I grabbed the ashtray my father always used and sat it on the table before I turned to the coffee maker and got it going. "Are you going to tell me why you're here?"

"You're always straightforward. That's what I like about you, Calix. It takes a lot of balls to talk to me the way you do."

"Not really," I said. "I don't trip all over myself for anyone. You included. That's all." I grabbed two mugs and set them on the counter. "How do you like your coffee?"

"Just cream." He walked toward me and leaned against the sink. "So, do you have the money?"

I swallowed past a huge lump in my throat. "Um, no," I said, not trying to beat around the bush. "Not all of it."

Not even half of it.

"That's too bad," he said with a sigh. "I guess that means we need to move on to other options."

My body tensed. *Other options? I didn't like the way that sounded.*

"Okay," I said as I poured the coffee and added cream to Gabriele's. I opened the cabinet above the stove and took out the bourbon my father kept stashed there. I had a feeling I was going to need it. "What are these other options?" I asked as I picked up my mug and took a long, deep sip, ignoring the way the hot liquid burned my tongue.

Gabriele's eyes ran up and down my body. For the second time in his presence today, I shivered. His gaze was a dark and dangerous thing. It felt as if he was opening up and examining every part of me. Every alarm bell in my head screamed 'run' but I was stuck to the spot, staring, and waiting for his next words with a knot in my chest.

"I've worked out a way for you to keep your gym." He sipped at the coffee and hummed lightly. "Good coffee."

I frowned. "What did you work out?"

"Right, that," he said as he sat the mug down and watched me closely. "I could use an assistant. Nic has other things to do and I need some muscle, someone that can handle a fight. That's where you come in."

Nope, no, no. I didn't like the way that sounded at all.

"What?"

"You know," Gabriele said, waving a hand. "You'll be my personal errand boy until your debt is paid off. Help with debts owed, make my coffee, hell shine my shoes if I tell you to." He grinned and it unnerved me. "So, what do you say?"

I stared at him as if he had two heads. Being his errand boy? There was no way it wouldn't involve some illegal and shady shit. Not to mention the way he said it. I squeezed my fists tightly trying not to let my temper get the best of me. *He wants me to be his dog. That's what he's saying.*

Fuck. I didn't want to tell him no, but working for Gabriele was a one-way ticket to ending up in a jail cell or dead. No one in the history of ever had joined in with the mafia and walked away with a peaceful life. And I didn't want or need that stress. MMA was working out for me, I had a real chance at a good future. A nice big house, continuous food, fame, everything someone like me who came from nothing could ever want.

"Tick-tock," Gabriele said as he took a step toward me. "Yes or no?"

"I can't kill anyone," I said, shaking my head. "That's never something I'm going to do."

Gabriele raised a brow at me. "Are you telling me what you will and won't do? Do you remember you're the one that owes the money and I'm the one in charge?"

My eyes narrowed. "I don't care. I'm not going to steal someone else's life for my own. So, if you're going to kill me then do it. But that's a line I'm not going to cross."

Gabriele looked me up and down before he let out a short laugh. "You have a ton of balls," he said as he stepped closer to me, once again invading my space. "I like that. But not directed toward me. I need an answer, Calix. And this thing is my rules, my way."

I gritted my teeth. "I won't kill."

Gabriele grabbed me by the front of my shirt and yanked me forward sharply. I reached up, my hand wrapping around his wrist as I dug my nails into his skin. He didn't even flinch as I glared at him.

"I said what I had to say," I ground out. "You can make me do anything else, but if you expect me to kill an innocent person, then you might as well kill me now," I said as my heart raced. "Because I won't do it. That's the only thing I'm asking."

Gabriele scoffed. "You're so naive. There's no such thing as innocence." When I didn't waver, he released me. "Fine. Be ready by tomorrow." He looked me up and down. "Dress better than that. I have a reputation to uphold."

I glanced down at my gray sweats and a black t-shirt. *What's wrong with the way I'm dressed?* By the time I looked up again, Gabriele was drinking down the rest of his coffee. He nodded toward me and sat the mug in the sink.

"Eight tomorrow night. Don't keep me waiting," he said as he turned on his heels. "I'll let myself out."

I stared after him until he disappeared. Shortly after, the door closed and I was finally able to draw in a proper breath.

"*Jesucristo,*" I muttered. "Fuck!"

There was no escaping the psychopath that was Gabriele Bianchi. No matter what, tomorrow night I was going to be his little bitch.

And there was nowhere to run.

Chapter Four

Gabriele

WHAT THE HELL HAD I BEEN THINKING TELLING CALIX HE COULD work under me? The thought had popped into my head in an instant and spewed from my lips. I groaned long and low as my hands tightened around the wheel.

I'm a dumbass.

As I drove to Calix's house, all I could think about was that I would be crammed into my car with him for the rest of the night. *Goddamn Ama.* It was his fault that I'd put forth the proposition in the first place. But I hadn't come up with anything on the entire drive over and that was the first thing that popped into my head.

"Goddamn, this is a pain in my ass."

I should be doing something more important like looking for the assholes who tried to put Amadeo in a grave. But since we had no new leads, I was stuck babysitting. The only people I didn't mind working with were my family members and even then I still preferred to strike it out on my own. There were no distractions, no unnecessary bullshit. And then once work was done, I could find somewhere to relax and enjoy what little free time I had.

Why couldn't I have come up with another solution? There had to be a million other ways to handle this, but it was done now and Amadeo knew about it. And he liked it.

Of course, he does. That bastard.

My phone rang and I snatched it up. "What?"

"Someone's irritated," Six said with a chuckle. "Are you with Calix?"

"No," I grumbled, not in the mood to talk to Six when it was his fault I was stuck in this predicament in the first place. "Why?"

"I just wanted to tell you to be nice to my friend. He's all tough on the outside, but Calix is a good guy. Don't break him."

I scoffed. "We're working together. What do you think I'm gonna do to him?"

"Well your brother likes breaking fingers," he muttered.

"How many times do I have to tell you to stop telling people that?" Amadeo growled. "And give me my phone. You're still grounded."

Six groaned. "You need to get laid," he muttered before he sighed. "Just be nice, Gabriele. Okay?"

"As long as he doesn't give me any shit."

He let out a laugh. "Calix? He's going to give you shit for days. I don't know why you think I would associate with anyone who doesn't have a solid backbone. They'd never be able to handle me."

"Six!"

"Fine!" Six snapped at Amadeo before he grumbled under his breath. "I gotta go, but I mean it. If you mess him up, I'm going to be pissed. And another thing you-"

Six's words were cut off as commotion filled their place. The call ended and I shook my head. *Well, he's dead.* Amadeo was going to have his ass for yelling at him.

They're both chaotic.

Amadeo had loosened up a hell of a lot around Six. It was a good thing. Before he was so rigid I was sure he would end up snapping, but now he laughed. He talked to us. He doled out assignments and didn't try to juggle it all himself. I could tell it was still difficult for him, but he was trying. All because of Six.

My heart squeezed and I rubbed at my chest. *Was that jealousy? There's no way I'm envious of them.* I didn't mind being alone, having men and women hanging off of me wherever I went. But...

It's not the same as actually having someone you give a damn about.

I shook my head and cleared those thoughts away. There was no time to be daydreaming about things that weren't in the cards right now. Instead, I pulled up to the curb and climbed out.

Oh well. At least I know Calix can hold his own when it comes to a fight.

If I was honest with myself, he would make great muscle. And he wouldn't kill anyone so I wouldn't have to cover tracks and spend my night getting things cleaned up like when I worked with my psycho cousin Nic. Maybe this wouldn't be such a bad thing.

My eyes swept the area looking for Calix. Instead, I found his neighbor from the day before sitting on her porch. She looked at me with those same judgemental eyes from the day before and had the nerve to glare.

I raised a brow. "Is there a problem?"

"What do you want with Calix? He's a good boy and you shouldn't be trying to hurt him. How much does his old man owe, huh?" When I stared at her she laughed dryly. "Yeah, I know what you are. Everything about you screams gangster from a mile away." She shook her head. "Why don't you leave him alone?"

I scoffed. "Why don't I make you disappear and then I won't have to look at that sour expression on your face again? That sounds like a much better plan to me."

"Hey!" Calix stormed out of her house, the door banging against its frame. "Sorry, Mrs. Lopez. I'll finish taking a crack at that leaky faucet tomorrow."

Calix jogged down the stairs, his shirt in his hand and his black sweats hanging off of his hips. Sweat rolled down his brown skin and my eyes tracked the movement, my annoyance temporarily forgotten. His long hair was sticking to his skin and it took every ounce of self-control in me not to push it off of his shoulder and take a nice, long lick.

What the fuck is wrong with me?

My thoughts were broken when Calix's hand wrapped around my arm and squeezed. "Come on," he ground out. "My house."

I stared at the man in surprise as he dragged me to his house and up the stairs. Did he know who he was touching like that? Once the door was open, he led me inside and I finally shook him off easily.

"You don't have to be mean to Mrs. Lopez. Why would you threaten a sweet old lady?"

"She was being a pain in my ass. A lot like you," I said as I narrowed my eyes at him. "What have I told you about grabbing me? Do you want to lose one of those precious hands?"

Calix frowned. "I'm just saying you don't have to be a dick to her. She doesn't like you for good reason and we both know it."

I took a step toward Calix and he took one back making me grin. *He's scared of me.* I could see it, a flicker in his eyes, but apparently, that wasn't enough to make him behave. Or to shut his mouth.

"Move your ass and get ready to go. Didn't I tell you to be ready when I came to retrieve you today?"

"Mrs. Lopez had an emergency and I wanted to help her," he said steadily. "If you can wait twenty minutes, I'll be ready."

I looked him up and down. "Nope, I can't wait. Let's go."

I grabbed his arm and Calix's eyes widened. Turning on my heels, I dragged him through the house opening doors until I found the bathroom. I turned on the shower and shoved him toward it.

"Get undressed or I'll help you with that. And you won't like the way I do it."

Calix turned to me and glared. "Get out."

"What? You don't want me to see you naked?" I asked.

"No, I don't," he said evenly. "So get out or I'm not going to do shit."

I stared at him and felt my jaw tighten. *Damn, he makes me want to strangle him.* That smart mouth of his was going to get Calix in trouble and it would be no one's fault but his own. I took another step toward him and my hand shot out, wrapping around his throat and squeezing.

"You seem to be under the impression that you have any say when I'm around you. Let me make it clear, you don't. I know I can seem like a light-hearted guy sometimes, laughing with Six and Ama or joking with Nic. But if you keep pushing me, Calix, I will make you know pain in ways you could never even dream of." My hand tightened and he whimpered. That sound shot straight to my cock. "So lose the fucking attitude before I make you lose it. Do you understand?"

He nodded hard, his pulse racing against my palm. My cock stiffened even more and I was half tempted to keep choking him, to pick him up and fuck him on the counter of his dingy little bathroom until he came for me over and over again.

What is wrong with me? Back off, Gabriele.

I released his throat and Calix coughed hard before he yanked away from me sharply, his back colliding with the shower door. He stared at me with wide eyes, but there was still a flicker of defiance in his gaze that I wanted to devour.

"Five minutes. And like I said before, dress better."

Calix didn't respond. Instead, he nodded his head and started stripping off his sweats. My throat tightened as I took in the sight of his muscled back. I forced myself to walk out of the bathroom or I really would jump him and that wasn't at all what I was supposed to be doing.

I closed the door behind me and leaned against it. Reaching up, I rubbed my eyelids and blew out a long, slow breath. Ever since the night I laid eyes on Calix, I had been drawn to him, curious. But it was getting so much worse now.

I pushed off of the door and let myself out to the front porch. Digging into my pocket, I pulled out a cigarette and popped it into my mouth before lighting it. Smoke curled into the air as I stared at the quickly darkening sky.

"Come on, Gabriele. Hold it together."

I was losing my mind. Every single thought was becoming consumed with images of Calix. No matter how much I tried to block him out, there he was again.

A few minutes later, the door closed behind me and I turned. Calix locked the door before he turned and looked at me. His long, dark hair had been pulled up into a bun and instead of his usual sweats and t-shirt that I was getting all too used to seeing, he was wearing a pair of dark slacks with a silver buckle and a black button-up. I could see myself ripping the shirt off of him and watching the buttons fly and the shock that would decorate his face from me doing it.

"What?" he asked, a sharp edge to his voice. "You told me to dress better. Is this not okay?"

"It's good enough," I said, shaking myself out of my trance. "And lose the attitude. We have a long night ahead of us. If you're going to be an asshole the entire time, it's going to get old very quickly. Understood?"

"Yeah," he muttered, shoving his hands into his pockets before he glanced away from me.

"No," I said as I walked closer and gripped his chin. "You work for me now. Yes, sir is the acceptable way to answer me. Now, do you understand, Calix?"

Calix's tongue darted out and swiped across his lower lip making it shine. *I bet it would be entertaining to bite that plump lip and make him squirm.*

"Yes, sir," he said finally before he pulled his chin out of my grip and nodded. "Can we go?"

I gave him one last look over before I turned and walked down the stairs. There would be plenty of time to teach Calix how to behave, but we had work to do and it wouldn't be accomplished by standing around. Or thinking of all the ways I could fuck him. That was all Calix would be to me. Another one-night stand.

I jerked my chin in the direction of my car. "Get in."

Calix moved past me and slipped into my car. I watched as he stared straight ahead and his jaw ticked.

At least both of us would be annoyed tonight.

Chapter Five

Calix

I don't want to do this.

Every second that passed with me sitting beside Gabriele, my stomach tightened. I could still feel his hand wrapped around my throat, his hot palm squeezing against my flesh as he glared at me so hard I thought I would melt under his intense gaze. I stopped myself from reaching up to touch my neck only because I didn't want him to see me do it. There was no need for him to know that I was still on edge about it.

Men like Gabriele thrived on chaos, control, and fear. I wasn't going to give him anything. I gripped my thighs tightly, my fingers digging into myself as I felt his eyes lingering on the side of my face. But I refused to turn around and look at him.

I need to do this. I need to do this. I need to do this.

Maybe if I repeated those words to myself enough times it would make me feel better. For now, I was stuck with a lump in my throat and my stomach twisting into knots. Being too close to Gabriele was bad for my health.

I let out a slow breath trying to regulate my pulse. No matter how much I didn't want to do this I had to. Tallia, Sam, and everyone who came to the gym to learn and grow and be themselves, they would suffer if I didn't do what I had to do to keep my gym.

I wish I could tell someone what was going on. But talking about it wasn't going to fix the problem. I had to suck it up, get the job done, and hopefully move on once it was all said and done.

"Don't pout so hard. You act like I'm driving you out to the woods to put a bullet in your head."

I tensed. "Shit." *He could be.*

"I'm not!" Gabriele scowled, shaking his head. "What? You see what I do for a job and you figure I must be the type of guy to drop you in a ditch and put two in your skull?"

I glanced at him out of the corner of my eye. "Do you want me to lie? Or be honest?"

"*Saccente,*" he mumbled. "If I wanted you dead you'd be in the ground already. Loosen up."

Gabriele flipped on the radio and turned it up. *Guess that's the end of the conversation.* I couldn't say I wasn't happy to end our chat. Everything about the man made me squirm and feel odd. I adjusted my collar in the side view mirror and tried to tune everything out.

Until he stopped on one particular song.

Upbeat Korean music came over the stereo and I slowly turned and stared at Gabriele. His thumbs drummed against the steering wheel, his head bobbing back and forth as he mouthed the words. He looked over and froze when he saw me staring.

"Really?" I asked over the music. "Kpop?"

"This is BTS and the song is called Dynamite. And it's good."

My mouth dropped open and I couldn't stop staring at him. *What kind of big, bad mafia guy listened to fucking kpop?* He glanced at me sharply before he growled.

"Is there a problem?"

"N-no," I said, shaking my head and trying hard to stifle a laugh.

"This is good shit," he argued. "Don't laugh!"

"Who would have guessed?" I mused. "You and kpop."

"Yeah, and if you open your mouth and tell anyone I'll kick your ass," he said, narrowing his eyes at me. "Got it?"

I threw my hands up. "Who am I going to tell?" I asked as I turned and glanced out the window again. "Besides everyone," I muttered under my breath.

"What was that?"

I jumped. "Nothing."

God, Six is rubbing off on me.

I knew better than to antagonize this man but for a second I couldn't help it. Biting my tongue, I stayed staring off into the distance until I was sure Gabriele wasn't looking at me anymore. I took a moment to search his face.

Gabriele watched the road, swerving in and out of traffic like he didn't have a care in the world. His dark suit clung to him like a glove. Gabriele's dark hair brushed his collar, looking so silky I wanted to reach out and touch it. He reached up a hand and rubbed his chin before his eyes cut to me. Gabriele raised a brow.

Stop staring at him! Jesucristo. What's my problem?

It wasn't my fault that he was so good-looking. But he was also dangerous as hell. Gabriele Bianchi was the kind of man that could make you disappear if you weren't careful. I didn't want to be one of his victims.

"We're here," Gabriele said as he turned down the radio and looked at me. "You can stop staring now."

I scoffed and frowned. "I wasn't."

"Sure. Whatever you gotta tell yourself to sleep at night," he said as he climbed out of the car. "Move your ass."

I rolled my eyes and slipped out of his car. We were in a pretty rough neighborhood, but Gabriele didn't seem concerned. Instead, he adjusted his suit jacket and nodded toward a tall, dirty brown building.

"First collection is here. Jeffrey Salinger. We're going to go in, ask for the money nicely, and if he doesn't have it, well... that's what you're for. No reason for me to lift a finger."

I shook my head as I followed him into the building. "I told you, I'm not killing anyone."

"Did I say anything about that?" he asked, his gaze narrowing. "Times like this, at most you'll have to punch someone a few times. But it might be good enough for you to be standing behind me. Just try to look menacing. No one wants to fuck with us so they're more likely to pay than put up a fight."

"Even if it's their last few dimes?"

Gabriele stepped onto the elevator and raised a brow at me. "We don't force people to take out loans. They do it themselves, get in over their heads, and then when it's time to pay they like to shove a big middle finger up at us. What's the bigger sin? Collecting what's ours? Or some asshole running up debt and expecting to get off without having to pay it back?"

I shook my head. "You don't want me to answer that."

He scoffed. "Probably not."

The tension was so thick between us, I could choke on it as we exited the elevator. We moved together to the door and after Gabriele nodded to it, I knocked. *Let's get this over with.*

***

I was surprised things had gone smoothly all night. One after the other, money was handed over to Gabriele and all I had to do was stand by and look tough. I wasn't going to complain. The sooner the money was collected, the faster I could go back to my place, crawl into bed, and get ready for my next fight. If I kept winning, I could get the sort of money that would easily wipe away what I owed and I would be free of the Bianchi's, my father's failures, all of it.

Ugh I'm still worried about Dad though. That bastard. Where is he? Is he still breathing? I was pissed, but he was all I had. I didn't want to think of him floating facedown somewhere.

"How many more to go?" I asked as we pulled to a stop.

Gabriele looked at his phone. "This is the last one."

I nodded. "How come you're doing things like this? I mean, isn't it kind of...beneath you? Don't you have people who can collect for you?"

He paused and looked at me oddly. "Yes, we do. But there are other things I have to look into and I can do it better with my own eyes. Other people make mistakes. I don't."

"Everyone makes mistakes."

Gabriele shook his head. "Not me," he said before he climbed out of the car. "Move your ass."

I groaned and dragged myself out of my seat. Gabriele was hiding something. *Mind your own business. There's no need to get mixed up with it.*

I followed Gabriele into the bar we'd parked down the street from. The sound of country music and the smell of beer were the first things that hit me. Cigarette smoke filled the air obscuring my vision and making me crinkle my nose. Cigarettes and MMA don't mix and I didn't want to screw up my training. But lately, I couldn't get away from it.

"Who are we looking for?" I asked.

"Seth Hills. He's usually hanging out around here. I'm damn sure this place is where all the money he borrowed went."

I nodded and shuffled after Gabriele. A man glanced up at us and his eyes widened to the size of saucers. He jumped out of the booth he was sitting in and ran in the opposite direction.

"Goddamnit," Gabriele growled. "Go get his ass!"

On instinct alone, I took off after the guy. Glasses fell to the ground and the sound of them breaking barely registered as I raced after the man. I burst through the back door after him and into the dark alley. Even if I hadn't been able to see him anymore, I would be able to hear his heavy, panicked breathing. He ran for a closed fence, but I was faster. I grabbed him and tackled him to the ground.

"Let me go, please!" he shouted. "I-I don' t have it. I don't have it I fucking swear!"

"Get him up," Gabriele said as he appeared in my peripheral. "On your feet, Hills."

I grunted as I stood and yanked the man to his feet. He was scrawny as hell, all bones, and loose skin. There were dark circles under his eyes and the gray in his dark hair was pronounced under the yellow light of the flickering bulb above us.

"Where's the money?" Gabriele asked.

"I-I don't have it, Mr. Bianchi. I tried to get it but-"

"But you have enough money to be drinking at this shit hole of a bar every night, right? I feel like you could have used your funds in better ways."

"It's not that simple," he muttered.

"Hit him," Gabriele said calmly, his dark gaze flickering to me.

I swallowed hard. *Hit him?* They were simple words but my brain was having a hard time processing them. I glanced at the man and he looked so frail I was sure if I did hurt him he'd break every bone in his body without it taking much effort.

"Please, don't," the man begged as he sagged in my arms trying to wiggle himself free from my grasp. "I-I got a little bit, but that's all. Here just let me..." He awkwardly reached into his pocket while I kept a hold of him and yanked out his wallet. Seth dumped the contents into his palm and held out a shaky hand to Gabriele. "That's all I have I swear to God. Look," he said showing off the now empty wallet. "I swear. I swear."

"Take it," Gabriele said.

After I let the man go, I counted the money before I passed it to Gabriele and took hold of the man's arm again. "It's not every-thing, but...."

"It's all I have," the man pleaded. "Please. I'll get you more next week. I work a few double shifts and I can afford it after I pay the rent. Please."

Gabriele took the money and counted himself. As he took his time, I felt the trembles in the man's arm. My stomach turned and I released him.

"Thank you, thank you," he muttered before he turned on his heels and ran back into the bar like his heels were on fire.

"Did I tell you to let him go?" Gabriele asked once we were alone. He took a step toward me. "At what point were my orders to release him?"

I took a step back. "You didn't."

"Then why did you let him go?" He asked.

"It was all he had," I said moving back again to put more distance between myself and Gabriele. "What was I supposed to do? Beat him up? How is putting him in the hospital going to get you more money?"

Gabriele glared at me before he turned on his heels. I watched as he stormed back toward the bar and I sank against the brick wall of the opposite building. I let out a shaky breath and ran my hands over my hair.

I felt as disgusting as the dirty alley I was standing in. That man was someone's son, brother, friend, or maybe even someone's father. The fear on his face, the way he shook. *Is that how my father looked whenever they came to collect from him in the office?* I gripped my stomach trying to steady my breathing, but I couldn't.

I can't do this.

Chapter Six

Calix

EVERY MILE WE DROVE IN SILENCE MADE MY STOMACH TIGHTEN more. I had never been so nervous in my life. Not when I started school as a kid, not when I got my first job, not even before my first fight. *He's going to kill me.* Gabriele hadn't said a word since we'd gotten back to the car. Not even the radio was playing, just eerie, charged silence.

I bounced my knee up and down, my mind racing a mile a minute. What if he was taking me somewhere to kill me? What if when we stopped he pulled a gun out and shoved it to my head? I had fucked up. And Gabriele's threatening words weren't lost on me. I tried not to think about my brains being splattered over the ground and my body ditched somewhere dark.

The car stopped and I glanced up to see my house. I let out a heavy breath and grabbed the car handle and opened the door before a hand clapped around my arm.

"Next time I tell you to do something, you do it. You don't get to make decisions. Ever."

I turned to look at Gabriele. "He didn't have anything more to give you," I said evenly, trying not to show I felt about as scared as that man had looked. "What was the point of hurting him?"

"You don't need to worry about thinking. Until your money is paid back you belong to me," he growled, sending a shiver up my spine. "To the Bianchi's. You belong to the Bianchi's," he said, his brow furrowing before he shook his head and looked at me pointedly. "Do you understand?"

"Yeah," I muttered.

"Try again."

I gritted my teeth. "Yes, sir."

When I tried to pull away, he yanked me back again. This time, he leaned over his seat and grabbed the front of my shirt before he jerked me close. Being so close, I could smell his cologne and something underneath, a natural musk that was all Gabriele.

"You need to wake the fuck up," he snapped. "Just because that man gave you some sob story you believe him, but these people aren't innocent. There is no good or bad. No black and white. Everything in this world and I mean fucking everything is shades of fucked up gray. If you'd like to lose your gym or your life, keep putting their bullshit before your new job."

I opened my mouth and snapped it shut. "Yes, sir."

"You have something to say?" he asked, tilting his head. "Say it."

"Nothing," I said, shaking my head. "I'm ready to go to bed."

Gabriele searched my face before he released me. "I'll be in contact shortly. Don't worry, I already have your number."

I stared at Gabriele for a moment longer and bit my tongue. Saying anything to him was pointless. Gabriele thought he knew how the world worked when really he was just a bastard.

I climbed out of his car and slammed the door so hard I was surprised the damn window didn't shatter. He'd gotten to me, talking to me like I was some kind of idiotic child. I didn't need to be told how people were, I saw it every day of my life. Especially when I was around him.

As soon as I stepped inside, I locked my door and thumped my head against the wood. What was I doing? I was being forced to betray everything I believed in. All so I could pay off this debt and be stuck with a man who didn't have a damn heart. How could he look at people and be so...cold?

I slammed my head back against the door again before I turned and punched it. Every bit of frustration, disappointment, fear, and anger poured out of me as I rammed my fist into the door again. Pain shot up my arm, bright pinpricks of hurt splintering over my hand as I pulled it up and flexed it.

Blood decorated my knuckles, and I swore under my breath. *How much more am I supposed to take?* I watched the dark droplets roll over my skin and drip to the hardwood floor. There was no one here with me, no one to talk to and confide in. No one could help me with this situation. And the one person who could had left me to deal with it alone.

***

I dragged myself into the gym the next morning even though it was the last place I felt like being. It used to be the place I went to express myself and let go. Now? It was like a prison. I felt the four walls closing in on me, the weight of the Gonzalez legacy crushing me day by day. If I failed, we all failed and my family would have scrimped, saved, and sacrificed all for it to end because of me.

"There he is," Tallia called as she climbed out of the ring and hopped down. "Where you been?"

"I'm late again, huh?" I asked, not even bothering to check my phone. Ever since my night out with Gabriele, I had been out of it. "Sorry."

She shook her head. "You're dealing with a lot. It's okay." She glanced around and waved a hand at me. "Let's talk in your office. I want to tell you something."

I nodded and followed her back. She turned the lock as I sat my bag down on the desk and waited. Tallia shifted from one foot to the other while she looked anywhere but at me.

"Tal, what's up?" I asked.

She finally glanced up. "I found a way to make a little money for the gym. Well if I do good, it's a *lot* of money."

I raised a brow. "I'm pretty sure your girlfriend will kill you if you start stripping."

She placed her hands on her hips and looked at me as if I was the stupidest man alive. "I'm not stripping, dummy. It's something else." She licked her lips before she scratched her temple. "I heard about these fights from my cousin. All underground stuff, pretty illegal, *but* you can make some serious money. Especially if someone bets on you."

I stared at her. "What are you talking about, Tal?"

"I'm talking about me entering some fights and you betting a shit ton of money on me," she said. "Come on, it would be easy money and we could save this place! Sam won't risk the underground fights anymore after last time, but I can do it."

She's lost her damn mind.

There was no way in hell I was going to let Tallia do underground fights. Sam had done them for a while and ended up in the hospital with a fracture in his skull. After his fiance banned him from ever doing it again, he stayed away. And for good reason. Underground fights were dangerous, unregulated, and could get you killed.

"No," I said firmly.

Tal groaned. "It would only be a few fights and then I would stop."

My stomach clenched. "It doesn't matter if it's just a few fights. When has anything good ever come out of easy money? Besides, we both know Titan doesn't allow its fighters to participate in that shit. You want to end your career when it's just starting?"

Tallia sighed. "No," she muttered. "I know they're really strict, but I can't see any other way out, Cal." She plopped down in a chair and shoved her fingers through her hair. "This shit is stressing me out. Losing this place would be like losing a piece of me," she said as she laughed dryly and gazed up at me. "I've been here since I was thirteen. Everything I know is this gym and the people who love it here."

I frowned, my heart squeezing in my chest at her distress. "I'm sorry, Tallia. But it's not over. I'm working on getting this place out of the shit as best I can." I rounded the desk and laid a hand on her shoulder. "Let me try to handle this."

She laid her hand on top of mine and squeezed. "It's more than that. I don't want *you* to lose this place, Calix. You've worked so hard and I can't stand the thought of you suffering."

A lump formed in my throat as I leaned down and pressed my head against Tallia's. I didn't have words for her and even if I did I didn't trust myself to speak. Tallia didn't need to see me crying like a moron.

When we pulled away from each other, she gazed up at me and the worry in her eyes made me sink. She wiped away a stray tear and sniffled sharply.

"I better get back to work."

"Yeah," I said quietly. I watched as she stood up and headed for the door. "Tal?" When she turned to face me, I gave her a tight smile. "I'm going to fix this, okay? Please, let me handle it."

Tal frowned. "You're not going to try to take all of this on yourself, are you? I mean, you should let us help if we can."

"I know," I said with a nod. "I just have one more question. What were those fights your cousin was talking about? I'd like the details."

"Oh no," she said quickly. "If I can't do it, neither can you!"

I laughed and waved a hand. "No, it's nothing like that! I'm going to keep them on my radar so I can check up on you. And if I find you at one, I'll kick your ass myself."

Tal grinned. "There's that fighting spirit. Fine." She dug into her pocket and laid a card on my desk. "But I won't go. Unless you ask me to."

"Never going to happen," I said as I picked up the card and tossed it into my desk drawer. "Do you mind looking after things out there while I get settled in?"

She nodded. "Sure thing."

"Thanks."

As soon as the door closed, I sat behind the desk and pulled out the drawer. The white card stared back at me, beckoning me to take it. *I shouldn't.*

I finally snatched it up and examined the details. Tallia shouldn't have to risk her career and her life for my father's sins and the Bianchi's greed. I was going to make things right and pay Gabriele off as soon as possible so he would get off my back.

As long as I don't get caught everything will be okay. I can do this.

All I had to do was attend my regular fights in the evenings and then attend the late-night underground rounds. I stared at the number listed on the card. Before I could second guess myself, I snatched up my phone and dialed the number.

Every time it rang my stomach clenched and my pulse skyrocketed. *This is insane. Hang up. Am I any better than my father doing this shit?*

I hated to admit it, but I was starting to realize why he had done the crazy things he had. Fear was a powerful motivator. I didn't want to get back into a car with Gabriele and terrorize people. And I didn't want to lose the place that felt most like home.

I don't have a choice. Hope it doesn't bite me in the ass.

"Hello?"

My heart raced as the deep, accented voice on the other end greeted me. Frozen, I gripped the phone flipping through the pros and cons. Either way, I was about to be put onto a road that might lead to my downfall.

"Do you want something?" the voice asked, annoyed.

"Yeah. I got this number from Tallia. I want to fight."

The words tumbled out of me as I clenched my hand against my thigh and stared ahead. If I didn't find my own way out, I would belong to Gabriele Bianchi forever.

Chapter Seven

Gabriele

I PULLED UP IN FRONT OF CALIX'S HOUSE AND SHUT OFF MY lights. Through his curtains, I could see his shadow moving around, pacing back and forth. I'd already let him know that I was on my way and he was waiting for me.

My eyes tracked his movements. He was like a caged tiger ready to be set free so he could maul someone. *Why does he have to act so damn naive? He would make an amazing killer if he stopped pretending the world was good.*

Calix had the wrong idea if he thought the people we collected from were upright people. He seemed to believe what I did was wrong, but the truth was that I was the balancing of the scales in the world. I was karma incarnate. What was wrong with setting things straight?

I watched as he picked up his phone and stared at it. My heart skipped a beat as he brought it to his ear. *Who the hell is he talking to?* I gripped the steering wheel tighter, the leather protesting my hold until I released it.

Ever since the night Calix bumped into me, I had been watching him. Not all the time, but usually when he was at the gym or when he had a fight. He was an interesting person. A hard worker who took no shit and yet was constantly walked on, a worrier, a loner. The only people he hung around were his father, the people who worked for him, and Six. Other than that, he came home alone, cracked open a single beer, and relaxed for forty-five minutes before he went to bed.

"For someone so young you act like an old man, Calix," I muttered. "What the hell happened to you?"

No one without a shit ton of trauma would volunteer to be a hermit at his age. Back then I was partying, being a moron, and still taking on jobs for the family. The only thing he seemed focused on was working, MMA, and sleeping when he got the chance.

My hear sank. It looked sad. And lonely.

Stop sympathizing and get to work!

I pulled out my phone and stared at it. Right, we had a job to do and the sooner it was taken care of, the sooner I could go back to living my life and not watching Calix.

Gabriele: Let's go.

Calix: You're here?

Gabriele: No shit. What do you think? I like texting you for fun? Come on.

Calix opened the curtain and stared out before the lights went out and he jogged out of the front door. This time around he wore a red button-up and black slacks. The first two buttons of his shirt were undone and I was sure it was because he had forgotten and not because he was trying to be sexy and draw my attention to the hair I caught peeking out of his clothes.

"What?" he asked when he slid into the car. "Why are you staring at me?"

"I'm not," I grumbled, clearing my throat harshly as I turned forward again. "Be quicker next time."

Calix scoffed. "It took me two minutes!"

"Next time make it one," I snapped. "Why do you like talking back to me so much? Do you need me to show you what happens when you keep running your mouth?"

I glanced over at Calix and his teeth were buried in his bottom lip as if it was taking every ounce of self-control he could muster to stay quiet. Something about that look made me want to laugh. *He's trying hard.* I knew he hated me, hell a lot of people did, but he was also trying not to die which I admired.

Smart move.

When Calix went quiet, I knew I wasn't going to get much more out of him. I pulled away from the curb and floored it, peeling out of the neighborhood and hitting the highway. The overhead lights flooded the road, and as I glanced at Calix out of the corner of my eye, I could see the frown on his lips.

"What's your problem?" I asked.

Calix glanced at me, raised one shoulder, and let it drop. "Nothing. Just thinking," he muttered before he glanced out of his window. "Who's on the list for tonight?"

I didn't respond. Instead, I took in the way he slumped forward and the frown on his face that had only intensified. Something was on Calix's mind. Was it more complaints about having to collect? That I couldn't do anything about. But if it was anything else...

"No, really," I asked, focusing on the road. "What's the matter with you? Is it the job? Or something else?"

Calix laughed dryly drawing my eyes back to him. The frown had disappeared and in its place was a sneer. "What the fuck do you care?"

My stomach clenched and I gripped the wheel tightly. "Fine," I spat. "Fuck you too, brat."

"I'm a brat?" Calix scoffed. "I think most people would be upset if they were hurting people just to save their fucking property. The one they'd worked their ass off for since they were thirteen. So yeah," he said as he faced me and glared, "I'm a brat."

My blood pressure rose as I stared at him. "You know what kills me? What just absolutely burns me the fuck up, Gonzalez?" When he simply looked back at me, I shook my head. "People like your dear old dad come to us askin' us for money and we give it to him. Fine. But then they can't pay it back and suddenly we're the fuckin' bad guys? Give me a fuckin' break," I muttered as I snatched up my pack of smokes and fumbled them as my hand shook. "People like you? You're always looking for a villian when most times it's just your own bullshit that trips you up. Fuck!" I dropped the pack and sucked in a deep breath. Amadeo was the calm one, and I liked to think I was the same. But I had a breaking point too. I stared at the pack on the floor of the car beside Calix's feet before I focused on the road again. "Pick those up, pull one out, stick it in my mouth, and light it for me."

"Are you serious?" Calix asked.

I glared at him. "Do I look like I'm a fuckin' joking?"

He shivered and reached over to snag the pack of cigarettes. Calix tapped one out and his long, sturdy fingers took it and slipped it between my lips. I held it in place as he looked for a lighter and found one in the glove compartment. As he lit my smoke, I glanced at him, the concentration on his face as he worked.

And my cock jumped.

Obedient when you want to be, huh?

Calix put the lighter in a cup holder and let his window down a bit. I let mine down as well, took in a long, slow drag, and blew smoke out the window. The car went back to being silent, but I couldn't stop thinking about fucking the man beside me. It had become a carnal desire that infiltrated my every waking moment. I forced myself to calm down before I did something stupid and kept driving.

"Are we close?" Calix asked after several long, silent moments.

Ignoring him, I pulled off of the freeway and found a spot in the back of the dingy little bar. Our guy still wasn't there and we had time to waste. But I didn't want to spend that time beside Calix. He'd gotten me to break character and show the temper I tried so hard to suppress. I needed another smoke and a walk.

Stepping out into the warm night air, I lit up again and walked around the car. My feet crunched against the gravel and I stopped to take a moment to breathe when I heard footsteps behind me. I turned around and Calix was standing right there.

"What?" I asked. "You following me around like a good little puppy?"

Calix frowned. "I'm not a goddamn puppy."

I stopped and raised a brow at him. "Say it again."

"I'm not a goddamn puppy," Calix repeated, standing his ground. "So stop calling me that."

You're too much fun, Calix.

It was easy enough to break a cowering, simpering thing, but a man like Calix? That took time, skill, and talent. And he made me want to prove that I could do it. I tossed my cigarette to the side and lunged forward. My hand gripped soft brown hair and I yanked downward.

"Fuck!"

Calix cried out as he was pulled to the ground. His nice, black slacks were mired with mud, but it felt as if that's how they should be. This work wasn't clean and put together. It was messy, difficult, and ugly. And Calix needed a serious reality check.

"You think the world is so black and white," I said as I gazed down at him. "I can guarantee it's not. No!" I snapped when he tried to stand. "If I say you're my dog, then that's exactly what you are. You need to learn your place. Do you understand me?"

I watched as Calix's Adam's apple bounced in his throat. There was a fine shade of red settling onto his cheeks and I could *feel* the words trying to escape with him telling me exactly what he thought about me.

"Say something ridiculous if you want to," I said shaking my head. "It'll only bite you in the ass."

"You're an asshole," Calix barked.

"Bad dog," I said as I gripped his hair tighter. "All I want to hear is your respect. Do you understand me?" I repeated.

The conflicted mask on Calix's face was delectable. He wanted so badly to rebel, but he knew the penalty for doing it would be harsh. Seeing him on his knees, that fire burning in his eyes made my cock so hard it was damn near painful. I wanted to see him there for hours, begging and pleading for more.

When am I going to get over this little obsession? I need to get control of it.

But that was a hell of a lot easier said than done. Seeing Calix up close made things worse. Shit stirred in me that hadn't in a long damn time.

I reached out and gripped his chin, yanking it up roughly. "I asked you a question twice now, mutt," I said. "Answer me or I can show you what it's like to be on the receiving end of my anger."

Calix groaned, but to my ears, it was tinged with... a moan? *Did I really hear that?* He gazed up at me with his chocolate eyes and licked his lips. I sucked in a breath wanting to taste his mouth desperately.

"I understand," he finally said, his face even redder than before. "Okay? I understand."

"You understand what?" I asked, pushing him even more. Even though I knew he was at his breaking point already. I wanted him to fully rebel so I could put him in his place. The times we would have together would be legendary.

"I understand, Sir," he said, his eyes narrowing. "Can we get back to work?"

I searched his face for a moment before I released his chin. "Yes, we can. But remember what I said, Calix," I told him as I walked away. I stopped and glanced back at him. "The sooner you stop viewing me as the bad guy and open your eyes, the easier this job will be." I turned on my heels again. "Hurry up, puppy. We've got shit to do."

Calix's shuffling footsteps filed behind me as I walked around to the entrance of the bar. I glanced over my shoulder to find him frowning and deep in thought.

What's going on inside your head?

Chapter Eight

Gabriele

THE WAY I COULDN'T GET CALIX OUT OF MY MIND WAS STARTING to become a problem.

I sat outside the gym, across the street, staring inside and watching him. He smiled at *everyone*. The more he did it, the more I wanted to march over there and ask him what the hell he was in such a good mood for. Wasn't he so fucking tortured every time we left his place?

Technically, it wasn't time for us to do collections. But it had been a few days since I'd last seen him in the yellowy overhead lights of the bar's parking lot on his knees and frustrated. *He really did look like a puppy.*

Calix walked away from the woman he'd been talking to who I recognized as Tallia and started speaking to someone else instead. This time, it was a guy with dark hair and a wide smile. And every time Calix turned around, the man stole a long gaze at his plump ass.

My heart rate skyrocketed as heat rushed through my body. I let myself out of the car and slammed it shut behind me. I'd been sitting there long enough and I was sick and tired of seeing that bullshit. Six wasn't there and I was thankful for that. If he saw me all amped up, he'd be on my ass about being nice to his friend again. But I couldn't help that his friend was flirting with every dude that crossed his path.

I walked into the gym and made a beeline to Calix. As soon as I drew closer, he looked up, his eyes wide. I moved between him and his client and stared Calix down.

"We need to talk," I said.

The man he was with scoffed. "Excuse me, buddy. But I was here first. I paid for this session."

I turned on my heels and looked the man up and down. "Beat it."

"What the fuck? No! Why don't you beat it, dumbass?"

That's a mistake.

I reached out and grabbed the man's wrist. Before he could even register what was happening, I yanked his arm up behind his back and pushed him to the floor. He let out a strangled noise that made me smile as I held him in place with my knee.

"Let go of him!" Calix yelled. "What are you doing?"

"Talking to you," I said as the man beneath me squirmed and tried to wriggle away. "If you keep moving you're going to break your own wrist and I won't be responsible for that. Stay still, asshole."

Calix's mouth dropped open. "Are you serious?" he hissed when he finally regained his composure. "Let Joshua go and come on," he growled.

"Joshua," I said as I glanced down at the man on the floor. "What's your last name?"

"Don't answer that," Calix cut in before he grabbed my upper arm and tugged. "Come on!"

Reluctantly, I let Joshua go. But I committed his face to memory. All it would take was a last name and he would end up lying in a puddle of his own blood. Calix tugged again, his hand so warm I could feel it through my clothes. This time, I listened and turned around as he dragged me into the back office.

I could have stopped Calix. Pulling away would be nothing, but I let him take me away from the man. When I glanced over my shoulder I glared at the guy just to let him know that I wasn't done with him yet. He stayed on the ground, his eyes huge as he stared at me. A grin curled my lips. *Right where you belong, you insect.*

"What is your problem?" Calix asked after he pulled me inside and slammed the office door. "I'm trying to teach and you're assaulting my clients!"

I scoffed. "Some clients you have. All that guy was doing was staring at your ass every time you turned around."

Calix frowned. "What? How would you- Are you following me?"

"I'm doing my job," I said, sidestepping the question altogether. "I needed to talk to you so I came here. It's as simple as that."

His dark eyes narrowed and I stared back with a straight face. Whatever he was searching for, he wouldn't find it. Lying came easier to me than breathing. And no way in hell was I about to admit that I liked to stalk Calix Gonzalez in my free time.

"What do you want?" he said, finally giving up and sitting on the edge of his desk. "We can't go around collecting money in broad daylight."

I could and had done just that before, but I wouldn't bring Calix along for that. Part of him becoming a fighter was that he couldn't have a messed-up record. Drugs, gun charges, and assault; all things he needed to avoid if he was going to keep growing in the Viper Fighting Championships.

"We have more collections to do tonight. This is me giving you a heads up."

Calix raised a brow. "This couldn't have been sent in a text?"

Yeah, it could have. Fuck.

"I was already in the neighborhood," I lied knowing damn well I had come forty-five minutes to his gym to see what he was doing. "We're up against more high-profile clients tonight and they're not as easy to deal with. They like to squirm their way out of everything."

Calix pinched the bridge of his nose. "This could have waited. You're interrupting my job to tell me about something that's happening hours from now. What the hell?"

I grinned. "Hey, you gotta be prepared. Besides," I trailed off as I realized the white bandage wrapped around his fist was stained with blood. My chest squeezed and I stepped toward him. "What happened to your hand?"

Calix uncrossed his arms and shoved the injured one behind his back. "Nothing."

I frowned. "Do you think I'm some kinda moron? I can see the fuckin' blood. Give me your hand."

He groaned. "It doesn't matter what happened! You've told me about tonight's collections. Can you go now? *Jesucristo,*" he muttered under his breath. When I continued to stand there he waved a hand. "Well? I'll see you tonight so you can go."

I closed the space between us and my hand wrapped around Calix's throat. "Don't dismiss me like I work for *you*." I squeezed a bit and he grunted, his Adam's apple dancing against my palm. "What the fuck happened?"

Calix licked his lips and I followed the movement. "I, uh, got hurt, but it's fine."

"How?"

"Doesn't matter," he answered.

"You're stubborn as hell," I snapped as I shoved a hand into my pocket and pulled out my phone. I scrolled through the contacts until I landed on Doc and dialed her number. "It's Gabriele. I'm about to send you an address. Come here and bring your kit."

"Sure thing. I'll be over as quickly as I can."

I hung up and laid the phone down before I released Calix's throat. He tried to move away, but I gripped his arm and yanked it forward so I could see his hand. When he tried to tug it away, I growled at him.

"Move that fucking hand and I will beat your ass, Gonzalez."

Calix sucked in a sharp breath, his eyes wide as he stared at me. Somewhere in my gaze, he must have seen that I wasn't fucking around. He kept his hand still and I finally looked down to examine him.

"Good boy," I said as I started unwrapping the bandages. I gazed up to make sure I wasn't hurting him too much but Calix had turned away and was staring off into the distance, a slight pinkness on his cheeks.

Fuck. Why is he so perfect?

I stared for what felt like ages until he looked at me, confused. Quickly, I redirected my attention to his hand and continued to undress his wound. I could see where the cut on his knuckles kept trying to heal, but it was too deep.

"Where did this come from?" I tried one last time.

"It was an accident."

I stared up at Calix, but his lips were pressed tightly together. Whatever had happened, he wasn't going to tell me. I laid his hand on the desk carefully.

"Our family doctor is coming to take a look at you, but you definitely need stitches."

"How do you know?" Calix mumbled.

"I've been in my fair share of fights," I said raising a brow. "I know what it looks like when a wound needs to be stitched up. And if I had the right supplies, I could do it myself. But I don't, so I'll let Doc come check you out."

Even though I want no one to touch him but me.

Calix nodded. "It's been bleeding on and off for the past few days so I guess it can't hurt."

"The last few days?" I glared. "Why didn't you go to the doctor?"

He laughed dryly. "Who has money for that? I don't have insurance and a trip like that will take away funds from more important things," he said looking at me pointedly. "So I didn't go."

I gritted my teeth and clenched my fists tightly. Calix was the definition of a moron. He would rather bleed out than get fixed up so he could keep fighting for his stupid gym and his life? It made me want to kick his ass until he gained some common sense. But strangely, it also made me want to grab him in my arms, hiss at the world, and protect him fiercely.

There was a knock on the door and Vanessa breezed through with a bag in her hands. She sat it on the desk and smiled at Calix.

"Hello, you must be the patient."

"Calix," he said a hell of a lot more politely than the way he talked to me.

"Vanessa," she said as she shook his good hand. "Let's see what we're looking at and I'll fix you right up."

"Thanks," Calix said as he blew out a breath and held out his injured hand. "I need to be able to fight so hopefully it's not too bad."

She looked at his hand and frowned. "It's not horrible, but you'll need to give it a rest for a little while I'm afraid. At least a week." She took out a few supplies before she filled a syringe with clear liquid. "I'll give you a local anesthetic and stitch you up. Shouldn't take too long at all, but you have to promise me you'll rest it or we're going to be here doing this again."

Calix nodded. "Yes, ma'm, I understand. A week is okay. I can take that off." He gazed at me. "I think."

I nodded shortly, but my bad mood had already settled in. He was cooperative with Vanessa and respectful. But when it came to me, he was like an untrained mutt. I never thought I'd be jealous of the good doctor but I briefly fantasized about snapping her neck. The only thing that stopped me was the reality that Amadeo would be pissed.

"That's it," Vanessa said, her voice cutting into my lurid thoughts. "He's all done." She turned to me and paused before raising a brow. "Don't give me that look. I did what you asked."

I frowned. "Yeah."

Vanessa patted me on the arm. "Call me if you need anything. Make sure he takes the antibiotics I gave him and the pain meds."

"Yeah."

She peered at me cautiously. "Are you alright, Mr. Bianchi?"

I nodded, but the truth was that I was far from okay. Whatever was happening to me was bad and it was affecting me in ways I never expected. I sucked in a breath and turned to Calix who was staring at me.

"What?" I snapped.

"Nothing," he said throwing his hands up.

"Let's go."

"Wait, what?" he asked, his brows knitted in confusion. "What do you mean let's go?"

"You heard Doc. Rest, medicine, and more rest. Let's go."

Calix scoffed. "Are you high? I have a business to run!"

I gripped a handful of his hair as my temper snapped. "You have employees, don't you? They'll take over for you. Get your ass to the car."

Calix shoved me away. "Fine! You're such a-" He grunted and censored himself. "Shit!"

He stormed out of the office and slammed the door after him. I stared at it, shocked at how little fucks he gave about the way he talked to me. I was used to grown men pissing their pants when confronted with me, but even after all he'd seen, Calix didn't seem to give a fuck.

I ripped the door open and followed after him. Calix talked to Tallia and she gazed at me before her eyes cut back to him. Once Calix was done, he joined me and we walked out of the gym together. He let out a short hiss as he slipped into the car before he stared out of the window refusing to look at me.

"I'll do collections alone tonight," I said as I started up the car.

Calix turned and stared at me. "What? No, I can go."

I shook my head and pulled out of my spot. "No."

"I can go," he said again. "I don't want to miss a night and owe you or your family anything more than I already do."

My eye twitched and I resisted the urge to push down my lid and stop the involuntary spasm. Calix was going to be the death of me. Everything the man did drove me insane. And I had no idea why. He was correct that he owed the family, but for some reason, I couldn't stop envisioning his debt as *mine* and mine alone.

"You're a fuckin' liability," I snapped at Calix as he tried speaking again. "The only thing you're gonna do is go home and stay out of my goddamn way. You got me? Do you?"

"Yes, sir," Calix spoke through tight lips.

We went back to the awkward, charged silence that stayed between us as I drove to his house. As I gazed down at his hand, I sighed.

I don't want you to get hurt because of stupid collections. Once you heal up, we can go right back to business. But not now.

Everything in me screamed to say the words out loud, but my silver tongue became lead whenever I was around Calix Gonzalez.

Chapter Nine

Calix

I FUMBLED MY KEYS AND THEY FELL IN A HEAP ON THE PORCH. Groaning, I bent over to pick them up but Gabriele scooped them up first. He pushed the key into the lock as I stared at him before he opened the door for me.

"Are you going in or not?" he asked when I continued to eyeball him.

"You can leave," I pointed out. "I'm home."

Gabriele glared at me. "Seriously if you keep talkin' to me like I'm a fuckin' moron..."

There was that accent again. Every time Gabriele got irritated the small hint of Italian accent I normally heard amplified. *I wonder if he even knows he's doing it?*

"Get in the house, Gonzalez."

"Calix," I said as I walked past him and stepped inside. "And I'm inside so you can-"

"Shut up," he said as he closed the door and locked it. Gabriele shed his suit jacket and tossed it over the back of the couch before he unbuttoned the sleeves of his shirt and rolled them up his strong forearms. I stared at the veins prominently displayed on his skin and swallowed hard. "You need to take that medicine with some food or you're gonna feel like shit."

I blinked at him trying to focus on what he was saying. "Okay? I'm capable of making myself-"

"Sit down," he said pointing to the couch. "Now."

I groaned. Shit, I hated being treated like a child. But I could tell by the look in his eyes that there was no room for negotiation. I rounded the couch and sat down slowly before I toed off my shoes. The shot the doctor had given me at the gym was slowly starting to wear off and those pain pills were looking better and better.

Gabriele nodded when I gazed at him before he disappeared into my kitchen. I heard him rustling around in the refrigerator and cabinets and my stomach tightened. There was hardly anything in there. The Bianchi's had major money and knowing that Gabriele was seeing I had nothing filled me with embarrassment.

"Listen, I can make a sandwich for myself," I called out. "It's no big deal."

"Have you eaten today?"

I frowned. Come to think of it I hadn't. I'd woken up late after my fights the night before and while I had more money, I had also hurt my hand. I thought it would be fine so I'd just grabbed a cup of coffee and headed off.

"Calix?"

"No," I answered. "I didn't."

"You need more than a sandwich."

I stared in the direction of the kitchen, confused as hell. *Why is he acting like he gives a damn about me?* I toyed around on my phone for a minute before I couldn't sit still anymore. When I walked into the kitchen Gabriele had four pans going on the stove and he was chopping onions as he moved around the kitchen as if he belonged there.

"What are you making?" I asked slowly.

He turned around and glared. "Didn't I tell you to sit down and rest?"

"I wanted to know what you were doing," I said as I walked further inside and my stomach growled from the amazing aroma. "You actually found stuff to cook in here?"

Gabriele turned back to what he was doing. "You had just enough to make penne arrabbiata. It won't take long."

I had no idea what penne arrabbiata was, but it smelled so good I didn't care. I sat at the table and watched Gabriele as he worked. Seeing him the way he was at that moment, moving around my kitchen almost gracefully, I let my mind wander. If he wasn't a grade-A asshole, he would be hot. Underneath his fancy clothes I imagined was a body that I would appreciate, all hard muscle and tanned olive skin. Heat raced up my back and my cock throbbed.

Gabriele turned to me and I stopped daydreaming fast. *Reality check time. This man is a killer. If I wasn't working for him, he wouldn't hesitate to take me out.* I stored my fantasies back where they belonged as Gabriele poured water out of a pitcher in the fridge and sat the glass in front of me.

"Here you go," Gabriele said as he put a plate in front of me. "Eat it while it's hot." He sat another plate across from me and went back to dig around in my fridge before he returned with a beer.

"I want a beer."

"No," he said as he cracked it open. "You're about to take medication."

I scoffed. "Are you trying to tell me you've never taken pain pills with a drink?"

Gabriele rose a brow. "I have, but you won't be. Not while I'm here."

I huffed. "Who asked you to be here?"

He stopped, the beer halfway to his lips before he lowered it. "I just made you a meal. The least you could do is say thank you, eat it, and be appreciative. I don't cook for just anyone."

I picked up my fork and toyed with a piece of penne. He was being…real. I felt like shit for what I'd said. "Why *did* you cook for me?"

"You needed to eat and you have a fucked up hand," he said before he took a swig of beer.

"Okay..." I frowned as I looked up at him. "Or is it because you want me to heal up so I can go back to being your little slave?"

Gabriele stared at me without saying a word. I shifted in my seat under his intense gaze, my stomach tying itself into knots. *Shouldn't have said that.* I searched his face to see if he was about to lose his temper, but he didn't. Instead, some other emotion flickered over his face. Gabriele stood up and grabbed my plate.

"Don't eat it then," he grumbled.

My good hand shot out and I grabbed his arm. "Sorry," I said, the word spilling out of my lips quickly as my stomach dropped. "I'll eat it."

I think I hurt his feelings. Do Bianchi's even have feelings?

Gabriele didn't look at me, but he put the plate in front of me none too gently and sat down again. I had to switch to using my right hand to eat. Food spilled off of my fork multiple times before I was ready to give up.

"Here," Gabriele grumbled again as he used his fork to feed me. "Take your time."

I blinked at him. Gabriele Bianchi was feeding me in my little kitchen. I didn't know what to do with that.

"That's good," I said as I stabbed at another piece. I couldn't take him feeding me again without melting. "I didn't think you could cook."

"What? Because I kill people I can't have other interests?"

I nearly choked and pounded on my chest to make the food go down. "You say that so casually," I said as I shook my head. "How are you cool with it?"

Gabriele shrugged. "Death is a part of life. We all have to go some time." He nodded toward me. "Finish your food and take your medicine."

I frowned. "I might just take some Tylenol or something. Pain meds make me a little crazy."

He narrowed his eyes. "You're going to take those pills Doc gave you or I'll shove them down your throat."

"Does everything you say have to be a threat?" I snapped.

"When it comes to you? Apparently fuckin' so."

I caved and shook my head before I moved around in my seat. The bottle hit the floor and I sighed before I reached over to get them. I winced a bit as my fingers grazed the bottle and a pair of shiny, leather shoes entered my field of vision. Gabriele snatched up the bottle and pushed me upright in my seat.

"Finish your food."

"I can take pills by myself."

"Keep protesting," he said as he opened the bottle and tapped out two pills. "Do you really think it's going to work for you?"

My shoulders slumped as I held out my hand and took the medicine from him. He was right about one thing, there was no point in arguing with him. When Gabriele wanted to do something, that was exactly what he did. And I was tired of fighting with him. My hand hurt, my mind was a mess, and all I wanted was to take that rest that I'd been ordered to.

I tossed the pills into my mouth and chugged them down with the water Gabriele had sat out. His eyes stayed trained on me until I started eating again. Satisfied, he put the medicine away on the counter before he joined me again.

"Once you're done you need to rest," Gabriele pointed out. "I'm giving you some time off, but it won't be forever. You'd better take advantage of it while you can."

"Yes, sir," I said with a hint of sarcasm in my voice. "Thank you for the generosity."

Gabriele sucked his teeth. "That's it. I've had enough." He walked over and yanked me up by my upper arm, his grip tightening. "Move."

"Where are we going?" I asked, my heart drumming in my ears so hard I could barely hear him. "Gabriele?"

He was silent as he pulled me from the kitchen, up the stairs, and pushed open my bedroom door. *How the hell did he know where my bedroom was?* I didn't have time to wonder too much longer before he pushed me toward the bed.

"Go to bed. When you wake up, maybe you'll lose the attitude."

I stared at him. "Wait, you're making me go to bed?"

"Yes," he growled. "Is that a problem?" he asked as he crossed his arms over his chest.

"I thought you would do something more...mafia-y."

Gabriele stepped toward me and I moved back. "Like what?"

"Nothing," I muttered, cursing myself for talking too much. But he'd taken me by surprise. "I'll go to bed."

"No, you wanted me to do something more to you, right?" He pushed me back until I fell into the bed. I stared up at him with wide eyes as he climbed on top of me and pinned my wrists to the mattress. "Is this what you had in mind?"

Shit. Shit. Shit. That wasn't at all what I had in mind. I felt my cock harden and I tried to shift so I could close my legs. So *he* wouldn't feel how turned on I was. But as he glared down at me and his eyes widened I knew that he felt my erection.

"Oh? So that's what you like," Gabriele said, a grin appearing on his lips as he ground against me.

"No! It's not because of you; it's been a long time and I'm-" I licked my lips. "It's the pain meds. Relaxing me and stuff. Get off of me."

Gabriele leaned down and I felt his stiff cock pressing up against mine. He rubbed against me and I sucked in a sharp breath. I tugged my wrists against his hands and he tightened his grip.

"Hold still or you'll hurt yourself," he muttered as he gazed at me. "Don't pretend you don't like this."

My cock twitched and I cursed my stupid body as my brain began to get floaty and tingly from the pain medicine. I hated the way it made me more vulnerable, weaker. Grunting, I tried to pull free, but Gabriele laughed at me and ground his cock against mine even more.

"Is that why you have such a nasty attitude, Gonzalez? Do you need your cock milked so you can think straight?"

"D-don't touch me."

"I haven't touched a thing," he purred as he picked up speed, the friction of his cock against mine making me suck in a sharp breath. "And you're already panting."

"Fuck you!" I snapped as I strained to get him off of me.

"Bullshit," he growled. He captured my wrists with one hand and I heard my zipper come undone as he continued to stare at me. "You can lie all you want, but your face and your body are betraying the fuck out of you. Spread your fucking legs."

I shook my head. *No, I don't want this.* Gabriele was the kind of man I would have happily climbed into bed with if I didn't know who and what he was. But I did and I refused to sleep with someone who killed without a single care in the world.

"What? Do you like being forced to do things?" Gabriele asked as he rubbed my cock over the fabric of my boxers. "Is that what you need? To be taken?"

"No," I panted as my back arched and I bit my bottom lip. "Gabriele, stop it."

"Are you sure?" he asked. "It seems as if you need to be touched." He pulled my boxers down and the cool air of the overhead fan kissed my aching cock making me shudder. "But if you want me to stop then I will." Gabriele tilted his head at me. "So tell me, is that really want you want, Calix?"

Jesucristo.

My name shouldn't have sounded so good on his lips. The little smirk he wore was smug as if he knew what I was going to say. I wanted to open my mouth and tell him that he could fuck off, that no I didn't want him or anything to do with him. But my hips jerked upward looking for the missing friction and I let out a pathetic whine.

"Really?" He chuckled. "Does that mean you want more?"

I couldn't say yes. Telling him he could touch me was admitting that he wasn't someone I would never want. It would be like I was accepting what he was.

"You don't have to answer," Gabriele cooed as he wrapped his hand around my cock and I let out a moan. "I can tell you want it because you've stopped fighting me. All that barking has calmed down now, hasn't it? Good boy."

I shuddered. "Fuck you," I moaned as I writhed underneath him. "I'm not a dog!"

"You're right. You're not just any dog, Calix." His hand squeezed around my length and he stroked me faster before he slowed down. Gabriele leaned forward and spat on my cock before he started stroking again and I trembled. "You're *my* dog. Isn't that right, boy?"

I shook my head. "No...no it's not right," I tried to catch my breath but my body was heating up as he picked up speed.

"Liar," he hissed. "Tell Daddy you're his dirty little mutt."

"Fuck!" I cried out as my hips shot upward again and I found myself practically humping his hand. "Stop, Gabriele."

"Stop what? Making you confront what a pathetic little whore you are?" He chuckled and a shiver worked its way up my spine. "Come on, let go. You're so goddamn uptight no wonder you're always freaking out. I know you want to release all of that tension."

Gabriele Bianchi was a bastard. I'd always known that, but now I was up close and personal with a side of him that I'd never seen before. I tried to close my legs to stave off the pleasure, but he used his knee to open them back up and continue to jerk me off.

"I asked you for something," Gabriele said as I stared up at him. "Tell Daddy you're his dirty little mutt. I want to hear you say it."

I shook my head, wishing he'd stop calling himself Daddy. It was getting to me in ways I couldn't begin to explain. "No."

"Say it," he growled as he picked up speed. "I can feel how close you are. Your cock is throbbing in my hand."

"No!"

"Fine." Gabriele removed his hand and I panted as I stared up at him in shock. "If you don't behave, then you don't get rewards." He stood up and started rolling down his sleeve. "You can bring your arms down. I'll see myself out."

Right. He's not holding me down anymore. For some reason my arms had stayed in the same position, my wrists still crossed as if waiting for him to come back. My cock throbbed and pulsed, my balls painfully sore. I'd been so close I could taste it.

"Wait," I whispered, hating myself until he turned around and looked at me curiously. "Please."

"Please, what?" he asked.

"K-keep going."

Gabriele smirked. "Are you ready to play by my rules?"

Shit. The bastard wasn't going to make it easy. I just wanted some relief that didn't come from my own hand. Everything had been so busy between matches, the gym, and helping my father, I hadn't had time to go out and meet anyone. And now I was even busier. There was only so much of my own hand I could take before I craved the warmth of another person. But I never thought that person would be Gabriele Bianchi.

"Going once. Going twice-"

"Yes, sir," I answered quickly.

Gabriele looked me over before he moved back onto the bed. His hand gripped my wrists again and I was finally able to breathe. He leaned down and wrapped his mouth around my cock giving it a few long, deep sucks and leaving it wet and slick once more. I gasped, my toes curling as he sat up and began jerking me off once more.

"Fuck..." I groaned as I pushed my head back against my pillow and shook my head. "So good. So...so damn good."

"Good boy," Gabriele said as he picked up speed slowly but surely. "Tell Daddy exactly what he wants to hear."

Pleasure surrounded me and I couldn't hold back. I pulled against his hands and he pressed down harder. My cock jumped in his hands and I gave up.

"I'm Daddy's dirty little mutt!"

The words barely left my lips before I came so hard I saw stars. I jerked upward, fucking Gabriele's hand as I rode out the orgasm that crashed into me, stealing my breath and making me moan so loud I was sure the neighbors could hear.

Panting, I fell back against the bed and twitched lightly. Finally, I opened my eyes and gazed at Gabriele. He grinned at me before he stood up.

"Good boy. *Now* you'll get some rest. I'll see you again soon."

I was too out of it to say a word to him. Gabriele turned on his heels and walked out of my room. I heard the sound of him in the bathroom cleaning up before he disappeared and the front door closed shortly after.

Sleepiness gripped me and I tried to stay up but it was impossible. Instead, I closed my eyes. My brain was on cloud nine. I could beat myself up for what I'd done with Gabriele later.

Chapter Ten

Calix

"Hey!" Six's loud mouth cut through the chatter of the gym as he walked in with his bag slung over his shoulder. "Where have you been?"

I forced myself to put on a fake smile, but it was an uneasy one. The last week I'd spent hiding out. I knew I couldn't get away from Gabriele forever, but I needed space. My eyes darted around the gym, looking for him, but he was nowhere to be found. Amadeo stood nearby, watching over Six, but I'd gotten used to his presence.

"Around," I said, finally answering Six.

He raised a brow. "What kind of fucking answer is that? You found a boyfriend or something finally?"

I paled and shook my head. "Hell no," I spat. "I don't want or need that."

Six let out a laugh. "Okay, something is going on with you," he said as he put his bag down and nodded. "How's the hand?"

"It's good now. All healed up," I said before I froze. "How did you know about my hand?"

"Gabriele told us a few days ago that you had to get some stitches."

I frowned. *Gabriele was talking about me?* My heart did flip-flops in my chest and I wanted to slap myself. Of course, he was talking about me! He was probably telling Amadeo why he couldn't harass me lately.

"Oh," I said as I moved over to a punching bag and held it steady. "Well, I'm all good now."

Six nodded and pushed his bag to the side before he raised his fists. We always started off with the same warm-up and he was getting better. I held onto the bag as he delivered a powerful jab to it.

"Good form," I told him. "Go again."

"Thanks," he grunted as he took another swing. "It's all because of you," he said before he paused to reach down and grab his water bottle. "So? What's it like?"

"What's what like?"

"You know, working with Gabriele. I know Amadeo put you two together. He's not being a dick is he?"

"Only every second of every day," I muttered.

Six frowned. "Gabriele? You're sure? He was always cool to me at Ama's. I mean he's still cool now, but lately, he's been cranky with this whole thing they're trying to figure out and having to babysit you as he calls it."

I gritted my teeth, my jaw ticking with irritation. "No one asked him to babysit me," I said. "He could let me pay the shit off my way."

Six shook his head. "He can't, Amadeo's orders." Six glanced over at Amadeo and smiled. The man barely raised a brow and Six turned back toward me. "I better shut up before he realizes I'm talking about him. That man gets so testy if he thinks I'm talking too much, but it's just you."

"There's also the fact that I don't *want* to know what's going on with the Bianchi's. The less I know, the less chance I'll get implicated in their bullshit."

"Don't think that's how it works at this point, but I guess," Six said with a shrug before he grinned a little. "At least he's good to look at right? The Bianchi's might be crazy, but I haven't met a single one of them that wasn't hot as fuck. If I wasn't with Amadeo..."

"What was that?"

Both of us jumped. Amadeo had suddenly appeared out of thin air behind Six and I hadn't even seen him walk up. I swallowed thickly and Six swore under his breath.

"N-nothing, Daddy," Six said in a sing-song voice. "I was only kidding around."

Amadeo crossed his arms over his chest. "Pack up your things. We're leaving early," he said shortly before he reached into his jacket and pulled out some cash. He handed it to me. "For today's session. I won't cheat you out of money because Six can't control his mouth."

Six gulped like a cartoon character. "Save me," he whispered.

I gave him an expression that said *what the fuck am I supposed to do?* Amadeo grabbed his arm and I watched as my friend was dragged out of the gym. Shaking my head, I headed back to the office.

Six had called Amadeo Daddy and it threw me right back into bed with Gabriele. The haze of pain medicine had taken over after I blew my load, but I could still remember the way he loomed over me, teasing and tormenting me until I gave in. He was a brute of a man, but damn did I come hard when he touched me.

I groaned and put my face in my hands. "I don't need to be focusing on that shit right now!"

Tonight was another big fight for me. Not in the VFC, but in the underground fights I'd started attending. My last match-up had me injuring my hand, but I wasn't used to the hard ground and the viciousness of the illegal fights. In MMA, there were rules and guidelines. But on the streets, none of that existed. It was fight until the other guy couldn't stand up and if you were unlucky and didn't get back up, well that was the end of that.

I shuddered thinking about it. The sensible side of me screamed to call it quits, but I had people who needed me. *This is the right thing to do.* I stood up and walked over to the wall safe where I had money stashed away. Usually, there were only a few meager dollars in there, but now there was a stack of cash waiting to be given over to Gabriele. If I kept going, I would be able to pay him off a hell of a lot sooner and I would never have to see the man again.

The thought made me smile, but my stomach twisted into knots. I laid a hand on it and frowned. "Must have ate something weird," I muttered, quickly shutting the safe and turning the lock.

I refused to acknowledge the fact that my one time with Gabriele was affecting me.

***

I arrived at the warehouse as close to the fights starting as I could. Hanging out around areas like this was a bad idea, and if anyone saw me here I would have my ass handed to me. My coach was still out of town visiting his daughter, but he would be back soon and I knew he liked to keep an eye on his fighters. As he put it, fighters were overgrown children with more temper and he didn't have time to be pulling my ass out of the fire.

As I moved through the crowd, I tugged my hoodie down and looked from underneath it. There was already a crowd, beer, and the heavy smell of weed smoke. I slipped through and headed off to the side to wait until it was my turn.

One by one, men and women filed into the ring and fought. I watched them, studying each of their moves as I warmed up. By the time I was called, my heart pounded so hard I felt dizzy. I sucked down some water trying to calm down.

"Carlos! Are you fighting or not?"

I put my water bottle down and jogged over. "Fighting," I said as I slipped off my hoodie and tossed it onto a box over on the side of the makeshift "ring".

My opponent, Mickey, stepped forward and sized me up. He was a bit taller than me, but I didn't mind. Being big didn't mean you were going to win. I was known for my speed and I could take on someone twice my size as long as I avoided their hits.

"Fight!"

That shout woke me up and I dodged as my opponent dove toward me. He tried again, but I kept moving.

"Hit him! Stop fucking dancing around!"

I ignored the crowd. What they were saying was irrelevant. I didn't care about putting on a good show, I only cared about winning. Once the man in front of me, Mickey, was down, I would walk away with the money to save my gym and get the mafia off my back. That was the only thing that mattered.

We came together and his fist connected with my chest as mine drove into his chin. The stunned look on his face made up for the pain that blossomed over my skin and vibrated through my chest. I went back in again but moved after he swung. As soon as he was too far to defend himself, I moved back in and kneed him in the side.

The crowd cheered and I felt the same sense of adrenaline that I felt when I was in a professional fight. My goal wasn't to become popular here, but there was nothing as good as a fight to get the blood pumping.

Mickey lunged at me and wrapped his arms around my waist. I refused to go down and instead, I punched him in the back repeatedly as I tried to force him to release me.

"Go down you fuckin' prick!" he yelled.

"Fuck you," I snapped.

I finally elbowed him in the neck and he hit the ground with a grunt. But he was up again in seconds, his face red as he huffed and panted. I still wasn't out of breath and I smirked at him. The growl that left his throat didn't scare me at all.

Gabriele Bianchi growled a lot harder than that.

He charged at me and I sidestepped him only for him to change course. Strong, calloused hands grabbed me and my back slammed against the concrete floor. All of the air whooshed out of my body and I sucked in nothing as I tried to curl up and fend off his blows.

Breathe. Goddamnit, breathe! I'm not about to let this big asshole take me out! If I lose, I don't get shit.

I forced myself to breathe and finally, I sucked in a shaky breath. But it was enough. As he wailed on me, I turned over and his fist collided with my face. I felt the blood run down as flesh split and I was half-blinded by the stuff.

But it didn't matter. He'd gotten too close and I was going to make him pay for that.

I wrapped my legs around his neck as he tried to fight me off. He panicked as he realized what I was trying to do, but I was already moving faster than he could stop me. I locked my legs around his throat and yanked his head down.

Triangle chokes were my favorite fucking move and I watched as he panicked to get out of it. He turned from a man to a snarling, growling animal. We both knew the truth.

He was done. There were only two options; tap out or pass out. And I was okay with either one.

I squeezed harder with my thighs and he finally tapped out.

"That's it! The fight goes to Carlos!"

The crowd erupted into cheers and I released my hold on Mickey. He sat there trying to catch his breath as I stood up and panted. I reached out a hand, and he took it reluctantly before he groaned.

"You're a fast fucker, aren't ya?" he asked. "Shit, thought I had ya for sure."

"It was a good round. You almost did."

Mickey grinned. "Aye. You're takin' all my money tonight so I expect a drink."

I laughed. "Sure, why not. One drink," I said before I shook my head relieved that he took it so well. "It's the least I can do."

He patted me on the back. "Good lad. I like you." He nodded to the side of the ring. "Let's clear out and watch the next bastards get beaten." We moved out of the way and he opened his bag before he tossed me a towel. "For your eye."

"Shit," I muttered as I reached up and hissed. "How bad is it?"

"You still got the eye haven't you?"

I burst out laughing and the tension dissipated. There had been a few people I'd gone up against who were angry and bitter when they lost, but this guy didn't seem too torn up. Instead, he hung around with me until it was time to pick up our earnings from the next few rounds and I decided to buy him that drink after all.

At least I had one person watching my back here.

Chapter Eleven

Gabriele

I couldn't stop looking at Calix. The shiner around his eye was prominent as hell and I gripped the steering wheel even more tightly. First, he'd been avoiding me. But that didn't matter because I kept a constant eye on him. However, I had to work sometimes too and I hadn't laid eyes on him in three days.

"Stop staring at me," he snapped finally before he sucked in a breath. "Jesucristo, you've been doing that all night!"

"I haven't."

"You have," he shot back, crossing his arms over his chest like a child. "I can see out of the corner of my eye you know."

"Can you?" I asked. "Cuz you have a big ass shiner that I was sure you couldn't see past."

Calix flipped me off. "Can you drive the car before we end up crashing into something? *Eres un dolor en mi culo*."

I glared at him. "Don't start your shit with me. I wouldn't have to be a pain in the ass if you wouldn't make me this way," I snapped.

He stared at me. "You know what I'm saying?"

"I'm trilingual. No shit I know what you're saying, asshole," I said as I switched lanes and glanced back at him. "Where'd you get the shiner?"

"None of your business."

I rolled my eyes. "Why are you acting like this, Gonzalez? Huh? Is it because you want me to pull over and fuck you in the back seat? Are you waiting for me to hold you down and make you moan for me again?"

He shuddered and turned away from me. "I didn't want it the last time and I sure as hell don't want it this time," he grumbled.

I laughed. "You're telling me you *didn't* want it? Seriously?"

He turned on me and frowned. "Yeah, that's what I'm saying!" he snapped. "You waited until I was all drugged up before you decided to take advantage of me."

There was no way he was serious.

I stared at Calix for what felt like ages. Every time his eyes cut to my direction, I continued to look at him between glances at the road.

"What?" he finally asked.

"You're full of shit," I answered. "I had you squirming for me and begging to cum before those goddamn pills even kicked in. Don't make it like I need to drug you to get what I want. We both know you were a dog in heat for just my hand."

"Fuck you," he growled.

I shook my head. "I didn't do anything you didn't want."

"Really? How many times does someone have to say stop and no for you to realize they might not want it?"

"I told you I would stop, remember? And I walked away. You *begged* me to come back."

"I was drugged," he argued.

My grip on the steering wheel tightened. No one could get under my skin, but apparently, Calix Gonzalez was the goddamn exception.

"You think I need to drug you to get some ass? I could have anyone I want, Calix, and they would be begging for my cock. So don't sit there and act like I need to force you into anything to get off."

"Okay, then go be a man whore somewhere else because it's not happening with me."

I wanted to strangle him. When I glanced at Calix he looked even more pissed off than he'd been before. And I couldn't leave it alone.

"Don't be embarrassed because you called me Daddy and came so hard you almost passed out," I said.

Calix turned completely in his seat and stared at me with huge eyes. "I didn't- You don't-"

I pulled over and parked. "We're here," I said cutting him off as he stumbled over his words. "Come along, mutt."

I climbed out of the car and shut the door as Calix commenced barking. He was a cute little mutt, but he really didn't know when to shut the hell up. I paused as I reached the front of the car.

Did I just think Calix was cute? When did I hit my head? I had to if I'm thinking Gonzalez is anything other than a pain in the ass.

Calix climbed out of the car with a frown etched on his face. He wouldn't look at me and I wanted nothing more than to shove him against my car and demand answers. Did he really think I'd drugged him to get him to sleep with me? If that was it, why the hell did I leave his house hard as hell? I'd been satisfied enough that he felt good and was going to get rest. If he was just another toy for me to stick my dick in, then I wouldn't have left until I'd gotten off too.

I closed my mouth as we headed for the bar. Even if I brought it up again, he was going to say he didn't want it, but I knew that was a goddamn lie. The look in Calix's eyes when I'd been ready to leave had been desperate and pleading. It was the whole reason I'd gone back to him so I didn't have to see that damn expression.

"Who are we here for?" Calix asked as we stepped inside.

"Seth Hills," I answered shortly.

He glanced at me. "Again?"

"Again."

Calix stared at me for a minute before his mouth opened and he shut it again. Whatever he was about to say, he cut it off and scanned the bar. I did the same and saw our target in the back, hunched over, nursing a beer.

I moved through the smoky crowd. Most people moved out of my way automatically and I slipped between the rest of them until I was approaching Seth's table. He glanced up just as I reached the side and bolted.

"This shit again, Hills? Really?" I called.

"Please, leave me alone!" he yelled as he made a beeline for the front door.

"At least he's not stupid enough to try the back again," I muttered as I turned on my heels and waved a hand at Calix. "Get that bastard!"

Calix took off after him. He was closer to Seth than I was and as he grabbed the man they both crashed through the front door. The bar owner shook his head at me and I reached into my pocket and tossed some bills toward him.

"Sorry for the commotion. We'll be out of your hair shortly."

The man snatched up the cash and nodded in approval after a minute. "Alright. Fine."

I nodded and turned on my heels. I walked outside and looked around for Calix. My heart raced when I didn't see him and I trekked around the side of the building before I saw him with Seth. My heart slowed once I saw he was alright. He had the man's collar gripped tightly in his fist, but he still looked unsure.

I'm going to show you what kind of trash we're dealing with here, Calix. Maybe then you'll stop seeing me as an asshole and nothing more.

As I walked toward Seth, he started breathing heavier. He pulled back as if he could get away from me, but Calix held him in place.

"Seth, here we are again," I said as I sighed. "You have the money?"

He made a strangled sound and shook his head hard. "N-no, I don't have anything," he said, his skin pale underneath the arc of yellow light from the streetlamps. "I-I thought I had more time."

"You don't," I said as I stepped toward him. "Especially when I realized those bills you gave me last time were forged."

I didn't think he could get any whiter, but the man turned as pale as a sheet of paper. His knees gave out as he tried to sink to the ground, but Calix held him steady and he couldn't give into his dramatics the way he wanted to. I looked at him as if he was nothing more than a bug to crush underfoot as he babbled about why he didn't have the money.

Finally, I held up a hand. "Seth, stop talking. I think we can come to an arrangement." I moved forward until he was right up against me. He stared up, unblinking and shivering so hard I could practically hear it. I reached into his pocket and pulled out his wallet. After searching for a moment, I found what I was looking for. "Who's this?" I asked as I took out the picture and showed it to him.

"Th-that's my daughter," he whispered before he stared at me with wet eyes. "Please, don't hurt her."

I waved a hand. "I don't want to hurt her," I said as I tapped the photo and tilted my head at him. "I want to know, how old is she?"

"Sixteen," he stammered.

I nodded. "Old enough," I said as I rubbed my chin. "Give her to me and I'll erase your debt."

Seth paused and stared at me, his eyes so wide it was almost comical. "Give you...my daughter?"

"Melissa, right?" I asked as I gazed at the picture. "She would fetch a good amount if I sold her. Yeah, I could erase your debt for her."

"Gabriele," Calix choked out.

I held up a hand and looked at Seth. "What do you say?"

He shook his head. "W-what would she have to do?"

I grinned. "I think we both know the answer to that, Seth. Besides, that would be none of my problem. Whoever purchased her could do whatever they wanted. But your debt would be gone."

Seth opened his mouth and closed it again before he closed his eyes. "Okay," he said shakily. "But I don't owe you a dime anymore, okay?"

I nodded. "Fair trade," I said as I stuck out my hand.

Seth shook it and I waved a hand. "Let him go."

Calix stared at me in shock before he finally released the man. We both watched as Seth started to scurry away before he turned back around to us.

"Um, if she would get so much money, can't I have some of it? I-I'm losing a daughter after all."

I laughed, the sound threatening even to my ears. "Disappear, Seth. Before I feel the need to bash your brains in, you parasitic fuckin' maggot."

Seth turned and ran away so fast he slipped and ate dirt. He picked himself up and kept running, scurrying right back into the bar that we'd snatched him out of. I shook my head until I was shoved and I stumbled back.

"What the fuck?" Calix asked, his face red with rage. "What the fuck was that!"

"Right," I said as I dug out my phone and dialed a number. I waited until my call was answered. "I need Melissa Hills picked up and taken to a new location. No, give her a good apartment, one of the ones under our name. If he's willing to sell her to us, I guarantee he's tried it before. Yeah. Look for next of kin."

"What the fuck!" Calix shouted once I hung up.

I slipped a cigarette out of the pack and lit it up before I exhaled smoke into the night air. "I told you before, Calix. Men like this aren't good people. They're not victims. You saw how quick he was to hand his daughter over even though he knew what would happen to her? Seth Hills is the tip of the iceberg when it comes to the goddamn scumbags I deal with." I shrugged. "You needed to see who he really was. Maybe next time, you won't hesitate to do what needs to be done."

Calix frowned. "W-what? But he might be the only one who would-"

"He's not," I interrupted. "Eventually, I give all these non-paying douchebags the option to sell their children, wives, mothers. And they all take me up on it. They want all the benefits without any of the consequences. Men like that? There's no hope for them."

Calix swallowed thickly. "The girl... You're not really going to sell her. Are you?"

I shook my head. "Fuck no. I don't deal in that shit. The whores we own are legal age and always will be. Amadeo would skin me alive if I even tried some disgusting shit like that and I would off myself if I ever even had a *thought* like that. I might be a murderer, but I'm not a pedo." I adjusted my suit jacket and nodded toward the car. "Now, move your ass. We've got more work to do."

Calix stared at me and I saw emotions flash over his face one after the other. Finally, he started to move, but he was quiet. I stopped him when we reached the car and laid a hand on his chest.

"Oh and if you ever push me like that again? I'll kick your ass."

He groaned. "You weren't an asshole for two whole minutes."

"Yeah, two. See that? It was a world goddamn record."

"I hate you."

As we climbed into the car, I chuckled before I winked at him. "Whatever you say, mutt."

As Calix protested, I pulled out of the parking lot. When I glanced back, I saw into the bar where Seth stood at the counter and ordered another probably shitty beer.

Enjoy it while you can, asshole. Soon you won't drink anything ever again.

Some festering limbs needed to be cut off completely. And Seth Hills was a gangrenous pile of flesh just waiting to be sliced away.

Chapter Twelve

Calix

Gabriele was set on trying to convince me that the world was shit. But I wasn't buying it. Yes, there were horrible people, but there were good ones too. I stared at the pan of food I was cooking and frowned as I thought about Seth Hills.

I shivered. *There are people who would sell their own children?* I thought about my father and my chest tightened. He hadn't sold me, but he had forced me to deal with the Bianchi's while he ran off. I still had no idea if he was alive or dead and while I was pissed, I prayed he was okay.

My phone buzzed on the countertop and I scooped it up. Gabriele. I groaned and stared up at the ceiling before I put the phone back down. *Not right now.* I needed ten minutes to myself before I was immersed in whatever ridiculousness Gabriele wanted me to get involved in. He wouldn't let me live it down how I'd cum for him, and between him dangling that in my face and making me be his muscle, I was done dealing with his crap.

The phone stopped buzzing and I sighed. "Thank God. I'm surprised you can take a hint," I muttered to myself.

"I can't."

I jumped, the pan slipping from my hand. The grilled cheese I was making hit the floor and I hopped out of the way barely avoiding taking out one of my toes with the pan. I grabbed the front of my shirt and turned on Gabriele.

"What the fuck!" I yelled. "How did you get into my house?"

"Don't worry about it," he said as he walked over and picked up the pan before placing it back on the stove. He shut it off before he bent down and discarded the grilled cheese. "Why didn't you pick up my call?"

I stared at him. "Why did you call me when you were already here?"

"To see if you would pick up," he said with a shrug as he walked closer to me and pinned me against the counter. "And don't try to sidestep the question. Though I do admire it. You pulled a classic me technique."

"Yeah, I'm learning horrible habits from the best," I spat.

Gabriele grabbed my chin and grinned. "Why are you always in such a bad mood? Didn't you miss me?"

I swallowed thickly before I rolled my eyes. "Hell no. And I just saw you last night, what are you talking about?" I planted a hand in his chest and shoved him back. "Get out of my house. You smell like a brewery," I said picking up on it for the first time. "Where the hell were you?"

"Taking care of business," he said.

"Did you drive here?" I demanded. "If you kill someone because you're driving around like a dumbass while you're drunk-"

"You could be worried about *me* you know," he said as he pressed up against me again. "What if I died?"

"Then the world would be a better place," I shot back.

Gabriele's face fell and he pulled back a bit. "Huh, you're probably right," he said as he turned around and pushed his fingers through his hair. "*Hai assolutamente ragione.*"

I stared at his back, but he didn't turn and look at me. Slowly, I stepped forward and laid a hand on his arm. Gabriele finally shifted around and stared at me as if he had no idea where he was. The recognition finally filled his eyes and he shook his head.

"Come have a drink with me," Gabriele said, the somber look still lingering on his face.

"Me?" I asked, incredulously. "Are you sure you want me?"

Gabriele nodded. "Yeah, come on Gonzalez. What the hell else do you have to do?"

Besides getting drinks with a dangerous, drunk, psychopath who's trying to get in my pants? Oh nothing.

Before I could even think of saying those words, I swallowed them down. *He's going through something.* I glanced around my kitchen and sighed. I hadn't been doing anything anyway. A sandwich, a beer, and bed had been the only things on my agenda. Besides, what I'd said was out of line. I felt like I should say sorry, but it was easier to except his invitation.

"Yeah, alright," I finally gave in. "But only because you look like a pathetic puppy right now."

Gabriele smirked. "But you're the puppy, Calix. Isn't that right?"

I shivered. "Shut up or I'm not going."

"Alright, alright. Let's go!"

Gabriele moved through my house as if he'd been there a thousand times. It was dark outside and I could barely see, but he had no issues navigating. *You've been in my house more than you let on, haven't you? Note to self. Change the locks.*

"Wait, I need to put some clothes on," I said as I glanced down at the workout shorts and t-shirt I wore. "Give me five minutes."

Gabriele groaned. "Fine. I'm gonna smoke."

He let himself out and a minute later I heard him fumbling with his lighter. A long, slow exhale followed and I shook my head. *I'm getting way too used to him.*

I climbed the stairs so I could change . I wasn't sure where we were going, but I went for something casual, but not too laid-back. A pair of blue jeans and a lavender button-up shirt, and a comfortable pair of sneakers. I stripped out of my clothes and redressed quickly before I pulled my hair up into a bun and jogged down the stairs. When I stepped onto the front porch, Gabriele sat on a chair blowing smoke into the air.

"I'm ready," I said.

He gazed up at me and froze. I waited for him to have some smart-ass thing to say, but instead, he continued to stare. Fire blazed behind his eyes and his lips parted as if he had something to say before he closed them again. I shifted from foot to foot suddenly self-conscious under his gaze.

"What?" I asked.

Gabriele opened his mouth and snapped it shut again. "Nothing."

He stood up and I followed him down the stairs. *What's wrong with him tonight?* It was like someone had replaced Gabriele with a doppelganger. My stomach twisted and I laid a hand on it.

Was I really worried about what Gabriele Bianchi thought of me?

***

"Another round!" Gabriele yelled over the loud music that thumped away in the club.

The waitress winked at him and he grinned back at her. I watched until she disappeared into the crowd, a frown on my lips. Gabriele slapped a hand onto my thigh and squeezed drawing my attention back to him.

"Isn't this better than your old man routine?" he asked a slight slur to his words.

I raised a brow. "What are you talking about?"

"You know," he said with a dismissive wave of the hand. "When you come home, grab a beer and a sandwich, sit in front of the Tv for a little while and then go to bed. It's your routine. Every night it's the same thing." He paused. "Except for lately. Where have you been going at night?"

I stared at Gabriele in disbelief. "You *have* been watching me! What? Are you stalking me?"

Gabriele waved his hand again. "No, just keeping an eye on you," he said. "Stop looking at me like that!"

I shook my head. "That's *stalking,*" I said. "You get creepier every damn day," I huffed as I crossed my arms over my chest.

"Don't be like that," he said as he leaned toward me until his shoulder brushed against mine. "Have a drink! When have you ever been to a place like this?"

I glanced around the club. Gabriele no doubt knew I'd never stepped foot in a place as fancy as Luxin. We were above everyone else in a private area and sat on soft, plush, red couches. The smell of smoke was heavy up here both weed and cigarettes and Gabriele only added to it. He picked up his pack of cigarettes and slipped one between his lips. Before he lit, it the woman from before dressed in the tiniest little skirt wandered back over to us with a smile on her face.

"Your Hanger 1," she said with a grin. "Want me to open it for you, Mr. Bianchi?"

Gabriele winked at her. "Do it, doll."

She giggled and I rolled my eyes. *He's not falling for this act, right?* People tripping over themselves had to be something he was used to by now. *So why the fuck is he flirting with little miss blonde and skanky?*

"How about your friend?" she asked as she gazed at me. "Think he wants a drink?"

"Calix is too uptight," Gabriele chuckled. "How about *you* do some shots with me instead?"

"Gladly," she said as she sat on his knee and poured. "Open wide," she exclaimed, that fake giggle spilling out of her pink lips.

I stood up abruptly as my face heated. "You don't need me to drink and flirt. I'm going home."

"Calix, come here," Gabriele called.

I shook my head. "No thanks. Goodnight," I said tersely before I turned on my heels and headed for the stairs. The sound of a shriek and cursing made me turn back around. Gabriele's waitress sat on the ground, rubbing her ass as she glared at us. But Gabriele wasn't focused on her as he jogged up to me. "What are you doing?"

"Keeping you company so you don't act like a little brat and leave," he said as he grabbed me and pulled me against his body. "What? You want Daddy's attention all to yourself?"

I narrowed my eyes at him. "Fuck off."

"Jealousy is a good look on you," he said as he grabbed my cheeks. "But I've only got eyes for you, Gonzalez."

I stared at him in shock. *He's drunk and screwing with me. That's it.* My heart pounded so fast I couldn't get it to slow down. I tried to pull away from him, but Gabriele dragged me back and pressed his lips against mine.

My eyes widened as he kissed me while my heart skipped a beat. I battled between pushing him away and staying right where I was. In the end, I stood there and my mouth moved against his. His hands slipped from my face to my sides and he held me tightly as his breath feathered across my lips.

And then he *moaned*.

My cock stiffened, and I shoved him away from me so fast he almost fell down. He stared at me confused, and I panted as I tried to think of something, anything to get my head back on straight. Instead, I stood rooted to the spot, panting as my lips tingled and my cock ached.

"That's it," I snapped. "I'm taking you home."

"You don't know where my house is." He laughed as he stared at me with glassy eyes.

"I'm sure your driver does."

Gabriele grabbed me tightly and buried his face against my neck. "Take me home with you," he slurred. "One more drink and then I'll go. Quietly. Otherwise, I'll cause a scene. You don't want that, do you?"

I groaned. "Again with the threats?" I'd almost softened for the bastard, but he somehow found a way to mess it up.

He pulled back and looked at me closely. "Okay, I take it back," he said as he gripped my shirt like a lost child. "But I want to go home with you."

I stared at him. *Say no. Say no. Say no!* My mouth refused to form the words as he practically pouted at me. *Who knew the man was even capable of making a face like that?*

"I'm not fucking you," I warned him. "If that's what you want, go get your waitress."

"I don't care," he mumbled. "We don't have to fuck," he whispered, his breath brushing against my neck. His lips followed and I felt the faintest kiss. "I don't want to go home tonight."

What the hell is his angle? Everything he did was calculated, but not this. When I pulled back, I stared at him underneath the muted lights and frowned.

"What's wrong with you?" I asked.

"Nothing," Gabriele answered as he avoided my gaze a bit.

"Alright," I said as I gave in. I couldn't take that sad look on his face for one more second. "One drink and then we're going."

Gabriele lit up. "Alright, but you have to drink with me."

I sighed. "If I have a drink, will you calm down?"

"I'll be a fuckin' angel." He grinned as we moved back to the couch, his eyes on me the whole time. He patted my cheek roughly. "Pour 'em up, Gonzalez."

"Calix," I said as I grabbed the bottle. Gently, I took his hand off of my cheek so I could focus. "Whenever you call me Gonzalez, it reminds me of my dad."

Gabriele nodded. "Calix, then," he said as he picked up the shot I offered him. "To a good night."

I stared at him for a moment before I clinked my glass against his. "To a good night."

We threw back our shots and my throat burned. I sat our glasses down and thought about it before I grabbed the bottle. Gabriele was right about one thing. My usual routine of going home and sitting alone wouldn't do anything for me. Dad was gone and I couldn't stand going back to that quiet, empty house. I wanted to live, just a little.

"I thought we were only having one," Gabriele mused.

"Another one can't hurt," I said with a shrug.

"Good boy," he cheered as he slapped me on the back. His hand lingered on the spot, but I didn't shrug him away. He smiled. "Let's have some fun."

My face heated and I forced myself to focus on pouring the drinks. If I looked at him for too long with alcohol pumping through my system, I would make a stupid decision. One would result in me cumming all over him again.

Chapter Thirteen

Calix

"I've gotta take a piss," Gabriele muttered as we stumbled out of the club.

"Then do it," I said as we rounded the building. "But hurry up." I almost slipped and burst out laughing. "Shit, I'm gonna kill myself."

Gabriele barked out a laugh. "Stop! I'm not trying to piss all over these pants. They're expensive."

"Idiot," I said as I shook my head. "Fuck your fancy pants and go already!"

I stared up at the sky while Gabriele fumbled with his zipper. The world was a bit spinny, but I felt good. How long has it been since I had a drink with someone?

Too long. I should do this more often.

"Ah, fuck," Gabriele swore, grabbing my attention. "I hate this goddamned zipper," he muttered before he started speaking rapid Italian. "You motherfucker," he growled.

I waved a hand. "Move, I'll get it." I reached down and fumbled with his stuck zipper. "Are you sure I'm not *your* Daddy?" I asked with a grin.

Gabriele shoved a hand beside my head and pinned me against the wall. "I'll show you exactly who Daddy is, *Tesoro.*"

I swallowed thickly before I shoved him away. "Do you want me to help you get this down or not?"

"Only if you turn around against that wall and let me fuck you afterward."

I groaned. "What did I say? Didn't I say I'm not fucking you?"

"You say that, but your eyes say you want Daddy's big, thick c-" I unzipped him quickly and he jumped. "Shit, you could have injured it!"

"You would deserve it." I laughed.

"Ugh, I'm way too drunk," he mumbled as he fumbled with his pants. "Hey, help me out."

I raised a brow. "How the hell am I supposed to help you out?"

"Grab my dick and aim," he said with a smirk.

"Fuck no!"

Gabriele clicked his tongue and wagged a finger at me. "Is that any way to talk to your boss? Get on with it, boy. Grab it and aim."

I groaned. "Gabriele..."

"What? Are you afraid that if you touch it you might want it?"

God, I hate him. He was the worst, but he looked cute with his stupid squinted eyes and the dusting of pink on his cheeks from the alcohol. I'd never seen him anyway but completely put together, but this side of him was so much more interesting.

"Fine," I said as I rolled my eyes. "But you owe me."

"Nope," he answered. "I think you still owe me."

"Aggravating asshole," I muttered as I reached out and wrapped my hand around his cock. "Go already before we get caught and end up sitting in jail for the night."

Gabriele chuckled as he leaned his face toward me. "What? You think there's a cop in this city who would even try that shit? You're so naive."

I groaned. "Please don't talk about bribing the cops to me. I want to believe there's not just scum in Atlanta."

He barked out a laugh. "Naive *and* optimistic. How cute, *Tesoro*," he said in that intoxicating accent of his. A moan left his lips and I heard the splash of his piss hit the ground. "Fuck, that feels so damn good right now."

My face felt like it was about to burst into flames. "Can you enjoy this less?"

"Fuck no," he groaned as he moved back and gazed down. "Your hand around my cock while I piss? Now, that's hot as hell."

"There's something wrong with you," I said, but I gazed down despite my protest.

My cock jumped hard. There *was* something tantalizing about holding him while he took his piss that made me squirm. It was as if he didn't have to do a damn thing, not even hold himself, because I was there to do it.

Shit. This vodka is making me think crazy crap.

"Are you going to shake? Or stare at my dick all night, *cane?*"

I coughed and cleared my throat before I shook his cock and released him. "You're disgusting. And stop speaking Italian to me. What the hell is *cane*?"

Gabriele zipped up and draped his arm over my shoulder. "It means dog," he whispered against my ear before he planted a kiss on my cheek. "*Perché sei il mio cane.*"

I glared. "I'm not your dog!"

"Yeah you are." He laughed, pulling me back as I tried to escape. "And I'll make you bark for me."

I rolled my eyes and stepped right past that sentence that did funny shit to my stomach. "If *cane* is dog," I said. "What is Te-te-"

"*Tesoro?*" he asked.

"Yeah, that."

Gabriele raised a hand when we hit the sidewalk. "Don't worry about that." As the car pulled up, he opened the door. "Get in."

I stared at him. "What does it mean?" I prodded.

"In," he growled.

A shiver ran up my spine. Even with the huge smirk on his lips, I still reacted to that growl. It was deep and primal. For a moment I imagined him making that sound against my ear while I was stuffed with his cock before I quickly dismissed the thought. I had put boundaries in place and I needed to abide by them. I slipped into the backseat and he moved in behind me.

"You can drop me off at my place," I said to the driver.

Gabriele turned and stared at me. "Are you going back on what you said?" he slurred as he grabbed onto my shirt with both hands and yanked me forward. "Let's try that again."

I stared at him with wide eyes. "Not until you let me go."

"I don't want to," he muttered. "Change it, Calix."

"Fine, fine, you can still come over!" I huffed before he released me and fell back against the seat. "You're a terrifying and crazy drunk."

Gabriele dug into his pocket and popped a cigarette in his mouth. "Ama always said it's because I hold everything in day and night so when I drink, *pop* there goes the cork in my brain and all the shit spills out." He fumbled with his lighter. "Whatever that means."

I knew exactly what his brother meant. When I was younger, all I did was hold in my emotions until they boiled over. It was the whole reason I got into boxing and then Krav Maga and finally MMA. The only way I let out my stuffed down emotions was when I fought, and having that outlet stopped me from getting expelled from school.

Gabriele dropped his lighter and swore. I reached down and scooped it up before I rolled my thumb over the spark wheel. The flame danced on the expensive-looking lighter and I lit Gabriele's cigarette before I closed and looked at it.

"This looks old," I said, rubbing it a bit. "Surprised you keep anything old around."

"It was my father's." Gabriele stared at it before he glanced away. "He gave it to me when he died. In the will, I mean." He blew out a cloud of smoke.

Frowning, I laid a hand on Gabriele's leg. He didn't move it away but he wouldn't look at me either. My stomach tightened. But what made me stiffen was the way he let out a muffled sound and a shuddering breath. *Was he...crying?* Gabriele Bianchi wouldn't cry and definitely not in front of me. *Right?*

"I'm sorry," I whispered as I squeezed his leg. "About your father. What...what happened to him?"

Gabriele turned to look at me before he snatched the lighter from my hand. He shoved it into his pocket, rolled down the window and ashed out of it. I waited, my breathing burning in my throat, but he didn't say another word. For once, he was quiet.

We pulled up to my place and Gabriele leaned forward. "Take off," he told the driver. "But leave me the keys. Have someone pick you up or walk for all I care."

"Yes, sir, Mr. Bianchi," the driver said with a nod. He turned off the car and handed back the keys.

Gabriele took them and climbed out of the car. I followed behind him and trudged up the stairs as my mind raced. What was Gabriele hiding?

He flipped through the keys before he found what he was looking for and stuck one into my door. I stared, dumbfounded as he let himself in.

"Y-you need to give me that key," I snapped as I stumbled in after him.

"No way in hell," he said as he walked to the couch and plopped down. "Get me a drink."

I grabbed a handful of his hair and pulled his head back. Gabriele stared up at me with wide eyes.

"Get up and get in the shower," I said as I tugged. "Come on, you're not sleeping on my furniture in those clothes. You smell like smoke and whore perfume."

Gabriele burst out laughing. "You mean the girl you were jealous of?"

I released his hair. "I wasn't jealous."

"Liar."

"Fine, you stay down here. I'm taking a shower," I said as I turned on my heels. "Goodnight!"

I walked upstairs and left him with his cigarette. *He's dead wrong. I wasn't jealous. It's just fucking rude to have some girl all over your lap when you're the one that dragged me out of the house. Asshole.* I stumbled into the bathroom and righted myself before I yanked off my clothes. I turned on the shower and glowered at it.

"Hurry up, you slow fucker," I mumbled as I waited for my old water heater to do its thing. As much as he pissed me off, I thought about Gabriele and my body grew warm. I ran a hand down my body and wrapped it around my cock.

Gabriele was right downstairs. If he heard me moaning like a whore, he would never let me live it down. I released myself and let out a strangled sound as arms wrapped around my body.

"I'm taking a shower with you."

I tried to turn around, but those arms grew tighter. "Gabriele, no."

"Let Daddy take a shower," he purred against my ear. "I want to clean you up after you kept me company all night."

I shivered. "Stop calling yourself that."

"You don't like the word, Daddy?" he mused. "Why?"

I chewed my lip and the words spilled out before I could stop them. "I like it too much. I've never called anyone Daddy except in my fantasies, okay?"

As soon as I said it, I cringed. I waited for Gabriele to make fun of me like he always did, but it never came. Instead, he ran his thumb over my nipple before he tweaked it with his fingertips sending a delicious tingle across my flesh.

"I love being called Daddy," he admitted. "Never thought I would, but I'm figuring out there's nothing better than taking care of someone." Gabriele raked his nails down my chest. "Hearing it from your lips? It does things to me," he growled against my ear.

Fuck. What was this man doing to me?

"You're drunk," I panted as he pinched my other nipple and rolled it around.

"So are you," he pointed out. "Tell me what you want Daddy to do to you. Let me help you out like last time."

I sucked in a sharp breath. "W-what I want in a Daddy you can't provide," I answered honestly, the alcohol letting me talk freely. "Patience, care, someone to make sure I'm okay after a hard day and bandage me up or… hold me," I rushed out with a sigh as my cheeks burned. "Those are things that you can't do."

Gabriele's grip on me tightened. "How do you know that?" he asked. "You understand everything about me from what little I've allowed you to see?"

I opened my mouth to answer, but Gabriele turned me around and shoved me until my back connected with cool tiles. My thoughts came to a screeching halt as he dropped to his knees in one fluid motion and slipped my cock into his mouth. I reached down and pushed my fingers into his hair gripping it gently as I rocked forward.

"Gabriele," I groaned. "I said I wouldn't-"

"You said you wouldn't fuck me," he countered as he came up for air. "But you never said I couldn't taste you." He fondled my balls and gave them a squeeze making me groan. "Whatever you think of me doesn't matter right now. Close your eyes and enjoy it."

I gazed down at him. Did Gabriele's cheeks always turn red after he'd had a few drinks? And why did he look so good on his knees looking up at me through his long, dark lashes? *Fuck I'm losing my mind.*

Gabriele licked over my length before he ran his tongue along the bottom of my cock. I moaned, my back arching away from the wall as he traced over the vein underneath. My breathing picked up and I let out an embarrassing whimper.

"Good boy," Gabriele moaned as he kissed my cock all over. "The way you take it from me is so fucking hot." He grabbed my ass and squeezed, his nails digging into my flesh. "You're pretty much fucking my mouth every time I slide you inside." Gabriele winked at me. "Tell me you don't want me now."

I laid my arm over my mouth and bit it roughly. *No, if I don't shut up, I'm going to say something I'll regret. Like how good he feels. How fucking amazing he looks with his lips wrapped around me.*

He chuckled. "It's okay. This will be our little secret," he said as he spread my asscheeks and I pushed back against him. "No, you said I can't fuck you. Remember?"

I hate myself.

Damn, I didn't *want* to want him, but I did. Gabriele swallowed my cock down and I cried out, the sound muffled against my flesh. With my free hand, I tightened my grip on his hair and jerked forward sharply as pleasure overtook any shred of rational thinking I had left.

Fuck him.

Don't you dare.

Just once. One time and I'll never do it again.

My mind became a whirlwind that I wasn't able to slow. The more Gabriele twisted his tongue around my dick and sucked, his cheeks hollowing with his effort, the more I gave up and let him have me.

For now, he could take me apart.

But I couldn't sink to his level. I couldn't be what he was. And that meant there was no way for this to go beyond what we were doing now. Even if I wondered what he meant earlier when he said I didn't fully know him.

Maybe he could be the type of guy I dreamed about at night, one that would cherish me for everything I was and everything I lacked. The thought made my throat tighten. It was wishful thinking at best and toxic as hell at worst. My cock jumped at the wet warmth wrapped around my length as I stared down at him.

"Gabriele!" I cried out as my arm fell away from my mouth and I rocked into him harder. "Shit, shit, shit. S-so good."

His hand gripped my thigh and he picked up speed. It took everything for me to stay standing upright as an orgasm rocketed through me. Gabriele remained on the ground, his eyes fixed on me as he stuck out his tongue. Spurt after spurt splashed down his throat, but he didn't pull away or let any spill. He held my gaze as he swallowed every drop. My heart raced as I panted and drank in the sight of him. Gabriele finally stood and licked his lips.

"Gabriele," I whispered. "I-"

His lips crashed into mine, his hands all over my body as he pinned me against the wall. I gave in. My lips moved against his and I lost my breath. A symphony of moans spilled out of me as I held onto his shirt tightly and rolled my body against his. By the time he pulled back, my skin was a raging furnace and I was ready to let him do anything he wanted to do to me.

Gabriele pulled his shirt off and tossed it to the side. My eyes lingered on his tattoo. A skull with a rose and a pistol. When he caught me staring, he smiled.

"Family crest of sorts. You gettin' in the shower or what?"

I climbed into the tub, my legs still wobbly. There were a thousand things I wanted to ask him, but I couldn't force my mouth to form words when I felt like I could melt and disappear down the drain happily. I wanted a shower and then the comfort of blissful darkness.

Gabriele grabbed a bar of soap and ran it over my skin. When I tried to reach for it, he smacked my hand away and went back to work.

"Don't touch," he growled.

"Yes, D-" I blinked at him before I cleared my throat. "Okay."

Gabriele smiled, but he didn't make fun of me. Instead, he focused on getting me clean. Under his breath he hummed an upbeat pop song that I recognized as another Kpop hit from my time in his car. As he washed my back and I braced my hands against the wall, I couldn't stop the smile that tugged at my lips.

Maybe Gabriele wasn't so bad after all.

***

I rolled over to get away from the brightness that I could feel even through my closed eyelids. Groaning, I opened one eye and glared at the window.

"Fuck you too," I muttered at the sun.

My head throbbed as I sat up in bed and glanced around. My stomach dropped as I realized what was off about this picture.

I'm alone.

Did Gabriele take off in the middle of the night? My heart raced as I searched for him wildly and cursed him out in my mind for being a dog. I looked around for my phone and finally turned to the nightstand. My cell was there on the charger as well as a bottle of water and two Tylenol. I grabbed the pills and swallowed them down with the water before I allowed myself to smile.

Gabriele.

Bits and pieces of the night before came back to me, but I could barely think straight. All I remembered was Gabriele wrapped around me like a vice every time I woke up and me yelling at him that it was too damn hot for his shit. Of course, he hadn't listened. But I never expected him to.

I moved out of bed and padded around looking for some boxers. Apparently, I'd been too tired to even bother getting dressed after the shower. I shuffled over to the other side of the bed and found another phone on its charger. I clicked the side to check the time and a text popped up.

Glancing over my shoulder, I looked for Gabriele, but he was nowhere in sight. *He's still here.* The weight in my stomach lifted and I turned back around before I dragged my finger down on the screen curiously.

Ama: Are you coming to visit Dad's grave? Gabe I'm worried about you. Call. Or text. Or I'm going to send people after your drunk ass to bring you home.

Ama: Call me.

Ama: Seriously I will hunt you down.

Amadeo sounded worried. But what really struck me was the fact that they were visiting their father's grave. *Is he missing that while he's here with me?* I frowned and stared at the text. *That's why he was all messed up last night, isn't it?*

"What the fuck do you think you're doing?"

I spun around and the phone clattered onto the nightstand. Gabriele stood in the doorway wearing a pair of my sweats that were a size too small for him. In his hands, he carried two plates of food. But my eyes ultimately landed on his pinched expression as he narrowed his eyes at me.

"You're reading my shit?" he snapped as he stepped forward and sat the plates on the bed. Gabriele stormed over and I stepped back. He stared at his phone before he turned on me. "You have a lot of goddamn nerve, Gonzalez!"

My throat felt like it was clogged with sawdust. *Why can't I talk?* I opened my mouth, but nothing came out.

"Answer me," he demanded as he ripped the charger out of the wall. "What the fuck gives you the right to snoop through my shit!"

I swallowed thickly. "It was a mistake, Gabriele," I said quietly. "I went to check the time and I saw..." I closed my eyes and licked my lips before I tried again. "What I mean is uh... I don't know what I mean. But I know why you're pissed off. Your dad-"

"You don't know shit about my father," he sneered as he got in my face. "What's going on in my personal life is none of your damn business. Is it?"

I shook my head. "No, I know it's not. But after last night-"

"After last night you think you have a right to go through my shit?" he snapped. "I swallow your load and in your mind, we're going out now? Are you a moron? Huh?" He shoved a finger into my chest. "Stay out of my goddamn business."

I stared at him as a chill worked its way down my spine. "Gabriele, I-"

"Sir," he snapped. "I'm sir to you and nothing else."

The cold that shot down my back turned to fire. I shoved my hand against his chest and pushed him away from me. The terrifying danger in his eyes was enough to give me the reality check of the century. He was a criminal and a bastard. And I was going to stay far the fuck away from him.

"Leave," I demanded. "You bothered *me* last night. It was you that broke into my place and you that dragged me out and I'm in your business?" I scoffed. The more I talked the more pissed off I became. "I never wanted you around me in the first place. So grab your shit and get out of my fucking house. Now!" I yelled when he didn't move.

Gabriele moved toward me and I flinched involuntarily. He let out a scoff of his own before he turned and stormed out of my room.

A few moments later, I heard the thundering of feet and the slam of my front door. I closed my eyes and sucked in a shaky breath.

Fuck. What was that?

I laid a hand on my chest and tried to calm my racing heart. Anger blazed in my chest, but underneath it was something else. I stared at the door and even though I knew Gabriele wasn't coming back, I waited.

Like a dumbass.

Finally, I sat on the bed and choked back a sensation that I hadn't allowed myself to feel in years. I pushed my fingers into my hair and kicked myself for ever allowing myself to be vulnerable around Gabriele to the point of tears.

This is on me. Naive and stupid.

"Fuck!" I yelled. "Idiot. You damn idiot!"

I shot up from my bed and forced myself to put one foot in front of the other. Gabriele Bianchi was not going to be the reason I fell apart after all these years.

I refused to give him that satisfaction.

Chapter Fourteen

Gabriele

THE CHAOS OF THE FIGHT REACHED MY EARS BEFORE I EVEN entered the building. I tossed my cigarette to the side and stepped on it. A long, high-pitched whistle snatched my attention and I nodded at Nic as he grinned and waved at me like a lunatic.

"Hey, Gabe," he said as he walked up to me, hands shoved into the pockets of his too-tight jeans. "You've finally popped back up."

"Yeah," I said with a shrug.

"Does Amadeo know you're back?" he asked as he glanced around us. "He's been losing his shit for days."

He didn't need to tell me. Amadeo had been blowing up my phone every few hours. I hadn't even listened to the voicemails he left because I knew they would contain the words "motherfucker" and "dumbass" among many others. His text messages gave me a clear view of exactly what he thought about me taking off.

"Are you going in?" Nic asked, changing the subject. "The fight's about to start."

"Yeah, I'm coming."

Nic walked backward as he stared at me. "You're quiet. What's wrong?"

I shook my head. "Nothing. Let's go inside."

He held my gaze for a minute before he turned on his heels and started walking. I calmed down a bit when he did. I'd come out to the fight because Ama would be surrounded by people and I was a hell of a lot less likely to get into a fist fight with him.

We moved through the crowd and made our way to the seats that had been reserved for us. Nic slipped past Amadeo and sat on the other side of Six. Which left one spot for me. Right next to Ama.

Goddamnit.

"Sit down, Gabe," Amadeo said as his eyes slowly slid from the ring to me. "We need to talk."

I smoothed down my tie and took a seat. "I already know what you're going to say."

"Do you?" Amadeo asked as he stared me down, eyes blazing. "If you know what I'm going to say, then why the fuck didn't you get your ass back here faster? We're in the middle of a crisis and you decide to run off!" he hissed.

I tensed under his gaze. "I did. That was a mistake. It won't happen again, Ama. Trust me."

"*Can* I trust you?" he asked. "You left me to cover your mess. And Ma and Nonna? They're pissed off too. You know you can't disappear like that without making them worry."

I frowned. "Yeah, I know," I muttered.

"Why didn't you come visit Dad's grave? You know how much that means to them."

I shrugged, my throat squeezing painfully. How could I explain to him that I couldn't go this year? Every time we went to the cemetery, I broke down in ways they didn't realize. In ways I never allowed them to see because I waited until I was behind closed doors. I couldn't let them know how weak I was every year on the anniversary of Dad's death.

"Gabe," Amadeo called, his voice softer than it was before. "I know it's the hardest on you, but-"

"Don't," I snapped. "It's hard on every one of us. We all lost him."

"Yes, but that's not the point," Amadeo said as he frowned. "You don't take it the same way we do." When I didn't respond, Amadeo continued to stare at me. "You don't have to talk about it with me if you don't want to, but you need to talk to *someone*. I can't have you jeopardizing everything we're doing right now."

"I understand."

He watched me a moment longer and I felt his eyes as they tried to pick me apart. But I kept my face stoic. I wasn't ready to be seen.

"Are we done?" I asked shortly.

Ama raised a brow at me. "We're done. For now."

I felt his eyes linger on me before he turned to watch the fight. My body relaxed for all of five minutes before I tensed again. Calix walked into the ring, his hair pulled up into a bun. On the side of his face was another bruise. But I knew for a fact that he hadn't had a match while I was gone.

Where is he getting those from?

Calix glanced out into the crowd and his eyes met mine. My heart skipped a beat. I stayed still, watching him like I always did.

Our last meeting had ended in disaster. I'd tried to stop those nasty words from spilling from my lips, but they wouldn't. I snapped.

He turned away from me and my heart sank. *Fuck.* Calix was headstrong as hell. The next time, we talked I knew he wouldn't have a hell of a lot to say. Or he would tell me off. *Was it insane that I hoped for the latter? At least then he would be talking to me.*

The match started and Six jumped out of his seat as he cheered his friend on. I felt my insides twist as Calix turned and winked at Six before he threw his first punch. *It's like I'm not even here.*

I groaned. *What was I expecting? That he would be waiting for me?*

It was idiotic. Calix and I worked together, that was it. And once he finally made it big in MMA he would pay me off and that would be the end of our relationship. There was nothing there and I was acting like some love drunk teenager.

I remembered the way he looked at me as we drank at Luxin. For a moment, there had almost been something there. I could still taste his the vodka on his lips. His smile had been bright the more he drank and loosened up. And he had touched me of his own free will. A hand on my thigh, his shoulder against mine, his fingers against my cheeks as he brushed off a speck of something that I doubted had even been there.

And his cock. I adjusted my pants and squirmed in my seat as I remembered how amazing it had been to suck him off. That taste stayed burned into my memory. Even now I could imagine it as vividly as if I was transported back in time.

Calix grunted as he hit the ground and I jumped to my feet, my fists tightening as I was yanked from amazing memories to my boy getting hurt. The urge to run up there and beat his opponent into the ground until he stopped twitching came over me. I moved sideways, ready to cause a scene. But a hand wrapped around my wrist and tugged sharply.

"Sit down," Ama demanded. "You're letting your temper get the best of you."

I blinked and I was back to reality. Slowly, I sat down. Six stared at me, his eyes wide. Nic grinned from behind him before he chuckled. My jaw clenched and a sharp pain shot through it as I held myself back.

"What's gotten into you?" Amadeo asked. "You can't watch a fight anymore?"

I waved a hand. "It's nothing," I said as I tried to dismiss my emotions. "I'm good."

"You were about to go up there and cause a scene," he argued. "I'd call that something."

"No, it's fine," I said as I leaned back in my chair and watched the fight.

"If you need to leave..."

"I don't," I snapped. "Fuck, let me enjoy the fight!"

Amadeo glared at me. "I'll give you a pass since I know you're going through shit right now, but the next time you yell at me like that I'll punch you in the face. Am I clear?"

"Crystal," I muttered as I forced myself to calm down.

I turned back to the fight as Calix dodged a hit and came in with a knee that he drove into his opponent's stomach. The crowd erupted around me, but I barely heard them.

I was only focused on Calix.

***

"We're heading out," Amadeo said as he stood up and stretched. He pulled Six to his side. "Are you coming?"

I shook my head. "No. I need to talk to Calix."

"I'm sure you do," Nic mused before he winked at me. "I wasn't aware you could talk with your dick."

Six's eyes widened. "You're fucking Calix?"

I growled. "No, I'm not fucking Calix!"

"Watch it," Ama snapped at me. "Don't raise your voice at him. And I hope that's true. Mixing business with pleasure? That's how you get into trouble. I've warned you all about that."

I rolled my eyes. "Are you serious? Was it business or pleasure when you kidnapped Six?"

Six snickered. Amadeo grabbed him by the back of the head and smothered the man's face against his chest. Six struggled, but Ama held on tight.

"He's got a point," Nic said with a shrug.

"Nic, I will punch you in the diaphragm again," Amadeo ground out as a vein popped up on the side of his neck. "You two aren't an exception to the rule."

"But you are?" I asked.

"Yes!" my brother snapped before he sucked in a deep breath and finally let Six go. "We're leaving."

Six sucked in a breath. "Can you stop trying to kill me?" he scolded. "I wanted to say hi to Calix," he complained as Amadeo led him away.

I moved out of their way and they slipped past me. Six glanced over his shoulder with a grin on his lips and Nic slapped a hand onto my shoulder.

"Make sure you wrap it up," Nic said as he looked at me somberly. "If you knock him up, it'll be a pain."

"Nic, come!" Amadeo called.

I shook my head. "Yes, Nic. Leave."

He chuckled as he walked off with them and I was left alone. I turned and headed for the locker rooms. Security stood outside, but one glance at me and they moved aside. I walked inside and found Calix sitting on a bench. His eyebrows knitted together before he frowned.

"What are you doing here?"

"Congrats on the win," I said as I walked over and then thought better of getting too close to him.

Calix laughed dryly. "Thanks," he muttered as he unwrapped the bandages around his hand and hissed. "Shit."

I moved forward and grabbed it. "It's not as bad as before," I breathed with relief when I saw only bruises and some blood that clearly wasn't his own. "Thought you would need stitches again."

Calix yanked his hand away and glared at me. "I don't need you to be my doctor. I'm fine," he said as he tugged a shirt over his head. "I have to go."

"Wait," I said as he stood up and wavered a bit. "You should take it easy. That fight was brutal."

"I'm fine."

"No, you're not," I growled. "And I'm not letting you drive home like that. You can either get in my car and shut the fuck up or I can knock your ass out and carry you. Which would you prefer?"

He scoffed. "You're not going to come around here and start bullying me," he snapped. "We're boss and unfortunate employee that owes you a shit ton of money. That's it."

Calix tried to walk past me. Everything in me screamed to leave him alone, let him go, but I grabbed his arm instead and slammed him against the wall. He pushed against me, but I pinned him.

"Where are you getting the bruises, Calix?" I asked as I reached out and touched the spot on his face. He hissed and tried to pull away, but I refused to let him. "You didn't have this a few days ago."

"None of your business," he muttered as he tried to push against me again. "Move before I call security and have you dragged out of here."

I searched his face. "Calix, I-"

"Save it," he snapped. "I don't care what you have to say and I don't give a damn about what you do. The next time you have collections, call me. Other than that don't turn up, don't text, don't bother me. I don't care what you do to me. I don't have to speak to you when I'm not working."

My jaw ticked. Calix made me want to choke the hell out of him. I stayed still as I searched his face looking for answers that weren't there. He looked everywhere but at me until he finally couldn't help but meet my gaze.

"Where did you get the bruise?" I asked again. "Is someone hurting you?"

Calix blinked at me before he burst out laughing. "Did you hear what I just said!"

"I don't care what you said," I snapped. "I asked you about that bruise."

"You don't give up," Calix growled. "Get off of me."

"And what if I don't?" I shot back.

His eyes narrowed. "You think I can't kick your ass? I could, easily. But I wouldn't want to end up in a ditch somewhere. So I'm going to tell you one last time to let go of me."

My chest tightened. *He wants nothing to do with me.* I pulled back and he stormed away. I watched him go as my shoulders dropped.

I should lock him up like Ama did to Six.

Except I couldn't do that. Calix needed to fight and run his gym, he couldn't just disappear. And I didn't want to lock him in a cage. No, I wanted something a hell of a lot more impossible.

I wanted him to give a damn about me.

Chapter Fifteen

Calix

The last thing I'd expected to see the night before was Gabriele. He'd appeared out of nowhere and when we'd made eye contact, it took everything in me not to climb out of the ring and ask him what the hell his problem was. At least once I saw him there it spurred my irritation and I focused more than I ever had before.

Thanks for the win, Gabriele.

"Carlos, come over here!"

I glanced up and acknowledged Mickey as he raised his hand. *Maybe one day I'll tell him my real name.* I felt bad about lying to him, but considering I was meeting him in a seedy bar, I had no idea what he was involved with. And I couldn't let anything stain the name I had slowly made for myself in the world of MMA.

Mickey grinned as I walked over. He slid a bottle of beer toward me and I took it. After last night, finally seeing Gabriele after he went a-wall, I needed a thousand drinks. I could still feel his hand touching mine and see the concern etched on his face even though it had been twenty-four hours since I'd been anywhere near him.

He feels bad, but that's his problem.

I sat down across from Mickey. There was another man with him with red hair and a beard. He smiled at me and gave a short nod. I returned the gesture before I picked up my beer and took a long chug of it.

"You alright there, boyo?" Mickey asked.

I shook myself free of the melancholy that sat on my shoulders like stones. "Yeah, yeah I'm alright," I said with a small smile. "What are we doing here and who's this?" I asked, quickly turning the conversation away from me.

"This is Conor Kelley," he said with a nod. "My boss."

Conor reached out a hand. "Carlos, it's nice to meet you," he said and I noted his thick Irish accent that matched Mickey's.

I shook his hand. "Nice to meet you too."

"Skip all the pleasantries," Mickey laughed. "Carlos, you mentioned you needed money fast last time we hung out and I found a perfect solution for you."

I raised a brow. "What kind of solution?"

"It's nothing illegal," Conor cut in as he grinned. "Well, no more illegal than what you've been doing already. Although it's probably more dangerous."

"Okay," I said slowly. "What is it?"

Conor raised a hand. "Let's have another drink first. Do you want a beer or something stronger?"

"Well, I don't know what you're about to ask me to do so let's go with something stronger."

He chuckled. "I like you," he said before he turned to the waitress. "Two shots of your best whiskey. And Mickey, take a hike."

Mickey groaned. "You're so paranoid."

"Go," Conor said calmly.

Mickey gave me an apologetic look before he pushed out of the booth and walked toward the front door. It was just me and Conor now. My stomach clenched and it took everything not to show how nervous this man made me.

"Two shots of whiskey," the woman said as she sat down our drinks.

"Thank you." Conor pushed one over to me. "Can we drop the bullshit?" he asked.

I raised a brow. "I didn't know there *was* bullshit," I said.

Conor's grin widened. "Your name is Calix, right?"

I stiffened. "Does it matter?"

He shook his head. "Not really, but I want you to know that I'm aware of who you are and who you're working for as you pay off your debt. I'm telling you that first because I have a way you can get out of your predicament a lot sooner and if I'm truthful with you, you'll trust me."

"Sounds manipulative and too good to be true," I muttered before I snatched up the shot and downed it. Liquid fire burned my throat and warmth blossomed in my chest. "What do you want?"

"Nothing that will get you in trouble with the Bianchi's," he said. "You've been doing the underground fights and I have one that can make you a lot of money. On top of it, I'll pay you a generous fee just to take part. Win or lose."

"This is sounding more and more dangerous," I said as I gripped my empty shot glass.

"It is," Conor said. "Dangerous, that is." He picked up his glass and threw his shot back like it was nothing. "Amadeo and I both have had issues with someone messing with our livelihoods. They're targeting me as well and I need to know who's doing it." He stared ahead as if he wasn't there, but the expression on his face darkened. "I can't have them running around and going after my people."

I shivered. The look on Conor's face was enough to make a grown man pass out from fear. *Why do I end up surrounded by these terrifying men?*

"Sorry," Conor said as he blinked and glanced around. He leaned forward and I did the same automatically. "I need you to enter that fight and look around while you're there. These men are Russian. Usually, they're not a problem and they might not be. But I need to know what's going on with them. They've been cropping up like weeds." He reached into his jacket pocket and slid me a card. "That's the info for the fight. Ask for Lev. He'll get you in."

I took the card and stared at it. There was a phone number and a street address, but no other specifics. I glanced up at Conor.

I swallowed thickly. "What if I get caught and they find out what I'm doing?"

Conor raised a brow. "I would advise you not to do that. And if they catch you snooping around, find another thing to pin it on because I don't want it coming back to me. You point the finger this way and I'll have to kill you myself."

"That's a lot," I muttered as a shudder consumed every inch of me. When I was offered another shot, I took it.

"No risk, no reward," Conor said.

I frowned as I thought it over. Going where Russians hung out and getting involved in whatever shady shit they were doing didn't sound like my idea of a good time. But if I could save Gonzalez and Sons and get away from the Bianchi's sooner rather than later, wouldn't it be worth it?

"How much reward?" I asked.

Conor opened his hands in an "I don't know" gesture. "A hundred thousand for you to go and check it out. If you bring me good, solid information? I'll double it."

My eyes felt like they were going to fall out of my head. Two hundred thousand dollars! If I got my hands on that kind of money, I would only have a little over a hundred thousand left to pay off. My time working with Gabriele would be cut in half if not more.

"Shit," I mumbled. "I don't think I have a choice."

"There are always choices in life," Conor said. "You could say no and walk away. I won't make you do it. Or you could go, give me shit info and you would still make a lot of money." He grinned. "Granted, if it's all made up bullshit, I'll have to break an ankle or two." He shrugged. "Either way, what you do is up to you."

I slid another shot toward me when it was dropped off and swallowed it down. I coughed as it burned my chest, but I didn't care. This was to save my gym, my family, and my sanity. And if I solved the problem with the Bianchi's, maybe my father would be able to come back home again.

Conor didn't rush me as I thought things through and I appreciated that. Whoever he was, he knew a lot about me, about the Bianchi's, and I was pretty sure he was just like them. Making a deal with one devil to appease another felt like the biggest joke the universe could play on me. Conor insisted I had a choice, but the truth was that I didn't. Either I could drag myself out of my situation or I would end up drowning.

I stuck out my hand. "Alright."

Conor shook it and smiled. "That's what I like to hear. When you go, try to have a look around before and after the rounds. That'll give you more time to figure out what's going on. " He took out a picture and pushed it over to me. "That's what you're looking for. A tattoo. Check out anyone who has it. Keep your head down and your mouth shut and you should be fine."

"Should," I repeated. "I don't love the sound of that." I stared down at the tattoo. It was a skull with a snake bursting from the crown.

"It's the best I can do," he said with a shrug. "If I could send my guys in there without everyone knowing who they were, I would do it. Trust me, I prefer a professional, but I'm paying you this much because you're taking a risk."

"Don't think it will be worth much if I end up with a bullet in my head," I muttered and snagged one last shot. When I stood up I swayed a little. "You already know where I live, don't you?"

"Of course," Conor said with a nod and a smile.

I nodded. *Yeah, he's one of them.* The fact that he knew who Amadeo's family was would have been enough of a tip-off, but the creepy factor, the way they watched people, that was something the mafia apparently loved to do.

"Then I'll ask Mickey to give me a ride."

"Good idea," he said with a chuckle. "I'm sure he's out front smoking."

I nodded. "Okay."

"Carlos," he called and I turned back around. Conor slid me some money. "That's half of what you'll get if you just show up. Keep it safe."

I gawked at the stack of cash. "W-why would you just lay that out like that? Someone might rob you!"

Conor blinked at me before he burst out laughing. "These are all my people and this is my territory. No one would even try that shit," he said as he shook his head. "But thank you, for the laugh. Take it."

I snatched up the money and shoved it into the pocket of my hoodie. *Fifty thousand dollars.* The money felt heavy in my hand and I kept my fist tightened around it so it wouldn't fall out or disappear. Conor might be confident in his people, but I wasn't.

"Good night, *Carlos*," he said.

"Night."

I pushed my way out of the bar and stopped to suck in a deep breath. *Shit. Did that really happen?* Mickey waved me over and I trudged to him with my mind still replaying the conversation I had with Conor.

"Everything go alright?" Mickey asked.

"It went great." I paused. "So your boss, he's..."

"Yeah," Mickey said. "He's a dangerous man, but he's not a bastard. And he's my brother."

I paused. "You're...in the mafia."

Mickey nodded. "The mob. Mafia's the Italians." He chuckled. "I didn't want to scare you off. I told you, Calix. I like you. And I figured I could help you out."

"Thanks," I said. "It's terrifying, but I could use the cash. Can you give me a ride home?"

Mickey tossed his cigarette. "Yep, come on boyo." He slung an arm over my shoulders. "Tell me everything Conor said."

I stared at him. "No way.

"Good man, good man," he said as he shook me and barked out a laugh. "Keep that up and you'll fit right in."

My stomach twisted. *You'll fit right in.* I didn't *want* to fit in with gangsters and mobsters. But every day I was drawn in more.

What was I becoming?

Chapter Sixteen

Calix

My body throbbed as I laid in the bed and stared up at the ceiling. My instinct was to roll out of bed and hit the ground running, but if I moved an inch I would be in pain. I remembered the pills that Gabriele's doc had given me. I hadn't taken all of them and now I was grateful because I needed to take the edge off.

I reached into the nightstand and groaned as my body protested. Between training, MMA fights, and the underground bouts that I had agreed to, my body was ready to quit. I had never pushed myself so hard in my life and I regretted it.

"Oh shit, come on," I growled as I made myself move forward and dug around in the drawer. My hand closed around the pills and I flopped back onto my pillow. "Yes!"

Moments like this, I wished I had someone there to care for me. A warm hand and soft voice to soothe me and tell me to keep going. Because the truth was that I wanted to give up. If the people I gave a damn about wouldn't suffer, I would have disappeared by now.

I shoved the pain pill in my mouth and snatched a bottle of water toward me. As soon as the rim touched my lips, I chugged it down and only stopped when I had to take a breath. "Thank God."

My phone buzzed somewhere beside my leg, but I ignored it. Whoever thought it was a good idea to bother me was wrong. I wanted to lie in bed and pretend my muscles weren't on fire for a little while. I closed my eyes and sighed as I let the pain pill kick in.

"You look comfortable."

My eyes snapped open and my heart beat so hard I could barely breathe. Sunlight streamed through my window where it had been barely light before. *Did I fall asleep?* I didn't have time to think about it. As I looked for the source of the voice I frowned as I came face to face with Gabriele.

Shit.

"What are you doing here?" I snapped, shoving myself up and against the headboard as I glared at him. "I changed the locks!"

"That's a waste of time and money," Gabriele said as he glanced down at me. "I know how to find my way in."

"Like a roach," I sneered. "What do you want?"

Gabriele sat on the edge of my bed. "Where did you get those bruises?"

I stared at him like he'd lost his damn mind. "You're *still* on this shit? What is wrong with you?" I hissed as I turned to climb out of bed and cried out when my wrist lit up like it was on fire. I looked around wildly. Each of my wrists was circled with a cuff and they pressed together. "What the- Gabriele!"

He tapped a cigarette into his palm and slipped it between his teeth. "Yes?"

"L-let go of me!"

"Why?" Gabriele asked as he lit up and smoke curled into the air. "I've waited for you to give me a good answer for days and you refuse to cooperate. So, here we are." He waved a hand. "You can tell me or I find some creative ways to get the truth out of you."

I licked my lips and felt how dry my mouth was. *How long had I been asleep?* I couldn't My disoriented brain reeled.

"Let me go," I snapped. "I'll call the..." I trailed off as I remembered that Gabriele's family probably owned the cops. "Shit."

"Good boy," he said, as he chuckled and pet my thigh. "You're learning."

"Fuck you," I shouted as I kicked him in the side hard. I shoved away from him and the floor came up to greet me. I hissed as my knees slammed into the wood. "Shit!"

"That was a mistake," Gabriele said, his voice dripping with danger as I tried to get to my feet. Instead, I felt something in the small of my back and I was forced to the ground. "Where are the bruises from?"

"Fuck you!"

Gabriele went quiet and that scared me more than anything. I tried to glance over my shoulder when I heard clinking, but he shoved his foot against my back more firmly and pinned me in place.

"What are you doing?" I demanded.

My boxers were tugged down my hips and my eyes widened. I squirmed, but when Gabriele put more pressure on my back I gave up again. My heart pounded so hard I felt dizzy as I stared straight ahead.

Fire danced along my backside as I shouted and jumped. The feeling faded away in waves before it started all over again. A loud crack echoed through the room every time the pain flared and slowly the realization of what was happening dawned on me.

Gabriele Bianchi was spanking me with his belt.

I let out a gasp as it came down again and a whimper tumbled out of my lips. "Gabriele, stop!"

"You need to learn how to speak to me," he said evenly as the belt flicked against my skin. "When Daddy asks you a question, you fucking answer it. The first time."

I shook my head. "You're not my Daddy! Fuck you! You are nothing to- Shit!" I trembled as the next blow came down harder.

"No," he snapped. "Try again."

You crazy bastard!

I bit my lip and refused to give Gabriele what he wanted. He was the one that had told me I was nothing to him when I thought I could see a peek of something different. Now he wanted to be my Daddy? Fuck no. I wasn't about to go cowering to him for a damn thing, let alone scraps of affection and care.

Gabriele could go to hell.

"You're stubborn," Gabriele growled as he struck me again. "It won't get you anywhere. I can do this all day." He shifted and I felt his hand as it gripped my ass tightly. "Your ass is the most intoxicating shade of pink. Let's see how it looks red. And then maybe all bruised."

I blinked and shook my head. "D-don't," I choked out. "Gabriele, don't."

"Daddy," he corrected as he slapped my ass with his palm before he squeezed again, his nails digging into my flesh. "Say it."

"I-I..."

"Say it!"

"I can't!" I bit back and jumped as his palm connected with my flesh. "You don't have what I need and I've told you that already," I panted as I shook my head. "You will never be my Daddy."

Gabriele's hand against my ass made pain flare and my cock stupidly twitched. I shut my eyes and braced myself for the next blow. But it never came. Instead, Gabriele's calloused fingers stroked my flesh before he parted my cheeks. A digit prodded against my hole and I shot forward.

"Don't," I groaned.

Gabriele was back to being silent. He spread me open more and spat onto my hole before he wiggled a finger inside of me. I clenched around him and rolled over to my side only to be shoved back onto my stomach again.

"Gabriele," I shook my head. "I don't want it."

"Liar," he hissed.

My cock jerked and I rocked against the floor before I pushed back toward him. Apparently, my body had a mind of its own because I sure as hell wanted Gabriele off of me, but my body wanted him to keep going. To touch and stroke and fuck me into the ground until I couldn't take it anymore. I twisted my wrists and the metal of the cuffs dug into my skin, preventing me from moving too much.

Gabriele's finger sank deeper and I bit my lip so hard I tasted the familiar, coppery tang of blood. He hooked it and pressed against my prostate. A moan slipped free and my face burned. I'd tried so hard not to show him I was turned on but there was no hiding it now.

My thigh muscles squeezed and gave in. I fucked myself on his finger. A cloud of shame settled on my shoulders and I buried my face on the floor so he couldn't look at me like this. *Why did I become a desperate whore when Gabriele touched me?*

"What I said before," Gabriele growled out as he began to push against my hole with another finger. "That day... It had nothing to do with you and everything to do with my mental state. No, you should not have touched my phone and read my personal messages. But I shouldn't have snapped on you either. And then abandoned you after." Gabriele sighed, his voice softening. "I needed time."

I opened my eyes and frowned. *Was he opening up to me?* I didn't have any overwhelming urge to forgive Gabriele just because he was being nice, but... I never expected him to get so close to being a decent human being.

"What I'm saying is, I'm sorry," he rushed out. "Okay? Stop fighting me because I'm not going away. And you're going to be mine no matter how much you say otherwise."

I froze. *Did he just apologize to me?* I couldn't wrap my head around someone like him apologizing to someone like me or giving a damn. Was this really Gabriele? Or did he suddenly get possessed by a demon that was less of an asshole than he was?

I groaned and glanced over my shoulder. "Why?" I moaned out as he picked up speed. "Why do you want someone like *me*? You could have anyone."

"But I don't want just anyone," Gabriele growled and fucked me so hard I couldn't stay still any longer. "I want you, *Tesoro*. And if I have to lock you up and fuck you stupid every single night until you give in? That's what I'll do."

My heart rate tripled. I believed every word he said. His lips brushed against my back and I shivered. "Gabriele," I groaned. "I don't forgive your bullshit just because you say sorry. Words don't mean shit to me."

"I respect that," he said. "But I will still be your Daddy, puppy. And eventually you'll forgive me."

Shit. A moan left my lips and I couldn't take it anymore. I maneuvered onto my knees and pushed back against his fingers. I wanted more. My ass ached to be stuffed with Gabriele's cock. Yes, he was an asshole. And I couldn't stand him or the control his family had over me. But I also couldn't deny that I was attracted to Gabriele.

My mind was filled with images of him fucking me as I called him Daddy. That pushed me right over the edge, and without my cock being touched, I decorated the floor in spurts of cum.

"Daddy!"

The word escaped no matter how hard I tried to bite my tongue. Gabriele moaned, the vibration traveling over my back as his lips stayed pressed to my skin.

"Good boy," he growled. His free hand gripped my ass roughly before he soothed my skin softly. "Now that you've relaxed we need to talk."

I swallowed thickly. "About what?" I mumbled, my breathing still staccato as I glanced back at him. "Can you take these handcuffs off of me?"

Gabriele smiled at me. "Ask nicely."

"Please," I said through gritted teeth.

"Not nice enough," he said with a shrug as he stood. "I guess you can stay down there."

My heart skipped a beat and I licked my lips. Shit. I was going to have to suck it up and say what I knew he wanted to hear. Even though I'd just cum, my cock throbbed as soon as the words formed in my brain.

"Daddy, please release me."

Gabriele groaned, a small smile on his lips. He crouched down in front of me and gripped my chin. As his eyes searched mine I shifted under that intense gaze. He leaned forward and his lips pressed against mine. The man stole my breath away and I confronted the truth.

I never wanted him to let me go.

Chapter Seventeen

Gabriele

I stared at Calix as he sat at the table and squirmed in his seat. He'd been doing that since we came downstairs, and every time our eyes meet, he glances away. A smile curled my lips as I turned back to the stove. He might be uncomfortable, but I had never felt lighter.

Apologizing had always been like pulling teeth for me, but after I said it to Calix and he relaxed, I felt as if we were getting somewhere. Maybe he could see beyond all my edges and accept me for the lying, hardass, bastard that I was. And if he couldn't, then I fully planned to *make* him see the good parts of me even if I had to drag him kicking and screaming to my side.

The truth, that I would never admit out loud, was that I'd missed him. Every second I spent away from Calix had been torture. I thought I wouldn't give a damn if he wasn't around, but that was bullshit. I craved him in ways I had never craved anyone before. I was around for a hell of a lot more than a stupid loan.

"Gabriele," Calix called and I turned on my heels to meet his puzzled face. "Why didn't you go to your father's grave?"

I tensed as all the blood drained from my face. My father. It was the one subject I didn't want to broach. My throat tightened and I shook my head.

"No."

Calix frowned. "No?"

"No," I repeated more firmly as I turned back to the stove and flipped a pancake over.

Behind me, Calix scoffed. "You can't just say no! This is what I'm talking about, Gabriele. You think you can grunt one-word answers at me and I'll sit down and shut up, but that's not how this works."

My grip on the spatula tightened. Calix didn't understand what he was asking of me. There were some things I never talked about because if I did, I would go down a long, dark path that I had just found my way off of. I didn't have time to break down and drop off the grid once more when I knew Amadeo was counting on me to keep things going. Me and the rest of my family had demanded that he let us into his life. And he had. Now I needed to do my part to be sure everything didn't fall onto his shoulders alone.

"Gabriele."

"Enough," I snapped. I stopped to take a long, deep breath. "You like to push me when I've already told you I don't want to fuckin' talk about it. Stop. Now."

Calix gazed at me before he nodded. "Okay."

His shoulders slumped and I wanted to kick myself. I'd never talked about my father's death beyond attending his funeral and visiting his grave. What Calix wanted, I couldn't give him.

My phone rang and the charged silence broke. I snatched it up and groaned when I saw Amadeo's name on my screen.

"Yeah?"

"Where the hell are you?" he asked.

"Out," I answered as I plopped pancakes onto the plate I'd taken out. "Whatever you need, reroute it through Dar or Riccardo or hell, even Nic."

"No," Amadeo said firmly and I froze. "I need *you*. There was a fire at one of the houses today and we're carrying out bodies." Amadeo sounded close to the breaking point. "One of those assholes got caught in the blaze and there was the damn tattoo on his arm. This shit is escalating and I need answers. Now."

I tensed. "Right, I'll be there in twenty minutes." I checked the phone. "Which house?"

"Walnut Terrace."

"Okay."

I hung up and sighed. House was code for brothel and it was one of our big ones. No doubt Amadeo had already paid off the police. Our business wasn't legal, but we donated huge funds to the cops, the fire department, and local politicians so they looked the other way. Amadeo had probably tripled the cash output to keep it out of the news.

"I have to go," I said as I stuffed my phone into my pocket and carried the plate over to Calix along with a bottle of syrup. "Here."

Calix picked up the bottle and frowned at it. "This isn't mine."

"I know, you only had that artificial crap. This is real maple. Eat it." I poured the syrup onto his pancakes and placed utensils beside his plate. "We'll talk more when I return. For now, I have work to do."

He frowned. "Yeah, I can guess what kind of work."

"Don't try to guess. You'll give yourself a headache." I held my hand out. "Give me your wrist."

Calix hesitated. "Why?"

"You ask too many goddamn questions," I snapped. "Wrist, now."

His eyes narrowed. "You almost made me think you'd changed."

"Where did you get that assumption?" I asked as I waited for his wrist. "I was an asshole last week and I'll be one tomorrow. Some shit never changes."

"Tell me about it," Calix grumbled.

"Wrist, *cane*."

"I'm not your dog," he huffed.

"Aren't you? When you make that face you remind me of a frustrated little chihuahua. All bark and minimal bite." I rubbed my side where he'd kicked me earlier. "You're a little dangerous, but not life-threatening."

"Only to you."

We both froze and I stared at Calix. He blinked up at me as if he couldn't believe he'd spoken aloud. I smiled and took his moment of stunned confusion to grab his wrist. I pulled out the plain silver chain with the silver bar and fastened it on.

"There," I said. "My world is getting more dangerous by the day and I need to be able to protect you. This has our family crest engrained on it here," I said as I showed him the skull and rose wrapped around a gun. "People won't fuck with you if they see this."

"Except the ones that want to hurt you," he said, clearly having regained his voice. "Thank you," he said shortly before he glanced up from the bracelet to gaze at me. "Can I ask you something?"

"Quickly."

"Do you know where my father is?"

My stomach twisted. Yeah, I knew exactly where that asshole was. He had abandoned Calix and left his own son with the responsibility to pay it back. It made me want to grab and shake the man until he fell apart, but I simply kept a close eye on him. If I hurt him and Calix ever found out? I got the distinct feeling that Calix would detest me for the rest of my life.

"Gabriele?"

I cleared my throat. "No. I have no idea."

Calix shot out of his chair. "You do know, don't you? Is he alive?"

Amadeo had told me to keep my mouth shut when he found Henry. And besides, it was good to keep the man away from Calix. I shrugged.

"Where is he?"

I reached out and grabbed his chin. "I told you, I don't know," I stressed. "Leave it alone."

Amadeo hadn't gone easy on the man when he first found him. He'd gotten his ass handed to him and only stopped because I stepped in. If I'd stood by and done nothing, one day Calix would have found out. And he would never forgive me for that.

"Gabriele, wait." He shuddered as I smashed my lips against his before he blinked at me. "You have to-"

"I don't have to do shit," I warned him. "Stay here and don't leave this house. I need to straighten things out." I turned on my heels and forced my feet to move. "Eat!" I called over my shoulder.

"Wait!"

I couldn't. Staying around any longer than I already had might cost my family and those that relied on us a hell of a lot. Calix would have to take my word for now. Later, however, I knew there would be questions I would have no choice but to answer.

***

"You're late."

I stared at my brother and nodded. There was no point in telling him that I was only late by three minutes because he would ream me for it. And I didn't want to argue. My time with Calix had left me emotionally raw.

"They really did a number on this place," I said as I stared at the flame-licked bricks. "How many?"

Dario walked up and groaned. "There's fifteen dead. Eight of our girls, two guys, and five guards. It looks like someone locked the room with the guards in it first before they set the fire so they wouldn't be able to escape."

"*Jesucristo*," I muttered.

Amadeo turned to me. "Since when do you say that?"

I blinked at him, confused until I realized what I'd said. *Calix*. I was around him way too much. I shrugged at my brother. His gaze lingered before he turned back toward the building.

"So far I've found a few leads," I said redirecting the conversation before I could become the subject of it. "Whoever these people are, they're smart. They're covering their asses well and they have some powerful people in their pocket to be able move around Atlanta this undetected."

Ama rubbed his right temple. "Shit, shit, shit!" he snapped before he blew out a deep breath. "We need more than that, Gabe. Leave Calix alone and put your focus on this."

I jolted before I glanced at him. "Is that wise?"

"What do you mean?"

I shrugged. "You know, letting him off the hook could send a bad message to everyone else we loan to. If they see one person got away, they'll think they can do it too. That makes it a hell of a lot harder to collect debts in the future."

"Is that it?" Amadeo asked as he gazed at me. "You want to stay beside him because you want to uphold the ways of our family? Or is it because there's something going on between the two of you?"

Amadeo knew something was up. If he didn't, he wouldn't have said anything. I stiffened but tried to appear relaxed as I turned toward him.

"There's nothing going on between Calix and me."

"Hmm." Amadeo nodded, but his face screamed he didn't believe a damn word of what I was saying. "Don't get too close."

I scoffed. "I'm sorry, what is this? Fucking deja vu? Wasn't I the one that told you not to get too close to your boy toy a little while ago?"

"Yes, and I didn't listen," Ama said as he shook his head. "That almost got everyone I loved killed because I was distracted. Don't make the same mistake as me." He laid a hand on my shoulder. "We look out for each other, we always have. But you've changed lately."

"How?" I asked in disbelief.

"You're secretive and distant, Gabe. Not to mention you disappear for hours and you're not reachable. I could name a hundred other things but the truth is that you know you're different. Just...be careful."

I shrugged his hand off of me. "I'm always careful."

Amadeo searched my face, but he only shook his head and turned back toward the building. The tension between us built. Dario's head swiveled between us, but neither one of us spoke. The longer I stood there, the more anger crawled up my spine as I clenched my fist.

"Don't put these deaths on me," I said through gritted teeth. "I won't be told I'm responsible for this shit. We both know I'm doing the best I can."

"I never said you did," Ama snapped. "Don't put words in my mouth, little brother."

It took everything for me to shut up. One more word from Amadeo and I would swing on him. For once, just once, I'd let someone cloud my judgment and fill my time and now I would pay for that with unspoken words and accusatory gazes.

I shoved my sleeves up my arms. "I'm going inside to speak to the fire department and see what else I can learn," I said as I walked forward. "And I'm going to figure out who did this even if it kills me."

"That's not what I'm asking for," Ama said. "I just want you to remember your job and where your loyalties lie at the end of the day."

Like you did with Six?

The hypocrisy made me want to slap my brother. Apparently, only he was allowed to fall in love and live some version of a normal life. I had thought that future was impossible for me, but now that I had a taste I craved it.

I'd keep my head down and plow ahead. But when all was said and done, I would put Calix first.

Even if it got me killed.

Chapter Eighteen

Calix

A shiver worked its way up my spine and I tightened my jacket around me. I tugged up my hood and glanced around. The night air was still warm as spring tumbled into summer, but for some reason I was cold. My heart wouldn't stop pounding in my chest as I walked down the street and tried to keep my face passive. Showing fear would get me singled out and I wasn't in the mood to be a victim.

I pulled out my phone and stared at the screen. *Nothing. Where the fuck is he?* Gabriele had burst right back into my life as if he'd never been gone and ever since I'd been confused. It had been two days since he pinned me to the floor and made me cum so hard I'd seen stars, so where the hell was he? All I'd gotten were texts few and far between that said he was busy. And the latest one that pissed me off.

Gabriele: Go home after work. Don't stop off anywhere. STAY boy.

I ground my teeth as I stared at the message and shook my head. He was determined to call me his dog and I was going to kick his ass because of it. Why did he feel the need to torture me? Wasn't it bad enough that he had turned my whole world upside down and made me question everything I was?

No, I'm not going to think about Gabriele Bianchi. He's a bastard and a criminal. Focus.

That was easier said than done when I considered what I was about to do. Working for one criminal was bad enough, but I was currently employed by two. Conor Kelley needed me to find out what I could. And if I wanted that money, I needed real information and not bullshit.

It was time to stuff Gabriele into the back of my mind where he belonged. I forced down the odd feeling that collected in my belly as I thought that and pushed forward. Lev, Conor's contact, was waiting for me and he seemed like the kind of man you didn't want to make wait.

"You're late." A thick Russian accent greeted me and I turned to stare up at a giant of a man with a bald head and a severe frown. "The fights have already started."

"I'm not on until later though, right?" I asked.

"Doesn't matter. If I say be on time, be on time." He shook his head and looked me up and down. "You know what you're doing?"

I had a vague idea. But I didn't tell him that. Instead, I nodded once and then stepped into a dark building. The sound of fighting was nearby, the loud applause and yells of more violence. As soon as I was in that atmosphere, the chill fell away and excitement grew. Places like this were home.

"You'll fight and then no one will pay you any attention when you go into the bar next door. Have a look around, keep your head down. And if you get caught or something goes wrong? Don't fucking look at me. I'll pretend I don't know you so goddamn fast your head will spin."

I believed every word he said. When I finally gave him a nod in acknowledgment, he grunted and led the way. I kept my mouth shut as we moved deeper into the building. It looked like an abandoned warehouse, something no one looked at too closely at night. My eyes darted around as I tried to take in every detail I could. This was a one-time job that might set me on the course to freedom. All I had to do was play along for one night.

We stepped out of the darkness and the room opened up. There were people everywhere milling around a makeshift ring in the middle of the space. Electricity danced up my spine as I tightened my jacket around my body. The air here was different than the fights I'd been in before. There, it was a tinge of desperation. But here? It was danger, thick and heavy, ready to choke you and leave you discarded in a dark alley.

"If you keep cowering, they're going to smell your fear a mile away," Lev said as he nodded toward the corner. "The men here ain't your average fighters."

My eyes darted to the corner and I saw men three times my size lined up and itching for blood. That should have been what terrified me, but it wasn't. A challenge, a real and bloody challenge, was something I'd never run from. I liked being viewed as the underdog and showing everyone that I was the best.

But these men looked as if they killed on a daily basis. Everything about them screamed they weren't there for the thrill of the fight alone, but to take out their frustrations and do some serious damage too. They were all covered in various tattoos, some with a few discreet ones, and others bore marks all over their bare skin.

I glanced at each of them but didn't let my gaze linger. Conor had told me to watch out for a tattoo. It was distinct. A skull and crossbones with a snake bursting out of the top of the head. No matter how many people I checked out, however, no one had that particular mark.

"Fight starts in a while. Stay out of the way and sign the book," he said as he nodded toward it. "You can make bets over there. Collect cash there."

Lev turned and disappeared before I could even respond. And I was left on my own. I turned around and watched a man's heavy fist collide with his opponent's face. Blood sprayed, the crowd roared, and my stomach turned.

I'd never stepped foot in an underground fight once my father pulled me out of my last one when I was seventeen. He'd told me how stupid I was, berated me for throwing away my dreams, and for the first time in my life, he'd hit me. I still felt that punch to my chest to this day, but I knew I'd deserved it. He'd tried to save me.

So why the fuck had he thrown me to the goddamn wolves now?

And why was I flushing my dreams down the toilet again?

I'm becoming like him. Gabriele and his family. Seedy spots, dark corners, crime. Shit.

My stomach clenched tightly and I forced myself to stay put instead of getting the hell out of there. At the end of the day, my family had put the people I cared about in jeopardy. It fell on me to fix it.

I hung back and watched the fights. But every once in a while, I glanced around to take in the rest of the place. There were a few men I knew to stay far away from, the ones in nice suits with women on their arms and more than likely too much money in their pockets. I had no idea who belonged to what organization, but I already had one psychotic family on my ass. I didn't need another.

"Carlos!"

I came out of my daze and realized it was my turn. As I shed my jacket and laid it over a crate, I headed for the ring. I had to participate in the fight and truth be told, that was the easy part. At least while I wailed on my opponent I wouldn't have to be reminded that I was putting my life on the line in a completely different and terrifying way.

***

I plopped down on a cushioned stool at the bar and held up a finger. A guy walked down and nodded at me before he waited.

"Anything strong," I muttered.

"Cheap or good?"

"Cheap."

He disappeared and I wrapped my arm around my ribs. My body was sporting a ton of bruises and my lip still leaked blood. I knew there were other injuries, but I was too damn busy trying to stay on my feet to lick my wounds.

"Vodka," the man grunted as he set a glass in front of me. "Shit burns like hell, but it's cheap."

"I don't care." I dug into my pocket and passed over the funds before I grabbed the glass.

"You got your ass kicked."

It wasn't a question and he was correct. At first, I'd thought I stood a chance, but my opponent had been better than me. Much better. Every move I made, he countered. Every time I tried to dodge he put me on my ass so fast it made me dizzy.

"Yeah," I said as I downed the vodka and choked. I coughed, my chest aching as I rubbed the back of my hand against my mouth.

He nodded. "You win some. You lose some. Here." He refilled my glass. "One on the house. You'll do better next time."

I wanted to laugh. Next time? There was no way in hell there would be a next time. Conor was paying me to get information, but I wouldn't come back to fight even if he tripled the money he'd given me before.

That's a lie. For triple, I would lick his boots and take fifty punches without blocking.

Thinking about it made me shiver. I was changing. Every damn day I was getting worse, letting their world draw me in and turn me away from who I used to be. Was that how my father felt when he got mixed up with them? I'd been in control at first, but now I was spiraling.

Instead of responding to the bartender, I took my glass and threw back the shot. Heat swept through my body and I asked for one more. *One part of the job over. One more to go.*

Conor said he would pay me for good information. So far, what I had was a bunch of nothing. But if I was going to get that cash, I needed to find *something.* My eyes drifted to some men in the back and I froze. One guy's shirt was open. A tattoo peeked out of it and I recognized the shape of the snake and skull.

That had to be it.

"I'm gonna sit over there. Can I still get a drink?"

The man nodded. "I'll have someone bring it over."

I tossed a few more bills to him as a tip before I got up and sucked in a sharp breath. My body desperately needed a comfortable bed after I took a long, hot bath. But I had to focus.

Slowly, I limped my way back to a table and stayed as close to the little group of men as I could. They all wore dark scowls and thick brows and as I listened I could hear the Russian accents as clear as day. I frowned and when my drink came over, I sipped at it instead of throwing it back.

"When are we going to do more than start petty fires and rob these assholes? I'm tired of this bullshit. I want blood."

"Chill out," another, deeper voice answered. "The boss wants us to take them down before we take over."

"How long is that going to take? I'm sick of shitty bars and cheap whores."

"You couldn't afford expensive ones if you tried," deep voice barked back. "Shut the fuck up and do what you're told. If Andrei heard you talking like that..."

I glanced over my shoulder. As soon as the name was mentioned, Andrei, all of the men at the table stopped talking. They glanced around as if they waited for the man to appear and my stomach clenched. Whoever he was, they were afraid of him. And they didn't seem like the type of guys that were scared of much. Icy blue eyes met mine and I jumped.

"You," the deeper-voiced man stood up and knocked over his beer. "What the fuck are you doing?"

My heart leaped into my throat. I opened my mouth to lie my way out of it, but the look in their eyes made one-word pop into my mind. *Run.* I shot up and Ignored the pain that flared all over my body.

"You're sticking your nose where it doesn't belong. Come here."

"No thanks."

The words shot out of my mouth and I turned on my heels and ran. I heard yelling behind me, a loud crash, and then cursing. But I didn't stop to look behind me. If I stopped, I was as good as dead. I rammed my shoulder into the door and burst into the outside air. Looking around wildly, I spotted a gate I could scale or the open street.

"You're dead!" I heard.

A familiar sound clicked and I knew exactly what it was. Someone had cocked a gun. My heart rate tripled as I ran for the main road and darted toward the cars parked along the sidewalk. It wasn't the best cover, but it was better than being out in the open as rapid fire Russian filled the air and more footsteps joined the ones that came first.

I ducked behind a car when the first gunshot rang out, punctuating the night air. My head felt dizzy as I panted and I tried to stop myself from hyperventilating. I clutched my shirt and tried to will my heart to stop beating so damn fast when two shoes came into view. My heart froze in my chest and I knew all at once that I was going to die.

"I thought I told you to stay."

My eyes darted up and I stared at Gabriele Bianchi. The frown on his face didn't bother me because I knew I'd been saved.

Chapter Nineteen

Gabriele

I glanced up when I came face to face with four assholes. My boy would have to wait. I'd already pulled up with my gun in my hand and as my men swept out of the car behind me, we advanced.

"Hey, hey, wait a minute!"

He threw his hands up and I leveled my .22. One squeeze of the trigger and he dropped to the ground. I'd made sure I only shot him in the arm. He was a huge, burly man and something told me he was in charge of the assholes who had shot at my Calix.

I leveled off another shot and another. A bullet ripped through one man's head and another found his friend's stomach. More men poured out of the bar, but I didn't give a fuck. If I had to meticulously mow down each and every man in front of me, I would.

"Boss! Boss! They're down."

My ears rang as smoke filled the air. I shook my head. For a moment there I had been far away, but I was dragged into the present again. I turned from my spot on the sidewalk and marched back over to Calix. He was still on the ground, curled into a ball as he tried to protect himself from bullets.

"Up," I demanded as I grabbed his arm and yanked him to his feet. "Are you hurt?"

He groaned. "N-no," Calix whispered as he wrapped an arm around his stomach and grimaced. "This is from earlier. I'm fine."

I looked him up and down before I started to examine every inch of him. My fingers brushed over his skin while I lifted his shirt and tugged his pants past his hips to examine him. He hissed as I touched his abdomen and I yanked up his shirt higher to find bruises littering his skin.

"Gabri-"

"Shut up," I snapped. "I told you to goddamn stay, didn't I?" I yanked him against my side and glared. "Who did this?"

"It was a fair fight," he said. "I signed up for it and everything."

My grip tightened on him and he sucked in a sharp breath. "Do you think I give a damn about fair? Who did you fight? Where is he?"

Calix stared at me and kept his mouth shut. I wanted to pry his lips open with my bare hands until he spilled every detail about what the hell he'd been doing.

"Find out who he was fighting," I said as I looked over at my men. "I want any and all information on him."

"Gabriele..."

"Shut. Up."

"What about him?" Kris asked as he pointed to the man on the ground that I'd shot first. "What do we do with him?"

I zeroed in on him. "Take him to warehouse five and shove him into a room. Keep a close eye on him after he's tied up. We have a lot to discuss."

"Yes, sir."

I glanced at Calix and ignored the Russian that was being fired off from the man who was bleeding on the ground. We would have plenty of time to talk shortly. First, I needed to deal with Calix.

"Move," I said as I turned around. There was an audience gathering in front of the bar and I didn't need to be seen. "We need to talk."

Calix grunted. "Wait, slow down. Shit! Gabriele."

"No," I said as I opened the car door and shoved him into the passenger seat. "You don't get to speak to me except to say very specific things. Yes, Daddy. No, Daddy. Thank you, Daddy. Do I make myself clear?"

Calix stared up at me. "I-"

"No!" I snapped. "What did I just fucking say?" I gripped his cheeks hard and squeezed. "Say it!"

He shivered, his eyes wide. "Yes, Daddy."

I stepped back and slammed the car door shut. The fire in my chest rose and it took everything not to scream at Calix. Did he know how stupid he was coming here? How close he was to death? No, he'd charged into the situation and hadn't used his fucking brain and for that, I wanted to break every bone in his goddamn body.

But I couldn't.

I slipped into the car and stared at him. Calix was untouchable. Not even I could hurt him. I reached out, wanting to touch his face to make sure that he was alright. But Calix threw himself back as if I would do something terrible.

My blood ran cold and I turned back around. I shifted gears hard. My jaw tightened until pain shot up my face. I ignored it and drove faster. Someone was going to pay for this whirlwind of emotions that wouldn't shut the fuck up.

We pulled up outside of Calix's house and I moved quickly. I was on a mission. When I yanked him out of the passenger side, he grumbled.

"I can walk!"

"One more word," I warned him. "Just one and I'll do something I'll regret."

Calix shut up immediately. The look in his eyes held contempt and I didn't give a damn if he was angry at me right now. I would take all of his wrath if it meant that he was home, safe, and alive.

I unlocked his door and led him inside. As much as I wanted to take him upstairs, demand answers, and get him cleaned up, I had other places to be. I stood by the door as he started up the stairs. When I didn't follow, he turned and glanced back at me.

"What are you doing?"

"Going out," I said shortly. "What were you thinking, Calix? Who was that man?"

Calix frowned. "What man?"

"Don't test me," I said. "The one on the ground that I put a bullet in."

"Oh, that guy. I have no idea." He grimaced. "All I know is he's Russian."

"Why was he chasing you?"

Calix's frown deepened. "I heard something."

I blinked at Calix and waited. Talking to him was like trying to pull teeth and I was ready to drag him over my knee and spank his ass raw. He was hiding something.

"I heard a name. Andrei. The guy had that tattoo with the skull and the snake."

I froze. "How did you know about that tattoo?" I asked. "I've never told you about it."

Calix looked like he wanted to run and I narrowed my eyes daring him to. I would chase him down and tie him to the bed before I would allow him to get out of my questions. Someone had told Calix about that tattoo.

"Who told you?" I demanded. "And don't lie or even hesitate."

Calix must have seen how serious I was because he licked his lips and shuddered. "Conor Kelley."

Conor fucking Kelley. He had sent Calix into the belly of the beast to no doubt collect information. I wanted to kick his ass, but I knew the rules. We were in a state of peace with the Irish which meant killing them was off-limits. And even if it wasn't? Conor was a top dog. If we took him out, none of us would get an ounce of peace. It would be war and everyone would end up dead.

"Go to bed," I muttered as I turned around and gripped the doorknob. "Do not leave this house."

"Where are you going?"

I slammed the door behind me before I locked it. I wasn't in the mood to talk to Calix, not before I took care of what needed to be done. Afterward, I would come back and hold him until he tried to push me away, but even then I would hold him more tightly.

I tugged out my phone and made a call. "Get over here and watch his house. Two men at all times."

"Yes, boss."

I hung up. Time to find out who the hell Andrei was.

***

I walked into the warehouse and moved down to the basement. Men moved out of my way left and right. Whatever expression I wore must have been enough to warn them to stay the hell away.

Turning down a hall, I stepped into a room where the man hung suspended from the ceiling by his wrists. A box supported his feet and he swung back and forth as he tried to keep himself balanced on it. I looked him up and down before I opened up his shirt and spotted the tattoo.

"What do you know about the attacks on the Bianchi's?"

His icy blue eyes narrowed at me. "That's what this shit is about," he grumbled. "You're one of them."

"Gabriele," I said as I sized him up. "Who is Andrei?"

"I'm not telling you shit."

My pulse raced and I grinned. "I was hoping you would say that." I shrugged off my jacket and rolled my sleeves up. "After tonight I could use an outlet and I don't want to take any of this out on my boy, not the brunt of it anyway. He can't handle that. Not yet."

"О чем ты говоришь?"

I tilted my head at him. "I don't understand that shit so if you have something to tell me pick a different language. Who is Andrei?"

He hacked and a glob of saliva smacked against my cheek. I reached up and swiped the spit away. "It's too bad I need you to use your tongue for information or I would slice it out of your head."

"Lucky me," he grunted.

"Not really. I've got a ton of interesting ways to make you talk and there's plenty of you to slice off." I beckoned and a cart was wheeled to me. I ran my fingers over the shiny selection I had to work with before I gazed up at the man. "That man you were chasing down. What was the plan? Kill him?"

He stayed quiet, but I saw the pain that crossed his face as his muscles twitched. The bullet wound I'd given him in his arm had been patched so he wouldn't bleed out, but he was still in a hell of a lot of pain.

I kicked the box from underneath his feet and he screamed as he swung back and forth. The hook keeping him suspended yanked on the handcuffs and it looked like his wrists would snap at any moment.

"What's your name?" I asked.

He panted. "Why do you care?"

"I want to know who to send your body to when we're done. No reason your family shouldn't be able to bury you."

He glared. "Fuck you!"

I clicked my tongue. "You must really love pain to keep pushing me. I don't mind indulging you."

My fingers finally stopped stroking the weapons that had been supplied and I picked up a scalpel. Thin and precise, it would do a wonderful job.

"Are you circumcised?" I asked.

He blinked at me, his eyes knitting together. "What?"

"Are you circumcised?" I asked as I reached out and yanked down his sweats.

All at once, the truth seemed to dawn on him and I watched his chest rise and fall quickly. I grinned.

"You can't be serious," he stammered.

I ripped down his boxers and reached over to pick up a pair of gloves. Once they were on, I picked up the scalpel again and grabbed his cock.

"Looks like you are circumcised. Guess I'm going to have to keep slicing anyway."

He locked eyes with me and I saw the terror behind the mask. I ran the blade of the scalpel over his purple head and blood bubbled up.

"I would stop moving if I were you. My hands are real shaky and I might cut the whole thing off."

"Fuck, you're insane!" he yelled as he kicked and swung on the hook.

"You have no idea," I said as I ran the back of the scalpel over his flesh but kept my eyes on him. "Who is Andrei?"

He sucked in a shuddering breath as a vein pulsed in his throat. "If I tell you, he'll kill me."

I barked out a laugh. "If you don't tell me, I'll continue to slice and dice until you're nothing but a pound of blood and exposed muscle." I traced up to his abdomen and over his arm before I ripped off the bandage on his bullet wound. "And I'll have fun doing it."

I stabbed the scalpel into his wound and he screamed. The sound was music to my ears.

"Who is Andrei?"

"Fuck," the man panted when he stopped screaming. "I can't. I can't, man."

"You were going to kill someone I give a shit about," I said as I twisted the knife in the hole I'd made in his arm. Sweat rolled down his reddened face and he blew out puffs of breath. "So I'm going to try this one last time before I start gettin' real creative."

"This...isn't...creative?"

I grinned. "Not even close." He was wasting my time and keeping me away from Calix. "But I'm done talking. Start telling me who Andrei is and I might stop carving."

"Wait. Wait. W-wait ah fuck!"

I let my scalpel move the way it wanted to move. What felt natural. Every cut into his flesh brought on more blood and it rolled down his body before dropping to the floor below. I watched the color start to drain from his face and I reached up. I slapped him roughly and he panted at me as his eyes went out of focus and then returned to normal again.

"Andrei...is my boss," he said.

My skin tingled. His boss? I had just found the answer to all of Amadeo's problems. Once I dropped this news onto his lap, he would hopefully get off my back. I kept my face passive as I stared up at the man and crossed my arms over my chest.

"Where is this boss of yours?"

"Don't...know."

I sighed and stepped toward him again. The scalpel sank into his thigh like his flesh was made of soft butter. I turned it and felt the scraping of bone. The man's eyes rolled back in his head and he choked on air.

"No, no not yet," I demanded as I yanked the scalpel free and shoved it underneath his chin. "Where is Andrei?"

His words came out choked before his eyes came back into focus. "I-I don't fucking know!" He gagged and his head dropped forward. "Don't know. Don't know. *не знаю. не знаю. не знаю.*"

"Shit," I muttered. "Looks like you've reached the end of your usefulness." I snapped off my gloves and tossed them into the trash can. "Normally I would let one of my men have their fun before they finally slit your throat, but you almost took away the one goddamn thing I care about." I reached out and grabbed his cheeks roughly. Drool spilled from his lips as he stared back at me through glazed eyes. "I can't let *anyone* steal my *Tesoro*. He's the only treasure I have."

"Andrei will gut you," the man said as a smile tugged at his lips and quickly faltered.

"I look forward to him trying."

I shoved the scalpel against his throat and pulled. Hot blood arced from the gash in his neck and sprayed onto my shirt and cheek. But I didn't look away as he gasped, his eyes bulging out of his head. The light dimmed in his gaze until there was nothing left behind.

Once he was gone I stepped back and regained the part of me that had been tucked away. I washed my hands in the sink and watched the blood turn into swirls of pink before it ran clear and I didn't feel stained anymore. I took out my phone and texted Amadeo.

Gabriele: New developments. Meet tomorrow afternoon. Important.

Ama: Now

Gabriele: No

Ama: Gabe...

Gabriele: For once fuck off!

I shoved my phone back into my pocket and grabbed my jacket. What I needed was a shower and more than that I needed Calix. I needed to touch him, hold him, and know that he was safe and he wasn't going away.

A thought came to me and I fumbled as I dug into my pocket and pulled out my phone. I pulled up the tracking app that connected with Calix's bracelet and breathed a sigh of relief when I saw that he was still at home.

Calm down. He's okay.

My heart refused to believe that and the rising panic that clawed at my throat was just as sure. I had to go see Calix.

Nothing else mattered.

Chapter Twenty

Gabriele

I wrapped my arms around Calix and cursed the sun. Whatever time it was, I knew I hadn't been asleep for long. All I wanted to do was stay curled up around Calix and sleep a little longer. But I felt the way he shifted and his breathing became uneven. He would wake up soon and we would have a lot to talk about.

Calix groaned and pushed back against me. "Gabriele?" he asked.

I tensed. "Who the fuck else would it be?"

"Shit." He sat up slowly before he gazed back at me and frowned. "What are you doing in my bed?"

"Sleeping," I countered. "At least for an hour or two."

Calix pushed his fingers through his long hair and I admired the way the sun danced off of the smooth strands. His dark eyes looked like warm chocolate. And I couldn't stop admiring his plump lips and the stubble on his cheeks. I reached out and caressed his face.

Too bad I had to punish him.

"I told you to stay home," I said slowly. "Do you remember that?

Calix frowned. "Don't start this again," he muttered. "You yelled at me enough last night." He turned and I grabbed his arm tightly. He turned and stared at me, his eyes wide. "Gabriele."

"No, I told you already. It's Daddy. *Your* Daddy. I know you keep denying me because you don't think I can take care of you, but I can. I've protected you, watched over you, and today I'll punish you so you stop making idiotic mistakes."

He blanched. "What are you talking about?"

"I'm talking about making you realize how much I care about you, *Tesoro*. Even if you hate me for it. Because someone has to look out for you."

"I don't need anyone to look out for me," he said as he pulled back, panic rising on his face like a tidal wave. "Let go of me! I'm a grown man, I don't need this shit!"

"Try to keep it down," I warned him. "I still have a headache from all those gunshots last night and I'm not in the mood. But if you'd like me to gag you, let me know. That can be arranged as well."

Calix tried to shove away from me, but I was on top of him in an instant. Before, I'd gone easy on him. The truth was that I hadn't wanted to scare him away, but now I knew better. Calix left to his own devices was a danger to himself. And I wasn't about to lose him.

I pinned his wrists to the bed and straddled his body as he winced. "I know your body hurts. Before I got in bed last night I looked you over. Bruises, abrasions? You've been participating in underground fights."

He glanced away from me. "So what?"

I glared at him as heat swept through my body. *So what?* He said it with such an indifferent attitude as if what he was doing wasn't about to destroy everything that he'd worked so hard for.

My hand wrapped around his throat and his eyes widened. "Gabriele."

"No," I growled. "It's time for you to wake up, Gonzalez. What you're doing? It's as stupid as what your father did and you're following in his footsteps." My grip tightened and he gasped. "You won't participate in one more illegal fight. Do you understand me?"

Calix's lips parted. "Had to," he managed to get out. "Money."

My grip loosened and he choked. Instead of grabbing his throat, he reached out and took hold of my undershirt, his fist curling around it as he gazed up at me. His eyes looked...sad.

"I didn't want to do it," he finally spat out. "But they're relying on me and I can't let them down."

"Who?" I asked.

"Everyone."

My heart squeezed so hard I thought I was about to die. He wanted to protect the people closest to him. That I could understand because it was what I did every day of my life. But he was going about it in such a stupid way that he was going to lose everything and I didn't want that life for him. Even if it would make him even more dependent on me, I knew it would also make him miserable.

"That doesn't mean that you put your life in danger," I growled. "Where you were last night, do you realize that you could have died?"

Calix strained against me. "Your family put me in this situation and you're telling me to be careful?" He laughed dryly. "A few weeks ago, you and Nic were talking about killing me in front of my face. You can't tell me what to do when you're one of *them*," he hissed.

My blood ran cold and I gripped a handful of his hair. "You could be so much worse off," I snapped. "If your father had gone to anyone else he would be splattered on the ground and not off in New York hiding in some damp, dumpy basement with a friend. And you would be sold, your ass used to please whoever bought you."

"What?" Calix swallowed hard and I watched as his Adam's apple bobbed up and down. "You...you know where he is."

Ice shot through my veins. *Fuck.* I didn't want him to know that I was aware. But I'd known where his father was from the moment he disappeared. It was my job, my family's job, to keep tabs on people who were flight risks. I'd thought about killing the man, snapping his neck, and making him disappear, but then I'd thought about Calix, the way he smiled at his father when the man wasn't looking and the way he tried so hard to live up to his expectations. And I hadn't been able to pull the trigger.

"Yes," I said.

Calix struggled underneath me. "You motherfucker!" he shouted. "You told me you didn't fucking know! You're a fucking liar!"

"Calm down."

"Fuck you!"

I grabbed Calix's arm and pushed him onto his belly. He continued to fight with more strength than he'd ever used on me before. Calix bucked hard and I landed on the floor. Pain shot through my body making me hiss.

"Get out of my house!" Calix yelled. "I mean it. Right now or I'll kill you myself!"

Heat rose in my belly as I stood up. "Do it," I growled. "Kill me or shut the fuck up because you know what? I am tired, Calix. I'm weak, angry, and *tired*. So, I didn't tell you about your father? What would it have changed, huh?" I demanded. "He didn't want you and I did. *I fucking did*!" My eyes burned and I felt the foreign sensation of tears pricking the back of my eyes. "I'm not going anywhere. You still have questions to answer."

Calix crossed his arms over his chest. "I'm not answering shit," he countered.

My muscles jerked and I stared at him. Every instinct in me screamed to jump on him and beat his ass until he saw reason. That was the way I dealt with my problems. But I couldn't do that when he was the one causing the issues.

I'd tried so hard to stay away from Calix, to put up steel walls and keep him at bay. Maybe even back then, when I tried to pawn him off to Amadeo or anyone else who would take on the gym's debt, maybe I knew that I wanted him all to myself.

I jumped over the bed and grabbed hold of Calix. He tried to fight me off, but where he was trained I was pissed. I slammed him onto the bed and my mouth sought his in hard, fast, angry bursts. He cursed at me, his nails digging into my back, but I couldn't stop.

Right now, I needed him. I'd never craved anything the way I did Calix. And if I couldn't have him? The feeling of dread in my stomach grew. *I would die.*

"Stop," Calix moaned against my mouth as he clung to me. "I-I don't."

"No more lying!" I snapped before my shoulders sagged and I clutched him tightly as I stared into his eyes. "Calix, tell the truth. Or I'll walk out the door, erase your debt, and you will *never* hear from me again."

He trembled underneath me. "No!" Calix shook his head. "Shit, you piss me off and drive me crazy, but I...I don't want you to fucking leave me," he choked out. "But I'm pissed at you, Gabriele. You keep saying you want to be my Daddy but you fucking lie through your goddamn teeth and expect me to trust you? How can I? *Why* would I?" He slammed the side of his fist into my chest. "Fuck you for making me feel like this!"

"Right back at you," I growled. I took his mouth again and was drowned in the taste of him. "Fuck you for turning me into someone who gives a fuck." I yanked at his boxers and tore them down his muscular thighs. "You're right," I said as I gazed down at him. "I'm a lying piece of shit who kills and tortures without a second thought. You know what happened to that guy from last night? I slit his fucking throat and watched him die. For you," I growled. "I would do anything and everything for *you, Tesoro.*"

He gazed up at me and for the first time, I watched the conflict in his eyes. Calix had always been so sure of himself, but now? He wasn't. I had shaken his faith and part of me hated myself for that.

"What does that mean?" Calix asked.

I raised a brow. "What?"

"*Tesoro*. What does it mean?"

My heart pounded and I licked my lips before I spat it out. "Treasure," I said. "You're my treasure."

Calix's cheeks turned red as he stared up at me. "I thought I was your dog?"

"Can't you be both? I mean dogs are man's best friend." I grinned, my throat still tight and my eyes still wet. "I'll stop lying to you from now on as long as you stop lying to me. No more underground fights." As I thought about last night, my eyes narrowed. "And no more working for Conor fucking Kelley. I'm going to rip his tongue out through his asshole and set him on fire."

"No," Calix said as he reached out and cradled my cheeks. "Don't start anything with him. He gave me a choice and he made sure I *knew* it was my choice. I still took it. Gonzalez and Sons means everything to me. I can't lose it."

"I know," I said as my brows knitted.

We stared at each other for what felt like an eternity before I was drawn to kiss him once more. My tongue slipped into his mouth this time and Calix pushed back. His body arched up against mine and I felt his hard cock.

"I don't want to have sex," Calix said as he pulled back suddenly. "I want to talk about everything you've been hiding from me. And my father."

"Later," I answered.

He shoved his palms against my chest. "No, not later. Now."

I pushed his hands away. "Even with everything I've just admitted, please understand that you still belong to *me*. Not the other way around." I grabbed his chin and tilted it up. "And I still intend to punish you for last night."

Calix swallowed hard. "But then you'll answer my questions?"

"All of them," I answered. "Every last goddamn one."

I meant every word of it too. Usually, I kept my mouth shut and my head down when it came to work, but Calix deserved to know.

"He's fine if it makes you feel any better," I said.

Calix blinked up at me. "It does," he muttered. "Thank you."

"Don't thank me just yet." I climbed off the bed and gripped his boxers before I tore them roughly. "I'm going to fuck you, punish you, and show you exactly why you're my dog, Calix. And afterward when you're sore and exhausted? Only then we'll talk."

He tried to squirm away. "Wait."

"No more fucking waiting," I snapped. "I need you. Now."

Chapter Twenty-One

Gabriele

"Where are you going?" Calix asked.

"Get undressed and be waiting for me on the floor when I return. Kneeling." I gazed over my shoulder at his puzzled expression. "And I expect you to address me correctly for the rest of the day. Do you understand me?"

Calix swallowed hard and I saw a flicker of rebellion in his eyes. But when I raised a brow at him he slipped off of the bed and started moving.

"Yes, Daddy," he said.

I turned back around and walked downstairs where there was a box waiting for me on the front porch. I'd requested it the night before and sure enough there it was. I carried the box inside and went back upstairs.

When I stepped into Calix's room, he sat on his knees on the floor, his big, bright eyes gazing up at me. My cock throbbed. I hadn't taken him before and it had always been a struggle not to do it. But I knew he was ready for me now.

"Arms behind your back."

Calix hesitated and I snatched his chin upward. "Don't make me ask you for anything twice, *cane*."

"Yes, Daddy," he answered, his voice velvety deep.

"Now, I'm not a monster," I said as I sat the box on the bed and started to open it. "I won't ever hurt you past what you can take and you'll be given a safeword. Say it and we'll stop. Immediately."

"That sounds terrifying," Calix mumbled.

"Or exciting?" I asked as I stepped back and noted his hard cock between his muscular thighs.

"Both," he answered, a small smile tugging at the edges of his mouth. "What's my safeword?"

"Pick one. It should be something you would never say during sex."

"Um, helicopter," Calix said.

I grinned. "Helicopter?"

"It's the first thing that popped into my head!" he growled, his cheeks turning a shade of pink that looked attractive on him.

I reached out and caressed his cheek. "Helicopter it is." I leaned down and brushed my lips against his. "Now, kiss me because you won't get to do it again until we're done."

Calix's eyes widened in confusion as I crashed my lips against his. His tongue swirled around mine before I pulled back and nipped at his bottom lip. Neither of us could breathe right but I knew we didn't care. That kiss breathed life back into my body, and from the way Calix clung to me, I knew he needed it just as badly as I did.

Reluctantly, I pulled away and took in the sight of him. He panted, his chest rising and falling rapidly as he gazed up at me. There wasn't hatred in his eyes for once. *I could get addicted to that look, how calm and relaxed he looks with me. He trusts me and I wouldn't do anything to betray that.*

I straightened up and cleared my throat. There would be time for words left unsaid later. Right now, I needed to devour Calix. I reached up and pulled the ponytail holder from his hair. Chocolate brown locks cascaded over his shoulders and I admired how good he looked when his hair was down before I forced myself to focus.

"Didn't I tell you to put your arms behind your back?"

Calix gazed down at his hands in confusion. He quickly shoved them behind his back and nodded. "Yes, Daddy."

"Good boy." I smiled. "Tilt your head up and keep it that way."

I walked behind him and finally picked up the red and silver-studded collar that was in the box. It wasn't heavy in my hand, but it would be a noticeable weight around his throat. And it would contrast with his brown skin beautifully.

I put the collar around his neck and brushed his hair out of the way. Calix squirmed as I tightened it and fastened it in place. I reached into the box and pulled out a small padlock. Once it was slipped through one of the holes in the back, I fastened it and gave it a good tug. It wasn't going anywhere.

"A collar?" Calix asked.

"Shhh," I said as I turned back to the box of goodies and tugged out the next treat. "No more talking, *cane*."

"I'm not a-"

I shoved my foot against Calix's back and pushed him to the floor. He grunted, his ass in the air giving off a damn good view of his hole. I resisted the urge to sink a finger or two inside and instead applied more pressure.

"I said no more talking. Do you understand?"

Calix's hands were spread on the floor, his breathing mere pants. But he didn't move or try to run. "Yes, Daddy," he answered thickly. "Sorry."

My cock jerked and I wanted to throw him down and fuck him stupid. But I refused to give in that quickly. Even if his voice softly whispering *sorry* did impossibly hot things to me.

I let Calix back up and he pushed his arms behind his back without having to be told. There was a pair of handcuffs in the box, but I liked making him hold his position simply because I told him to. Forcing him to remember where I wanted him to be and how I wanted him to behave? That was a hell of a lot more fun.

My hand ran over the wire cage and I picked up the black muzzle. I pressed it against his mouth and Calix started to protest.

"Hey, wait a-"

I stopped moving and he shut up quickly. I grinned. *Didn't even have to say anything.*

The muzzle was fastened in place and I grabbed the red leash before I walked in front of him. Calix gazed up at me and I saw the questions in his eyes, but he didn't speak. I hooked the leash onto his collar.

"Good boy," I cooed as I tugged on the collar and he fell forward a bit. "See? I told you that you were my dog, didn't I?" I traced my fingers over the cool steel of the muzzle and groaned. "You look fucking amazing like this. Stay," I ordered.

I walked around the side of the bed and grabbed my phone before I returned. Calix's eyes widened and he shook his head as I held it up ready to snap a picture. I gripped a handful of his hair and tugged.

"I said stay, mutt."

Calix whined and I grinned. "Such a cute noise coming from you." I chuckled as I put his head back into the correct position and snapped off a few photos. They would come in handy later. I set the phone on video mode and hit record before I padded back over to Calix.

"It's too bad I won't be able to cram my cock down your throat and hear you gag. Next time though." I petted his hair and scraped my nails against his scalp. I gave his leash another tug. "Come on, boy. Up on the bed. I want you on your hands and knees."

Calix stood up and his gaze never left me. I wanted to laugh at the enraptured look on his face, but heat crawled up my spine instead and I knew I couldn't drag shit out the way I'd imagined I would the first time we fell into bed together. My patience was wearing thin and I needed him like I needed air.

He turned and crawled onto the bed. Calix positioned himself onto his hands and knees and I reached out to run my palm over his inner thigh. He twitched and sucked in a sharp breath, but he didn't pull away from me. I continued tracing every inch of his body before I shoved my palm into his upper back and pushed his chest onto the bed.

"Hips in the air," I said. "That's right. Be a good boy for Daddy."

Calix wiggled and I could imagine a tail plug stuffed in his ass. *Next time.* There was no time for that, not when I was craving the way he would feel wrapped around my dick. I walked behind him again and cupped my hand. Flesh collided against flesh and Calix cried out. His legs started to shake with every hard slap to his ass, but he kept himself as quiet as he possibly could.

"Good boy," I said as I ran my hand over his ass gently. "No more disobeying, *Tesoro*. Everything I do is to make sure you're safe and I can't keep you out of harm's way if you keep throwing yourself in front of loaded guns." My grip tightened, my nails digging into his flesh.

"Please," he cried out as he shook his head. "Shit. Shit."

"Quiet," I growled as I removed my nails and slapped his ass again. The vibration spread over my hand and I hummed at how good it felt. "It feels like your ass was made to be slapped by my hand."

He groaned and I reached between his thighs. Sure enough, Calix was hard. My fingers slipped over his slit and pre-cum kissed my skin. I pulled my hand back and tasted him as a moan echoed throughout the room.

"What? You like Daddy tasting you?" I asked as I spread his ass wide and examined his hole. He shuddered and shook his head hard making me chuckle. "Don't tell me you're embarrassed? Is it because I'm looking at your tight, throbbing hole, baby?" I ran a wet finger over his entrance and he jumped. "Uh uh, none of that. Hold still."

FIGHT ME DADDY

Calix shivered, his legs trembling now. I admired him for a minute before I reached into the box and pulled out what I was looking for. I laid everything out on the bed and Calix tried to turn to look which earned him a sharp slap to the back of the thigh.

"Shit!" he cried out. "Sorry, I'm shit. Sor-"

I slapped his opposite thigh and watched his flesh turn a beautiful shade of pink. He quickly realized his mistake and swallowed his next words.

"Smart dog." I grinned as I picked up the vibrating cock ring and rounded the bed. "On your back, mutt."

Calix shifted quickly. His pupils were blown as if he was high. He licked his lips, but he didn't glance down at the toys again or disobey. *I knew you could learn, Tesoro. You just needed me to guide you.*

"Spread your legs." Calix did as he was told and I nodded in approval. "Arms above your head."

The way he moved without a moment of hesitation made my heart squeeze with pure joy. Had I felt boundless exhilaration since I was a child? I couldn't remember a time that compared to this. I ran my fingers up his body and squeezed a hard nipple. His lips parted and he grunted as his eyes met mine.

"You're sensitive," I said with an amused smile. "That's too bad. You're going to have a rough go of it today."

Calix shivered and I drank in the fear that danced in his eyes. *Delicious.* I slipped the cock ring around his length. One strap wrapped around his balls and the other around his hard cock. He let out a whine and his eyes were huge when I gazed up at him.

"That's right," I said as I shook my head. "No cumming until I tell you to." I pushed the button on the side and the vibrations started slowly, but I didn't want slow. I ramped it up until Calix was a squirming mess. "Stay," I ordered as I pushed a hand against his chest.

"Better," I said as I wrapped my hand around his cock and stroked it once. I released him quickly and he gave me a pleading look. "Don't worry, Calix. You'll get all of my attention very soon and you'll cum until your balls are empty. That's a promise."

I grabbed the handcuffs and took one of Calix's wrists in hand. He yanked hard and panted. I paused as I gazed down at him.

"Do you trust me?"

Calix frowned. He shook his head slightly, then nodded, and shook it again. *He's confused and nervous. Can't say I blame him.* He wasn't used to seeing me like this. I'd always been aggressive with him, but this was different. The air felt thicker, more electrified and I had no doubt the expression on my face was the look a predator gave its prey before they were consumed.

"If you want to stop, use your safe word. Do you remember what it is?"

Calix nodded.

"Good boy. If you need to use it, then use it, but know that if you don't, we're going to continue *my* way. Your body, your moans, your tears," I said as I reached out and stroked his cheek. "They all belong to me and I will play with my boy anyway I fucking see fit. Do you understand me?"

He nodded again.

"Daddy needs your words this time."

Calix's lips parted. "Yes, Daddy," he whispered.

"Say it."

He swallowed hard. "I...I belong to you."

I smiled before I leaned forward and kissed the steel of his muzzle. "Yes, you do, Calix. You're mine and no one else's."

The look in his eyes softened and Calix raised his arms up. He stayed in place as I secured him to the bed using one of the slats of his headboard. I stroked my fingers through his hair and kissed his forehead before I feathered kisses to his ear.

"Daddy's going to destroy you." He whimpered and I shushed him softly. "But when we're done? I'll put you back together again."

I straightened up and opened the nightstand. I snagged a bottle of lube and a condom before I stopped and tossed the condom back into the drawer.

"No way in fuck am I sticking my cock in you wrapped in a damn thing," I said as I gazed at him. "Any objections?"

Calix opened his mouth but shut it again before he shook his head. I grinned and stripped off my boxers. I wasn't sure I could have stopped myself even if he said he *did* object. I had all of Calix's records, I knew everything about him medically and otherwise. Besides, I needed to feel all of him. I wouldn't accept anything standing between us.

I lubed up his hole and poured more onto my cock. As I stroked myself I stretched him a bit, but I didn't have the patience to wait anymore. From the look on his face neither did he.

I laid on top of Calix and pressed my cock against his entrance. His mouth fell open and his head fell back as I rolled my hips and pushed inside of him. He panted, his fingers clenching and unclenching as I shoved more of myself inside.

"Shit!" he yelled. "Daddy, wait. It's- *Jesucristo.*"

I thrust forward hard a strangled moan filled the room. "Look at me," I demanded. "Don't turn away again." I grabbed his legs and pushed them back until his knees nearly touched his chest. His hot hole squeezed around me and I groaned. "Fuck, baby. You're fucking tight."

I growled as I gripped his legs tighter and thrust inside of him hard and fast. Calix gripped the slats above his head and as he tugged and tried to pull away; I was glad I'd locked him up. He wasn't ready to take my cock without being restrained and I wasn't in the mood to chase him all over the bed.

"Daddy," he moaned. "It's hitting my damn prostate. Shit. Take it off," he said as he nodded toward the cock ring. "Please."

"Shut up," I growled as I reached out and wrapped a hand around his throat. "I told you this is your punishment. The only thing you're going to do is take my cock and keep your mouth shut. I don't want anything but your moans."

"Fuck you!" he panted out. "I can't do that shit. Daddy please!"

"Bad dog," I said as I squeezed and he choked. "You'll be lucky if you cum at all today with that attitude."

His eyes went wide with worry, but I drove into him roughly and he moaned. Calix trembled under me the longer I fucked into him. *Sorry, Tesoro. You feel too damn good to call it quits early.* From the first stroke, I was as addicted to Calix's body as I was to the rest of him.

There was no way in hell that he could ever get away from me now.

I pumped inside of Calix and turned up the cock ring. The vibrations rumbled away and his back arched as he gazed up at me. I grinned back, expecting him to tap out at any moment, but his eyes burned with determination.

You think you can beat me? That's what I get for chasing a fighter.

But I wasn't complaining. The more he fought, the better it would be when he broke down and couldn't take it anymore. I pulled out suddenly and he let out a squeaky whine that made me laugh. After a moment, I shoved myself back inside and worked him up into a frenzy. Once I saw him on the cusp of losing his mind, I pulled out again.

In and out.

In and out.

In and out.

Calix shook his head as frustrated tears lined his eyes. I leaned down and traced my tongue over a salty tear before I groaned and fucked into him hard.

"Now, apologize," I said as I picked up speed. "I think when you do it now, you'll mean it. Apologize for not obeying orders. For putting yourself in harm's way. For making me fucking insane."

"You were already insane!" he shouted before he sniffled and shook his head.

"Oh? You need to go longer?"

"No!" he shouted. "Please, please let me cum," he begged. "It hurts. Need to cum."

"So." I snapped my hips forward. "Apologize." *Snap.* "Now." *Snap, snap, snap.* I curled my hand around his leash and used it to fuck him with wild abandon.

"Sorry," Calix mumbled out, sweat on his brow. "I'm sorry, Daddy. I-It won't happen again, Sir. I swear it won't. It won't."

"Will you be in any more illegal fights?"

"No, please," he begged. "No more. I'll be your good mutt. I'll do whatever you want Daddy! *¡Fóllame, hijo de puta, fóllame! Solo fóllame por favor papi. Por favor, fóllame papi. ¡Déjame correrme!*"

I chuckled as he called me a son of a bitch and begged Daddy to fuck him all at the same time. Calix's words had turned to incoherent babbling. He couldn't take anymore. I pushed him past his limit for a few more rough strokes before I reached down and released his cock and balls from the ring.

"Cum for me, *Tesoro*. Cum all over your Daddy."

Calix's back arched. Ribbons of cum splashed against his body and mine. The warmth of his load on my body was the final straw. I grunted as I came hard, unleashing a torrent of cum into his spent hole. I hadn't cum in weeks because I knew nothing would feel as good as having Calix.

And I was right.

He laid against his pillow, his eyes glossy as he stared up at the ceiling. Soft Spanish left his lips, but it was a mess of jumbled words and I had no idea what he was saying. As I gazed down at him, I stilled and pushed in deeper. He jumped, moaned, and locked eyes with me as I relaxed. My hot piss filled his hole and his eyes widened to the size of saucers.

"Now you're marked by me in more ways than one," I moaned as I let out every drop. I licked my lips. "Clench your hole. You better not let a single drop out."

"Yes, Daddy," he moaned, his cheeks dusted with pink. "It's hot."

"The piss or the fact that I just did that to you?"

"Both," he whispered.

I chuckled and maneuvered around to the box. Handcuffs came undone and the muzzle was discarded as well. I leaned down and took his lips in a long, slow kiss before I sat up.

"I'm going to pull out now."

"Okay, Daddy," Calix whispered.

"Good boy," I said as I stroked his cheek. "You're perfect."

Calix beamed up at me and my heart sped up. I forced myself to focus on what I was doing and slid out of him. He gasped and nodded.

"Come," I said as I held out a hand. "Shower."

All of the fight had gone out of Calix in the best way. I held onto him to keep him upright as we padded to the bathroom together. I made a beeline to the shower and turned it on before I grabbed a glass sitting on the counter and filled it with cold water. I held it to Calix's lips.

"Drink."

He gulped it down without protest. I sat it to the side and pressed my lips against Calix's. He kissed me back, his hands gripping me tightly. When he stepped back he gazed at me.

"What now?" He asked.

"A shower, a rest, and then breakfast," I said. "And then round two."

Calix blinked at me. "No, you can't be serious."

I raised a brow at him. "I wouldn't joke about sex with you."

Calix swallowed hard. "Shit. I'm still being punished?"

"Oh *mio dolce tesoro.* Of course."

Calix groaned and I laughed as I led him into the shower. We had a long day ahead of us and I was going to enjoy every moment until I had to leave his side. Amadeo would demand I meet at some point, but until then I was going to hold the man that I was obsessed with.

The man that I was falling for.

Chapter Twenty-Two

Calix

I STAYED CURLED UP IN GABRIELE'S ARMS AND TUCKED BENEATH the blanket. He hadn't let me have any peace in the shower. And after he'd made me cum again with his mouth wrapped around my cock, he carried me into the bedroom. My body still twitched and my cock pulsed. The stinging in my ass made me shudder.

No one's ever fucked me like that before.

I'd always assumed that the sex I had in the past was good. Back then, I'd enjoyed it. Now? If I compared what Gabriele had done to me with past lovers, there was no damn competition. He stroked his fingers over my back in circles, his soft humming sending vibrations through my body as I stayed with my head resting against his bare chest.

"Can you move yet?" Gabriele's deep voice rumbled and I melted against him even more.

"Nope," I answered. "I'm in damn good shape and can't feel my legs," I muttered.

Gabriele chuckled. "Thank you. I take that as a compliment."

"It wasn't," I growled. I reached up and touched the collar around my neck. "When are you taking this off?"

"Never," he answered without a moment of hesitation.

"I have fights and stuff you know," I pointed out.

"And when we reach that bridge we'll cross it." His arms squeezed me against him more tightly. "But for now? It's not coming off," he growled.

I shivered. *He means it.* I decided it was better to leave it alone than to keep pushing him. Gabriele hadn't let me go since we'd fallen back into bed. If I didn't know any better I'd say he was being clingy.

Maybe he is. Would that be so strange? After everything he's told me and everything I felt when he fucked me, I don't think we're the same anymore.

I stroked my fingers over his chest. I pulled back so I could look at him and as I searched his face I saw something warm and inviting in his eyes. That hard edge that I'd gotten used to seeing had disappeared. My heart hammered in my chest so hard that I had trouble swallowing. *What is this?*

"You want to ask your questions now, don't you?" Gabriele asked, the corner of his mouth turning down.

I blinked at him. *What questions?* I racked my brain trying to figure out what he was talking about before it clicked. Before we had sex, he'd promised to answer my questions, any that I had. And I had completely forgotten.

What is he doing to my brain?

Gabriele had turned my mind to mush. And it wasn't just the way he fucked me like a wild beast. No, it was the way he held me and made me feel seen and cherished. Every time he called me *Tesoro*, I nearly came undone. It wasn't as if he was just calling me his treasure, it was as if he *meant* it.

I licked my lips. Asking questions was easier than confronting what was going on inside of me. That was something I was going to have to work through later.

"My father," I started. "He's safe?"

"Yes," Gabriele answered. "The moron doesn't know how to hide worth shit," he huffed. "But I made sure I knew where he was. He's been hiding out like I told you, not even going outside." He frowned. "Except for two times when he stepped out and called someone. I assumed it was you."

I frowned. Shit. There had been a few times I'd missed calls, mostly when I was working or training. I'd always assumed it was the normal bill collectors or scammers. I could kick myself.

"Shit," I closed my eyes. "I'm a dumbass."

"For what it's worth, I don't think he would have known what to say," I mumbled. "He always looks conflicted, but he should. Asshole. He abandoned you."

I stared at him. "You've watched him? Personally?"

"Yes," he grunted, no longer looking at me.

"For me?"

Gabriele shifted in bed and sat up. "Enough."

I moved with him and shoved him back against the headboard as he tried to get up. "You said I could ask any question and you'd answer it," I snapped. "Go back on it and I'll kick you out."

"You wouldn't," he said, his eyes narrowing.

"Try me," I bit back. "Even if that's not what I want, I don't give a damn. I'll put you out of my damn house."

Gabriele searched my face before he settled back against the headboard. "Next?"

I watched him for a while until he finally made eye contact. He sighed, his shoulders slumping. *That's better. Stop being so damn closed off.*

"He didn't abandon me."

"Bullshit," Gabriele snapped. "He-"

"He ran off because he was scared and overwhelmed. Ever since I started dealing with your family and collecting debts? I can see why he took off. Was it the right thing to do? Fuck no. I'd never do that to my kid if the situation was reversed, but I get it now." I sighed. "He's not good or bad, Gabriele. He's human and humans fuck up."

Gabriele frowned before he reached out and tousled my hair. "Why are you so smart?" he asked. "Feels like you're smarter than me most times."

"I *am* smarter than you." I grinned. "You're a hothead who doesn't think first and I'm the opposite of that. No shit I'm more intelligent than you."

He flicked my forehead.

"You're a child," I growled.

"True," he sighed before he shook his head. "Maybe you're right. I talk about you having views of black and white, but I'm the same with your father. I still think he's a piece of shit."

I shrugged. "I can't change your mind about that. I'm smart enough to know that." I laughed before I thought about something else. "What about my debt? Does it still stand?" I jumped out of bed and winced as I walked over to the floor and removed one of the boards. I dug up the cash Conor had dropped off after I reported to him the night before. He'd stopped by after Gabriele took off and thanked me. I scooped up the cash and laid it on the bed. "That's not everything, but it's most of it. A hundred grand is left, and if I can just go to a few more underground fights, I'll-"

Gabriele was up so fast I jumped. His hand wrapped around my neck and my back slammed against the bed. I stared up at him and reached out to grip his arm. He squeezed and I immediately pulled my hands away and laid them on the bed instead. Like a dog, I rolled over and showed my belly to the alpha in the room.

I never thought I'd be so pathetic.

"We agreed," Gabriele growled. "What was it?"

"No...more fights." I shook my head. "I know, Daddy."

My cock twitched when I called him that and I forced myself to calm down. *Focus.*

He searched my face. "No more underground fights," he said again. "If I catch you at even one. I'll chain you to my bed and you'll never leave again. And if you think I won't? Try me."

I didn't see an ounce of a lie on his face. He really would chain me to his bed and while that seemed like fun for an evening, doing it for the rest of my life would grow old fast.

"No more underground fights."

Gabriele loosened his grip. "Let's not have that discussion again."

I sat up when he allowed me to and touched my throat. Even when he wasn't touching me, I could still feel him. Lately, I could *always* feel him. And I didn't hate it.

More like I love it.

That firm grip, his warm hands, the look in his eyes. All of it made me feel like I was wanted. Maybe I was sick in the head, but when Gabriele manhandled me, I just wanted more.

He leaned down and kissed my neck. "I wish you'd stop pissing me off so much," he growled.

I grinned. "Yeah, I don't think that's going to happen. It's the thing I'm best at."

Gabriele grunted and then burst out laughing. "It is," he said as he wrapped his arms around me. "Why do I enjoy that?"

"We're both fucked in the head?" I asked as I sat back and stared up at him. "But seriously, what about my debt?"

He frowned. "I don't have the authority to erase it. But I have a meeting with Amadeo later and we're going to talk about it. Okay? If I have to punch him in the face repeatedly, he better listen to me," he said as he stared off.

I took his hand and Gabriele gazed back at me. "Don't do that. I feel like Amadeo would kick your ass."

He smiled at me. "He'd try."

Crash!

I jumped and Gabriele turned on his heels. He ran for the nightstand that had become his and dug around before he pulled out a gun. Normally, I would have protested. But someone had just broken into my home and I didn't feel like dying.

Heavy footsteps trudged up the stairs.

"Get in the closet," Gabriele whispered.

I didn't protest. As much as I didn't want to leave his side, if I got in the middle I might end up getting him killed. I slipped out of bed and quickly made my way to the closet. Once I slid inside, I closed it almost completely and stared through a slit in the door. My heart pounded in my chest and I struggled to take in a breath that wasn't loud as hell.

The door opened and I held my breath altogether as I heard Gabriele's gun cock. I waited for the gunshots to start, but they never did. After what felt like an eternal silence, someone sighed.

"Come out," Gabriele called.

I frowned and opened the door slowly. Once I stood in the open, I glanced at the person who had broken into my house.

Amadeo Bianchi. He stared at me, his eyes narrowed before he gazed back at his brother. The two of them didn't say a word, but I could feel the electricity in the air.

"I told you to meet me last night," Amadeo said.

"And I told you that I'd do it this afternoon. Last I checked, it's still morning."

"It's noon."

"Close enough." Gabriele shrugged. "What we need to talk about could wait. I put feelers out for more information, made sure my bases were covered and was going to report to you in a few hours. So, get off my back."

I shivered. *Don't say that shit. Fuck, Gabriele.*

Amadeo stepped forward. "Your mouth is going to get you killed."

"Not by you," Gabriele shot back. "You won't get off my ass about Calix, but I'm still working. I'm doing my part. And let's not forget how distracted you were when you were with Six."

"That was different."

"Was it?" Gabriele snapped.

"Yes, because I love him."

"And I love Calix," he growled. "So when I say back off I mean it. Because I'll kick your ass to keep him."

I froze and stared at Gabriele. *Did I hear him right?* The words I love Calix played in my head on repeat and I couldn't believe I'd actually heard it. I blinked at him, but he didn't look away from Amadeo. His fists were bawled up tight and I got the feeling they were going to come to blows if I didn't do anything.

Slowly, I reached out and took Gabriele's hand. He jerked, but when I tried again, he stayed still and let me pry his hand open. I slipped my fingers into his and when our hands grasped each other he finally glanced at me instead of his brother.

"You just said..."

"I know," he grumbled. "Don't make a big thing out of it."

I grinned, because what else could I do? Gabriele loved me. My own emotions were a tropical shit storm, but I knew I had feelings for him. Shit, I'd known for weeks now that something about him drove me crazy. I just didn't know that this was where it would lead.

"Gabriele," Amadeo started. "I think-"

"Get away from him!" The loud cocking of a gun drew our attention to the doorway where Mrs. Lopez stood with a handgun that looked way too big for her and pointed at Amadeo. "Get out!"

My heart nearly dropped out of my ass as I pulled away from Gabriele and held up my hands. "Whoa, whoa, put that down," I groaned as I walked over to her. "I'm fine, Sofia. This isn't what it looks like."

Her gaze darted from me to Gabriele, to Amadeo, and back again. "I saw someone kick in your door and I thought one of these thugs had come to hurt you."

My groan deepened and I pinched the bridge of my nose. "As sweet as that is, please, put that down. There's nothing wrong with me." I jerked a thumb over my shoulder. "That one spent the night for God's sake."

She raised a brow before realization hit her. "Oh, it's like *that*."

"Yes," I sighed. "It's like that."

Mrs. Lopez put the gun down and sighed. "Why didn't you tell me? And you," she said as she pointed at Amadeo. "You still shouldn't be kicking down doors in this kind of neighborhood. Anyone would think you're trying to rob someone blind! Especially if you walk around looking like thugs."

"Sofia," I whispered and shook my head hard as my pulse quickened. Did she know who she was insulting? "No," I mumbled.

Gabriele and Amadeo looked at each other before they both burst out laughing. I stared at them like they'd lost their minds. When I glanced at Mrs. Lopez, she shrugged, equally as confused as I was.

Amadeo shook his head and sighed. "Can you get dressed and get in the car?" he said as he looked me up and down. "Bring him too."

"Where are we going?" I asked.

Gabriele shook his head. "Closet. Clothes," he said shortly. "We'll be down in a minute Ama. And keep your eyes to yourself."

Amadeo whistled. "You really do love this one, huh?" he asked as he took another look at me. "I've never seen you be so overprotective."

Gabriele growled. "One more glance," he said as he shoved me behind his back. "And we'll go right back to being on the verge of killing each other."

"Fair enough," Amadeo said before he turned around. "Sofia, is it? Come on, I'll walk you back next door. I saw you on the porch when I pulled up."

"Yes, I watch the neighborhood," she said as she walked beside him. "Don't think I won't shoot you if you try anything funny."

Amadeo held up his hands. "I wouldn't dream of it."

"Well, that guy back there is always threatening me."

"Yes, he's the rude one of the family. I apologize on his behalf."

Sofia scoffed. "I'll tell you about rude ones. My sister Camila is the worst of them..."

Their conversation trailed off as they disappeared down the stairs. *Huh. Maybe Amadeo isn't so bad.* Gabriele turned to look at me and frowned.

"We have more to talk about, don't we?"

"Big time," I said as I grinned at him. "Why is he so nice to Sofia?"

Gabriele blinked. "That's what you want to talk about?"

I shrugged. "I'm curious."

"He's always had a thing about old ladies," he sighed. "I mean he's a complete asshole, but he's a respectful asshole sometimes."

I grinned. "I like that."

Gabriele grabbed a handful of my hair. "Don't smile like that while looking wistfully after my brother or I might take it as I need to fuck you all over again."

"I don't think we have time," I pointed out. "Your brother's waiting."

"And he can wait even longer for all I care."

Gabriele took my mouth in a punishing kiss. My lips ached and I sank against him as he moaned against my mouth. I had more questions for Gabriele, but now wasn't the time to ask him. Once I broached the big subjects, I needed there to be no one else around. I wanted all of his attention on me.

I'm becoming as possessive as he is.

The thought made my lips curl into a smile. For the first time ever, I gave enough of a damn about a man to be possessive over him. And I wouldn't change it for the world.

Chapter Twenty-Three

Calix

"I CAN'T BELIEVE YOU MADE ME WEAR THIS STUPID THING!" I snapped as I tugged out the collar around my neck as much as possible and glared at him. "Amadeo saw it *and* Mrs. Lopez too! What were you thinking?"

Gabriele smirked. "I was thinking you look damn good in it," he said as he laid a hand on my thigh. "And if you try to take it off, I'll yank you over my knee and spank your ass until you beg me to stop." He glanced over at me before he fixed his gaze back on the road. "Besides, what's wrong with people knowing you belong to me? Are you ashamed?"

My face burned. "No," I mumbled.

Gabriele rose a brow. "Are you trying to hide me from someone?" he asked, his grip tightening.

"Ow, no!" I groaned. "You fuck me one time and you become the clingiest man I've ever known," I said as I rolled my eyes.

His grip loosened. "Do you have a problem with that?"

"If I say yes?"

Gabriele grinned. "It won't change anything, but you can say it."

Of course, I had to go and attract the attention of a psychopath.

We pulled up to a huge house sitting behind an impressive gate. Gabriele sat there for a moment after he rolled down the window. The gate opened and he drove up to the house.

"How do they know who you are?" I asked. "You didn't even use the box."

"Don't have to. They know who I am," he said as he parked the car. "I'm going to have this meeting with Ama and I need you to keep your head down and stay out of the way, alright?"

I frowned. "Sounds like I'm just gonna get in the way," I muttered.

"Don't do that," Gabriele said as he reached over and cradled my cheek. "You're not in the way, but this is important. I don't want you caught up in the middle of my problems." He brushed his lips against mine. "My brothers will be here too so just...watch out for them."

I swallowed hard. "Watch out for them? Are they going to do something to me?"

"Besides get on your last nerve? Probably not. But they're idiots and I don't want to have to kill one of them if they hurt you." He frowned. "Or touch you."

"Clingy," I sang.

"Shut. Up."

Gabriele kissed me again and I moaned as he licked at my lip. I jumped as a loud knock rapped on the car window. My heart hammered out of my chest as I turned to see a woman smiling at me.

"You must be Gabe's new toy." She grinned. "He's cute!"

My face burned. "Um, who's that?" I asked as I turned to Gabriele who had furiously opened his door.

"Rayna," he groaned. "My sister."

Woah. She's gorgeous.

"Stop staring," Gabriele growled. "I swear you don't want to keep your eyes, do you?"

Rayna laughed as I stepped out of the car. She tossed long, dark locks over her shoulder and held out a perfectly manicured hand. "Don't let my brother bully you! He can stare all he wants," she teased, her smile making me feel at ease. "Rayna."

I shook her hand. "Calix."

Gabriele ripped our hands apart and yanked me against his body. I stared at him, but he was too busy glaring at his sister who continued to look amused. I shook my head.

"Sorry, he's kind of crazy," I muttered.

"It's a Bianchi men thing," she purred. "They're all nuts."

"Bianchi *men*?" Gabriele questioned. "Have you not met yourself?"

She stuck out her tongue. "I'm perfectly sane, Gabe."

"Enough you two," Amadeo said as he walked over to us from his car. "Let's go inside. Everyone else is already here. We were waiting for you to show up, Gabriele."

"Yeah, yeah, I know." Gabriele wrapped an arm around my shoulders and guided me inside. "Let's get this over with. We haven't even eaten."

Amadeo glanced at me over his shoulder. "I'll have Six order something for him."

"Thanks," Gabriele said, his shoulders relaxing a bit as we made our way into a sitting room where Six bounced up from the couch. Three other men were already there. One I knew and the other two looked related to Gabriele and Amadeo. "These are my cousins, Dario and Niccolo, you know him." He nodded. "And that Riccardo, my brother."

"Hey," I said.

Nic jumped up out of his seat. "Holy shit!" He burst out laughing. "What's going on, Gabriele? You finally bringing the boyfriend home?"

"Fuck you," Gabriele snapped.

"He didn't deny the boyfriend part," Rayna said as she breezed past us and sat on the couch.

"Why would I?" Gabriele growled at her. "Would you all lay off?"

"He's cute," Riccardo said.

Rayna chuckled. "That's what I said."

"Okay, that's it," Gabriele said as he let go of me and marched over to them.

Six walked over to me with a huge grin on his face. As soon as he opened his mouth, I held up a hand.

"Don't say it," I said. "I know what you're going to say and just-"

"How was the dick?"

I groaned. "Seriously?"

Amadeo snapped his fingers. "Six, take Calix out and go get breakfast from the chef. We'll talk about that little question later."

Six grinned. "I'm sure we will. But it'll be worth it," he said as he smacked me on the back. "Let's get out of here before we get in trouble."

I wanted to say there was no way in hell I would get in trouble, but the collar around my neck said otherwise. Discreetly, I tugged up the collar of my button-up and tried to make sure no one else could see it. Six seemed way too preoccupied to notice as he led me to a small dining area outside. He pulled out his phone and passed it to me.

"Order anything you want and she'll make it. There's a breakfast and lunch menu available right now but if you really want something different she'll do it for you." Six laughed. "She'll call you an asshole under your her but she'll do it."

I stared at him. "How is this your normal life?"

Six shrugged. "Beats my last one and the one before that," he said as he stared at me. "So seriously? How was the dick? Clearly, Gabriele had a good time if he brought you here."

"Amadeo told him to," I said as I shrugged. "It's not like he had a choice."

He laughed. "Are you kidding me? Amadeo says he never lets anyone in his home or around his family but Gabriele *let* you come here. Amadeo might have told him to bring you, but if he didn't want to, Gabriele would fight him on it. Did he?"

I thought back to my house and my lips curled into an involuntary smile. "No, he didn't."

"Exactly," Six said. "So the dick? Big? Small? Curved?"

I grabbed a napkin and threw it at Six's face. "I would never tell you that."

He groaned. "Come on, I need more details. I love a good storytime."

"You love to be a pervert," I said as I clicked on some random menu items and sent the order to the kitchen at the touch of a button. "He said he loved me," I blurted out. "In front of Amadeo."

Six's jaw dropped. "Fuck. Holy fuck!" he said as he laughed so hard he wrapped an arm around his stomach. "I never would have expected that from you two. Fucking I can see, but he's in love?"

"I'm as shocked as you are," I said, my face burning up as I flipped Six off. "Stop acting like an asshole already."

He grinned. "Hey, I'm happy for you," he said as he turned serious. "No, really. If anyone deserves to have someone on their side, it's you. And Gabriele Bianchi *is* pretty fucking hot."

"You just want your boyfriend to kill you, right? That's your whole thing?"

Six chuckled. "Every time he's jealous, he fucks me a hell of a lot harder and doesn't hold back." He winked. "I'm into it."

"I'm sure you are," I sighed as I pinched the bridge of my nose. "Freak."

"Says the one with a collar around his neck," Six said as someone walked over and dropped off two bottles of water. He picked his up and unscrewed the cap as he gazed over the top of it at me.

I wanted to sink underneath the table and hide. But Six would only make fun of me more. Instead, I shoved the bottle of water against my mouth and took a long, deep chug. The collar felt even heavier around my throat. *If I took it off for a second, Gabriele wouldn't know.* I reached up and touched it.

"Don't even think about it," Gabriele growled as he stormed over and yanked my hand away. "Didn't I tell you not to toy with that?"

I jumped. "I wasn't going to take it off."

"Yes, he was," Six said. "I saw him tugging at it."

My eyes bugged out of my head. "What the shit? Six!"

He smirked at me, but I didn't have time to look at him. Gabriele grabbed my cheeks and forced me to look up at him. "You've earned yourself another punishment tonight." A man came out and sat muffins on the table. Gabriele took one before he released my cheeks. "I'm going back into my meeting. Behave, *cane*."

"Yes, sir," I said on an exhale.

Gabriele grinned at me. "Good boy."

He ran his fingers through my hair before he walked back into the house. I reached up and touched where his hand had lingered. Before we'd left my place, I had tried to put it up into a bun, but he wouldn't let me. *I think he has a thing for it down.*

I blinked and realized I'd been staring after him for a long time. When I glanced at Six, there was a grin on his face. I cracked my knuckles.

"I'm going to kick your ass."

Six threw his head back and laughed. "I wouldn't recommend it," he said. "You'll be the one that gets in trouble."

I groaned and shoved back against my seat. *Shit, he's right.* If I did anything to Six Amadeo would definitely try to murder me.

"All I did was give you a little more fun for later. You're welcome." Food was brought in and we paused long enough to dig in. I'd ordered a bunch of baked chicken, pasta, and vegetables while Six had a bowl of mac and cheese. Once we dug in, he pointed his fork at me. "Do you love him?"

I nearly choked on a piece of chicken. I pounded my chest until it rolled down my throat and stared at Six. He looked back at me expectantly.

"Um, I uh-"

"You didn't say it back," he said after a minute. He frowned. "And Gabriele was...cool with that?"

It was my turn to frown. He hadn't said anything, but now that I thought about it I wasn't sure how Gabriele felt. When he brushed it off, we hadn't had time to go into depth with the conversation.

How do I feel about him?

I cared. That much I knew. Gabriele pissed me off and I wanted him to shut the hell up most times, but damn did I not want to be away from him. Every time I thought about him leaving me on my own, I felt like I was about to explode.

"Yo, pay attention," Six called as he snapped his fingers in front of my face. "Do you love him or not?"

"I don't know, okay?" I said as I went back to eating. "I'm still figuring it out."

Six nodded. "I get that," he said. "Just don't wait around forever. A guy like Gabriele isn't short of options."

I paused. "What do you mean?"

"I'm talking about Gabriele being a complete fuck boy not that long ago. Amadeo says he used to take home a different person every night. Well, not his home, but a hotel or whatever you know?"

My chest tightened. "Really?"

"Yeah," Six said. "I don't mean to make you upset or anything..."

I waved my hand. "No, actually I need to know this shit. Gabriele doesn't tell me much about him. He won't even tell me what's going on with him and his father."

Six sat up straight. "Oh, that."

I blinked. "You know about his father, don't you?"

He nodded slowly. "Yeah, I know."

"Tell me."

Six snapped his mouth shut and shook his head. For the first time ever, Six was quiet. An uneasy feeling settled into my stomach. I didn't push him to talk and we both sat in silence.

I need to find out the truth about his father.

Chapter Twenty Four

Gabriele

"Were you able to find anything else?" Amadeo asked as he sat back in his chair, his eyebrows drawn together. "What came back?"

I shook my head. I'd been checking my sources since we arrived at his house, but there was nothing. The name Andrei wasn't all that uncommon and the tattoo wasn't giving me any results either. As much as I wanted to find the bastard, there was nothing to go on.

"You're going to have to give me a few more days to shake something loose," I said as I scratched at my beard. "Whoever he is, the guy I sliced into last night was terrified of him."

Dario frowned. "You think he's running things?"

I shrugged. "Sounds like it." I went back to pacing so I could keep my thoughts straight. "Nothing else is giving us any results so let's keep following this lead for now."

Amadeo nodded. "Alright, but I still want every last one of us out there turning over rocks until we find this worm. Whoever he is, he's crossed the line several times. I'm not burying anyone else." He looked me over. "Anything else?"

"No, not now."

"Okay." Amadeo stood up. "Then let's talk about Calix."

I groaned. "Fuck no," I cursed. "I don't want to have a conversation about that."

"Too bad," he said. "So, you love him?"

Rayna whistled. "Love is a big word," she said. "You? The whore of the family loves someone?"

I rolled my eyes. "*I'm* the whore of the family?" I asked as I grabbed a cigarette and lit it. "I thought that was you, Rayna."

She smirked. "Sometimes." Rayna shook her head. "I never thought you'd be the type to settle down."

"Yeah well," I shrugged.

What was I supposed to say to them? I didn't think I wanted that either. Or at least I'd never admitted it to myself. I couldn't think of a single person who didn't crave having someone else beside them. But I'd never thought it was possible. Not until I met Calix.

"I noticed a large amount of money at his house," Amadeo said.

I glanced up at him. Oh yeah, the money. I had been about to tell Calix I didn't fucking want it when we were interrupted.

"Tell him to hand over every dime and we'll lose some of the paperwork on the interest," Amadeo said. "I'll consider him paid off and his father can come home. As long as he doesn't try to take out another loan, we're good."

"How can you be sure that isn't his plan?" Riccardo interrupted. "What if he's been trying to climb into bed with you so he can save his father?"

I frowned at my brother. Riccardo was always the cynical one, but I couldn't blame him. When it came to Calix, however, I knew that he wouldn't do that. He couldn't stand me at first and it was impossible to fake that kind of hatred.

"No," I said as I shook my head. "I believe him." I turned to Amadeo. "He'll give you the money. Calix is with me now, so he doesn't need money anyway."

"Glad we could come to an understanding." Amadeo held out a hand. "Sorry I was a dick about him. I'm protective. Over all of you."

I took his hand. "I understand," I said. "But I would have kept him anyway."

"I have no doubt you would have," he mused. "Regardless of how much I kicked your ass. That's how I know you really give a damn about him."

"Awww they're so cute together," Nic whispered loud enough for people down the hall to hear. "Kiss and make up. Kiss!"

I flung a pillow at his head and Nic grunted as he went down. "Someone needs to put you on a leash."

"Never!" his muffled voice echoed back before he yanked down the pillow and grinned. "I'll never become the two of you," he said pointing. "Riccardo and I are bachelors for life."

Ric nodded. "Yeah."

I couldn't take either one of them right now. Amadeo and I were square, Calix's debt was forgiven, and I was itching to get back to my boy.

"If there's nothing else..." I trailed off.

"Just be careful," Amadeo said. "Something's going on here and if anyone figures out you're the one that offed that guy, they'll be after you."

"I was careful," I said. "No one that stepped out of that bar was alive by the time I was done."

"Still," Amadeo insisted. "Watch your back."

I nodded. After the night I'd had, he was right. Someone had a target painted on all of our backs. *I need to keep Calix close to me.* We went our separate ways after the meeting and I walked into the backyard to find Calix and Six talking.

"Time to go," I said.

Calix glanced at me before he looked back at Six. "Text me later."

"Will do," Six said cheerily before he grinned at me. "I see you took my advice and went easy on my friend," he teased. "See? It all worked out for you because of me. You owe me one."

"I don't owe you shit," I growled. "You're the reason I got stuck with him in the first place."

"Hey!" Calix glared at me. "What the hell is that supposed to mean?"

Six chuckled as I stumbled over my words. Calix continued to glare at me and I rubbed the back of my neck. "Nothing," I grumbled. "Move your ass."

Calix crossed his arms over his chest. "Where the hell are we going?"

"Don't test me," I snapped.

"Fuck you."

I grabbed Calix's arm and yanked him against me. "What was that?"

The spark in his eyes was back. Instead of folding right away, he stared back at me without saying a word. Six snickered and I gave him a death glare.

"Stop it," Amadeo said as he grabbed a handful of Six's hair. "You're starting trouble."

"I'm bored." Six laughed as he was dragged away. "Ow, ow, come on. Ouch! Daddy," he moaned as they disappeared back into the house.

I turned back to Calix. "Don't pay that moron any attention."

Calix punched me in the chest and I grunted. "He's not a moron. An asshole, sure. But not a moron." I slipped my hand into his and he didn't pull away. "So what do you mean when you say you got stuck with me?"

I groaned. This was going to be a long ass day.

***

I pulled into my usual spot in the parking structure of my high rise. My heart sat in my throat as I climbed out and Calix followed. He looked around, confusion coloring his face as he walked over to me.

"Where are we?"

"Home," I said shortly. "Well, my home."

Calix didn't follow me so I turned to look at him. He stared at me and I threw up a hand.

"Your place? Like your real place?"

"What kind of stupid question is that?" I asked. "Of course, it's my real place. What? Do you think I have a fake place just waiting around?"

"Probably," Calix said. "I mean it's...you. I've heard about how you are with people."

I groaned. "Everyone needs to learn to keep their mouths shut." I took his hand and frowned as I turned on my heels and tugged him along behind me. "Yeah I have a reputation, but you've known that from the start."

"Kind of," Calix answered. "I didn't know how bad it was though."

"Does it matter?" I asked as we stepped into the elevator. Once the doors closed, I turned to him. "You're the only one that's here with me, right?"

Calix nodded. "Right," he said. But he didn't sound convinced.

I shoved my finger against the stop button and the elevator jolted. Calix glanced up at it before his eyes darted to me. I stepped in front of the panel and crossed my arms over my chest.

"You told me not to lie to you."

Calix blinked. "Yeah, I did."

"So when I tell you that you're the only person that's come up here, besides my family, that's what I mean. Do you understand me, *cane*?"

"Yeah," he said, his eyes wide as he realized I wasn't joking around.

"No, I want more than that," I said as I walked over and gripped a handful of his hair.

"Yes, Daddy," he choked out before I pushed him to his knees. Calix gazed up at me. "What are you doing?"

"Open your mouth, tongue out." I undid my pants and he opened his mouth like I'd told him to. I ran my cock over his tongue and he gazed up at me with big, round eyes. The sweet expression on his face sent a shiver up my spine. "When I tell you something from now on, it'll be the truth, Calix. Rather I want to talk about it or not. Even if it hurts your feelings or makes you hate me. That's what you asked for and that's what I'll give you."

"Gabriele-"

I gripped my cock and shoved it into Calix's mouth. "No more talking. Suck or I'll fuck your throat for the rest of the night."

He shivered and reached up.

"No," I slapped his hand away and ripped open the front of his shirt so I could see the collar around his throat. "Arms behind your back. Just your mouth."

Calix moaned and closed his eyes, but I didn't want that. I wanted to see every expression that crossed his face as he sucked me off. I scraped my nails across his scalp and squeezed his hair tightly.

"Keep your eyes on me, baby," I moaned as I jerked forward and my cock slipped to the back of his throat. He choked and gagged, but I held myself there until he stared into my eyes. "Good boy. Don't turn away. Not even for a second."

He bobbed his head once I pulled away and inhaled sharply through his nose. *Impressive.* He didn't even try to come up to choke down air. I admired that. I ran my fingers through his long hair and marveled at his gorgeous face. He was the most intoxicating man I'd ever met.

I dragged Calix along my cock and held myself in place. He gazed up at me, his eyes going wider and wider as he struggled against me. I saw the conflicted look on his face and grinned.

"It's hot, knowing that you need me to breathe. And that you still aren't trying to save yourself." He kept his arms behind his back as his eyes watered. "Fuck, Calix. You make me want to tear you apart."

My heart swelled as I pulled out suddenly and he choked. He sucked in a shuddering breath and wiped his mouth before his eyes tracked back up at me. *That look. The way he is with me. I love the fuck out of him.*

"More," Calix moaned. "Please, Daddy."

I slipped into his mouth and snapped my hips forward roughly. Calix's moaning hums wrapped around my cock and went straight to my balls. He gagged, but he didn't stop. Calix sucked harder as I braced myself against the wall with one arm and stared down at him. My balls tightened and I groaned as every sensation grew to a fever pitch.

"Fuck, yes," I groaned deep as my eyes closed and I pumped my cum down Calix's throat. "Good boy," I moaned. "Such a good boy."

I shivered as I slowly regained myself and gazed down at Calix. He licked his lips, his eyes full of warmth and fire that needed to be snuffed out all over again. I pulled him to his feet and took his lips in a punishing kiss. The taste of me still lingered, stoking the fire that was always in my belly ever since I'd met Calix. His moans against my mouth fueled me on and I couldn't wait to get him upstairs.

I turned and mashed the start button before I yanked up my pants. Calix leaned against my side and I wrapped my arm around him before I tilted his head up and gripped his stubbled cheeks.

"Do you believe me?" I asked. "Honestly?"

Calix sighed. "I want to, but it's going to take longer than a day, Gabriele. But if you say I'm the only person who's been up here then yeah, I believe that."

Relief flooded me as I brushed my lips against his. "Well, since you're the first, I think that means you're obligated to help me christen every single surface."

He burst out laughing. "I'm still sore from my fights, you know. You have to let me rest sometime."

I thought about it. "No." I gave him a quick peck on the mouth and turned as the elevator dinged, alerting us to our arrival. I took his hand. "But you can have small breaks for water and snacks."

Calix groaned. "This is going to be a long night, isn't it?"

I smirked. "Oh you have no idea."

Chapter Twenty Five

Calix

I STARED AT MY PHONE FOR THE FIFTH TIME IN A HALF-HOUR TIME frame. Gabriele had dropped me off at work and said he would text me later. And that he was picking me up. I'd insisted I had my own damn car to drive, but his answer was to kiss me, bite my lip, and smack my ass as I climbed out of his car.

And even though he was still a douchebag, I missed him. My mind drifted to last night's activities. The man had been true to his word and fucked me on every surface he could. When he couldn't pump me full of cum anymore, I'd thought it was over.

That was before he brought out the box of toys.

My body ached in ways I'd never experienced before and it wasn't unpleasant. Instead, I could feel where his hands had lingered, where his teeth had bitten me, and where he'd kissed every ache away before he curled around me and refused to let me go for the rest of the night.

Who knew Bianchi men were so fucking clingy?

"Boss." Sam walked into my office and I shoved my phone away. "I'm heading out for the day. You need anything?"

I shook my head. "Nope, not a thing."

He grinned. "You look happy as hell. Tal and I are proud of you."

My heart squeezed. Gabriele had given me the news the night before and after I handed over all my cash happily, I was free. The gym was mine, no more collections, no more mafia bullshit. I was ready to go back to my peaceful life. The only chaos that would be left behind was Gabriele, but I was willing to let him stay.

Not that I could get rid of him if I tried. He'd drag me right back.

The thought of falling for someone like Gabriele made my stomach twist into knots. He loved harder than anyone I'd ever met, but he was all-consuming. If I was with him, then I was with him. And I doubted I could one day say *it's not you, it's me,* and walk away with my life.

But that's part of what makes dating him so hot. I need deep therapy.

"Cal?"

I glanced up at Sam and remembered he was there for the first time. "Sorry, my head's a million miles away." I pushed back in my seat and stood up. "But I'm glad that we're able to keep this place." I glanced around, my chest pushing out as I admired every crack in the wall and every bit of chipped paint that needed redoing. It was *my* place this time. Not my father's. Mine. "I couldn't imagine life without it."

"Me either," Sam sighed. "I was worried there for a minute, but glad I get to keep the best job I've ever had." He grinned as we strolled out into the gym. "It's been a while since all of us have done anything but worry. How about Tal and I drag you out for a beer or five tonight?"

"Your girl will kill us both."

Sam chuckled. "Nah. As long as she knows where I am these days, she's fine. Besides, we owe you. So, drinks?"

I checked my phone again. "Let me answer that once I get a message back from someone. Then I'll know if I'm free."

"Someone." Tal laughed as she walked over and shook her head. "You mean that little boyfriend of yours."

"Boyfriend? What boyfriend?" I asked.

Sam and Tal exchanged a look and burst into laughter. I groaned and wiped a hand down my face. *Was I that obvious?* By the time they caught their breaths, I glared at them.

"Alright, alright fuck off and go home," I said. "You're both a pain in my ass."

"You love us," Tal teased. She patted me on the arm. "Go home and get some rest. Or don't." She winked. "You deserve a reward for putting up with this shit."

"I do," I nodded. "Go home."

They waved and headed for the door. I pushed the door forward to lock up after them when Gabriele's hand pushed against the glass and he smiled at me. Tal and Sam looked at him and Tal grinned.

"Go home!" I told her.

She chuckled as I moved back and let Gabriele inside. He locked the door after him and I opened my mouth to ream him out for not texting. I didn't get a word out before his lips crashed against mine and he tore at my clothes like a starving person. Breathless,

I resisted the urge to give in and kiss him back, but only barely. I shoved a hand against his chest and he panted as he stumbled back, his eyes full of lust.

"Come here, boy," he growled. "I wasn't done."

"You sure as shit were," I answered as I adjusted my disheveled clothes. "I didn't get a text from you."

"The day ran long," he said. "I was putting out fires left and right."

"And a text message takes five seconds to send."

Gabriele pushed his fingers through his hair and growled. "Alright, I get it."

"No, you don't," I said as I turned toward the office. "I'm getting my shit and going home."

"I made reservations for us."

"So you had time for reservations, but no time for a text," I said as I gathered up my stuff. When I turned, he was right in front of me. "Move."

"Why are you being such an asshole?" he asked. "Did you miss me that much?"

"Fuck you."

Gabriele gripped the back of my head and yanked me forward. "If you don't move your ass toward that car, then I'll bend you in half and fuck the stupid out of you."

I shoved him away again. "I said no."

"What do you want from me?" he snapped.

"How about a goddamn text!"

I shoved my wallet into my pocket and stormed out of the office. My stomach tensed and I swallowed hard. Seeing him triggered my irritation so quickly. And I knew why. *He was right. I missed him.*

Arms wrapped around me and I groaned as I tried to pull away. Attraction, lust, and care were different than what I felt now. Need. I *needed* him, wanted to hear from him, and I was disappointed that he wouldn't keep his damn word even when it came to something simple.

My damn feelings were hurt.

"I'm sorry," Gabriele said as he held me against him. "But I was in a basement all day, slicing into some asshole. I tried to text you, bloody hands and all I fucking swear. But I couldn't get any damn reception and torture is a delicate thing. You walk away and you have to start all over again." He sighed as he buried his face against my neck. "And I could have had someone text you for me the way I had those reservations made, but... I don't want anyone talking to you but me. It was selfish. I'm sorry."

My heart fluttered. I should be disgusted that he was torturing people, but some part of me had finally cracked because I didn't exactly care. I still wanted no part of it, but I knew Gabriele wasn't going to change. Part of being with him was accepting him. *All* of him.

Slowly, I turned in his arms and saw how sad he looked. He called me a dog, but he reminded me of a puppy. I sighed and touched his cheek.

"Fine," I mumbled. "Next time just say that."

Gabriele pushed his fingers into my hair and tugged my head back. "You make me fuckin' crazy you know that, baby? Such a pain in my ass and I put up with you."

"I know," I said.

When he kissed me this time, I let him. His lips lingered on mine for so long that I grew dizzy, but I didn't want him to stop.

***

I tugged at the collar of my shirt. Gabriele had picked a place that looked so fancy I was sure I couldn't afford to even *breathe* in there, but he looked like he was right at home. Soft music played through the restaurant and the smell of food made my stomach growl. I picked up the menu and stared at the words.

"French," I muttered. "I don't read French."

"Or speak it," Gabriele said as his eyes roamed over his own menu. "So, put it down and let Daddy order for you."

My cock stiffened and I shoved my thighs together. "Do you have to say that so loud?" I hissed.

"Yes," he answered before he gazed over at me with a smirk on his lips. "Because it makes you go all red and you start squirming."

I stopped moving in my seat and glared at him. "I change my mind. I'm ready to be pissed off at you again."

"Too bad. I allowed you one outburst for the day. The next one will result in me losing my patience and fucking you until we're both sore." He winked at me. "Not that you hate that."

"I literally tell you to stop all the time. You're just a pervert."

"A pervert you keep bending over for."

FIGHT ME DADDY

I groaned and Gabriele chuckled as he went back to perusing the menu. The little smirk on his face made me want to slap him and kiss him at the same damn time. He was so sure of himself. It was part of what made him hot.

The waiter approached and Gabriele rattled off our order in French so smooth I would have thought he was born in France. He handed the menus over when he was done and raised a brow at me as I stared at him.

"What?"

"How *do* you know how to speak so many languages?"

"My father had an interest in languages. He taught me most of what he knew and the rest he got me tutors for. It was what I wanted to do and he always gave me what I wanted."

I stared at him, surprised that he was talking about his dad. "So, he was nice?"

Gabriele picked up his glass of wine and laughed. "What? Just because he was a big, bad boss meant he couldn't love his kids?" When I shrugged, he gazed off into the distance. "Well, he did. He loved each of us, but I was probably the closest to him. We were inseparable."

I tried to approach the subject delicately so I wouldn't make him shut down. "Why were you the closest?"

Gabriele thought about it. "I guess because Amadeo was busy trying to prove that he could take over. He was always trying to show he was the best. Riccardo was always a mama's boy so he spent the most time with her. And Rayna is well Rayna." He laughed. "She was a wild child from the start and he always tried to reign her in. But she was his princess. They were probably as close as the two of us were. I was just older, that's all. I saw a lot more and took part in a hell of a lot more."

I picked up my glass and tried to pretend I knew what to do with such an expensive wine. One sip and I missed a cold beer. But I drank it anyway.

"Is that why you couldn't-"

Gabriele's fist tightened on the table. "No," he said evenly.

I sighed. "You keep avoiding the subject, but you did give me a promise. I could ask you any question and you'd answer. And I was interrupted before." Gabriele's brows knitted and I reached out and laid my hand on top of his.

"Yeah, that's why I couldn't go this year. I've done it for the past five and shook it off like it was nothing. But every time I go I come back and...I'm a mess," he sighed as he finally looked back at me. "Booze, sex, drugs, fights; whatever I can get my hands on, I do. And for some reason, I just couldn't handle it this year. There's already so much shit going on. I couldn't add to it."

I gave his hand a tight squeeze. "I'm sorry," I said. "I lost my mother when I was sixteen and I spiraled out of control. Nobody understood me the way she did. And nobody probably ever will."

Gabriele turned his hand over and held mine. "Yeah, that's the feeling," he grumbled. "Like there's a hole no one else can fix and they're just...gone."

I nodded as tears gathered in my eyes and threatened to spill. Knowing what I knew now, I wasn't so upset about everything Gabriele had said to me. He'd been raw and lonely. No wonder he wanted to hang out with me so badly that night.

"I'm really sorry," I said.

FIGHT ME DADDY

"Me too," he mumbled. "About your mother. What uh...what?"

"Heart attack. She was young, but she was born with a heart defect." I smiled a little remembering her. "She used to check my heart with a stethoscope every night when I was little. I think she was always worried she had given it to me."

"She sounds amazing."

I nodded. "She was." I reached into my shirt and tugged out the locket I'd slipped on before we left the house. I popped it open and showed it to him. "That's us. Mom, Dad, and me. We'd spent all day on the lake, fishing. Mom loved to fish and then she'd make my dad clean them for her before she cooked them up. They were a great team. When she died...the gym became all he had."

"That's why he took out the loan."

"Yeah," I said quietly. "It's why I can't hate him. What he did was idiotic, but the house and gym? It's the last pieces of her he had left. She used to love that gym and was always recruiting girls to learn how to fight to protect themselves. I loved her a lot."

Gabriele nodded and I watched emotions cross his face that I couldn't decipher. "My father was murdered," he finally got out, his voice choked. "Still don't know who did it or why. One minute he was there and the next? I was finding him on his office floor with two shots to the back of his head." He laughed dryly. "Something like that fucks you up for the rest of your goddamn life."

I didn't think, I just moved. I walked around the table and wrapped my arms around him. People looked over at us, but I didn't give a fuck. Gabriele was hurting. He reached up and gripped me tightly. A shuddering breath passed his lips before he growled at me.

"Sit down, *Tesoro*. If you make me cry in front of all these people, your holes won't get any rest for a week straight."

I barked out a laugh and stepped back. Gabriele's eyes were wet and I swiped at a single tear that rolled down his cheek.

"So what if they see you cry? I'll kick anyone's ass who says anything about it."

"*You'll* protect *me*?" he asked, an amused look on his face.

"Yeah," I said, firmly. "I'll protect you."

I kissed him hard and Gabriele's eyes went wide. He'd shared things with me I was damn near sure he'd never shared with anyone else. So yes, I would protect him the way he did me.

And I would never let him go.

Chapter Twenty-Six

Calix

I groaned. "Gabriele, stop humping me."

"Don't ask for impossible shit," he mumbled against the back of my neck.

I tried to pull free from his arms, but he dragged me back again. Gabriele feathered kisses over my back and shoulder. I smiled and gave up on trying to stop his antics. We'd been joined at the hip for the past couple of days and surprisingly neither of us had tried to murder the other.

"If you stop humping me, I'll let you fuck me instead," I offered. "But I get to get up and shower first."

"Fuck you? Yes. Shower first? No."

I groaned. "There's something wrong with you. Let me up."

"Nope."

Gabriele grunted as I started to fight him. He was strong, but I still knew how to put his ass into submission. At least when it came to fighting. He growled and I let him pin me to the bed with his hand wrapped around my throat. I grinned up at him and the ticked off expression on his face.

Six was right. It's way more fun to make a Bianchi mad in the bedroom.

"Spread your legs."

I licked my lips. "Go fuck yourself."

Gabriele was on top of me in an instant. He attacked my neck, his teeth biting into my flesh as he rolled his hips. I wrapped my legs around his waist and grinned. *Perfect way to start the morning.*

My back arched and I pressed up against him. I opened my mouth, ready to push a few more of his buttons when a loud beeping filled the air. I paused and sat up slightly.

"Did you get up before me and start cooking?"

Gabriele frowned. "No, I've been asleep with you." He sniffed the air. "Shit, I smell smoke." He hopped out of bed and dragged on a pair of sweats. "Clothes, now."

I moved over to the dresser and slipped into a pair of basketball shorts. By the time they were on, Gabriele was already heading down the stairs. I snatched up my phone and followed behind him before I froze.

"What the fuck?"

Flames filled the living room and were starting to spread. Gabriele glanced around before he frowned. At some point, he'd snatched up his gun and he cocked it. The flames grew as they ate up my curtains and the couch disappeared in a cloud of black smoke.

I stared. The fire was too out of control to snatch up the extinguisher and try to stop it. Both sides of the house were lit and the flames were coming toward us. I watched in horror as the home I'd lived in since the day I was born was consumed by fire. And there was nothing I could do about it.

"Back door. Now."

I heard Gabriele, but I couldn't move. Fear gripped my heart and I couldn't tear my eyes away as memories of my past were destroyed. The couch where my parents watched movies with me, the dining room where we ate huge meals together, and the floor where I played when my father was at work and my mother looked after me. All of it was being decimated and I was helpless to stop it.

"Baby, back door," Gabriele growled as he grabbed my hand and tugged. "You can't stop right now, you hear me? Think about it later! Move!"

Reality clicked back into place and I blinked at the fire before I felt my lungs burning. The heat was so intense the flames weren't even on me but I felt like I was going to burn. I turned on my heels and forced myself to move despite how much I wanted to cling to what little I had left in life.

Pictures, movies, and trinkets of my family were going to be obliterated. And I couldn't even stop to take that fact in.

Gabriele tugged me hard and I moved. We ran through the kitchen together as smoke filled the air. My lungs fought against it and I choked, the back of my throat burning. *Wait. There's smoke in the living room and not the kitchen?* My stomach knotted, but I didn't have time to think about it. I pushed on, covering my nose and mouth. The minute we burst outside, I doubled over as my lungs rejected the smoke.

"Shit, what is going on?" I wheezed out. I straightened up and flinched.

Gabriele was quicker than me. A man stood there with a gun trained on us. But Gabriele didn't even blink. He raised his and squeezed off two shots. Blood gathered on the man's shirt and he fell into the dirt. Loud Russian filled my ears and my stomach dropped.

Shit. Russians.

I didn't think I had to deal with them after our first encounter. But there were multiple men surrounding my house. Gabriele turned and shoved me down to the ground.

"Stay here. The closer to the ground you are the better." He stopped to return fire before he panted. "I should have known better."

"Known better about what?"

He didn't answer me as he stood up and ran for the shed in the back. My heart wouldn't stop pounding. The world around me was muffled like I was underwater. But the one thing I could hear, the one thing I concentrated on, was the crackling behind me. I glanced back and saw the flames that now burned even brighter as they consumed my house. Everything I owned was being taken away and I was lying on the ground. Like a coward.

Gabriele stumbled back into view. He took a punch to the face before he kicked the man in the stomach. As they fought a flicker of movement caught my eye. I glanced to the right and there was another goddamn Russian. He raised a gun and leveled it at Gabriele.

I'm not going to lose him too.

I jumped to my feet and ran for the man who was too focused on Gabriele to even notice me. When he finally did, he tried to swing the gun in my direction, but it was too late. I slammed my shoulder into his body and he grunted as he went down hard. But I didn't stop. I climbed on top of him, my fists so tight they would have hurt if I could feel anything but the raging inferno in my belly.

My fist connected with his face and his head bounced off of the pavement. I took his wrist and slammed it down once, twice, three times until I heard the cracking of bones and he yelled as the gun fell out of his hand. I threw it away from me and punched him in the face again.

The heavy sound of blows became wet. His face was covered in blood and I knew deep down I'd split my knuckles on his teeth. But I didn't stop. He reached out, his hand around my throat as his nails clawed at my face and neck desperately.

"Fuck you!" I screamed.

Every hit filled me with something I'd never felt before. This wasn't the same as standing in the ring and fighting an opponent. And it wasn't like being in the underground fights and knowing that you might die. No, this was something completely different. It was pure rage filled with the need to see him take his last goddamn breath.

Why should I be the one to hold back when he was ready to end my life only moments before? Gabriele's words sank into me and I knew he'd been right all along. There were some people that just couldn't be saved, that needed to be put out of their misery. And this man that had taken everything from me in less than an hour was one of them.

"Calix."

I heard Gabriele's voice, but I didn't stop. The man beneath me was still struggling, still clinging to life. His nose broke under the force of my blows. A tooth slipped out of his mouth, jagged and broken. But I couldn't stop.

"Stop, Calix. Stop!" Gabriele grabbed me and tried to pull me off of him, but I wasn't done.

I turned long enough and shoved him away from me. He stared at me, his eyes wide. I looked down at the mess of a man in front of me. He dragged in a rasping breath and his face was nearly unrecognizable, but it still didn't feel like enough. When was I supposed to stop losing? Hadn't I suffered enough?

His lips moved and the switch flipped once more. I gripped his hair and slammed his head against the pavement. The sound of skull breaking against concrete was wetter than I'd thought it would be. Somewhere, someone let out a primal, guttural scream and I knew deep down that it was me as I bashed his brains over and over again. Finally, he stopped moving, not even a twitch, and the rage I'd felt began to calm.

"Calix."

A hand touched my shoulder and I jerked away. I stumbled over myself and off of the man that had been pinned underneath me. When I gazed up it was into confused, but familiar eyes. I shook and Gabriele pulled me up and into his arms.

"Hold it together," he told me urgently. "You can fall apart later, but not here." He dug his phone out of his pocket and hit a number as the sound of sirens filled the air. "Where are you? Come and- Shit. Are you serious? Fuck me!" he snapped. "Meet us on the next street over."

Gabriele hung up and took my hand. I let him drag me away as I turned back and stared at my house. Or what was left of it. The fire was upstairs, flames licking the sky as ash rained down on the yard.

"We can't stop!" Gabriele snapped. "Come on, Calix. Now!"

I turned around and followed him with the image of my home permanently burned into my brain. The sirens were closer now and pretty soon they would find dead bodies in my backyard. A car pulled up in front of us and Gabriele pushed me inside before he climbed in and slammed the door.

"Go. Ama's house." He turned to me. "Are you okay?"

"I'm fucked," I said as I stared through him. "My career, my goals...All gone. I'll never be able to fight again when they find out I'm a...a..." I stared at the blood on my hands and felt bile rise in my throat. "*Jesucristo.* I'm a murderer."

"No, you're not," Gabriele argued.

I focused on him. "You saw what I just did."

"And I know you had to do it," he countered as he typed away on his phone and pressed it against his ear. "Yeah, get in touch with officers Houston and Calmes. Have them clean the mess up in the backyard. No one else steps foot back there and if they do collect some names and addresses. I'll talk to them. Personally."

Gabriele put the phone down and reached out to me. I yanked away and pushed myself up against the opposite door. Killing people, bribing cops, more murder if people didn't comply; where did it end?

I had become everything that I hated.

"Pull over," I muttered as I wrapped an arm around my stomach. "Now."

"We have to-"

"Pull over!" I yelled.

Gabriele glanced into the rearview mirror and nodded. The car pulled to the side of the road and I threw my door open and stuck my head out as last night's dinner made a swift return. I trembled and finally sat back up in my seat before I closed the door.

"Are you okay?" Gabriele asked.

"No."

I laid my head against the door and closed my eyes. I was worlds away from being okay.

Chapter Twenty-Seven

Gabriele

I paced back and forth. Calix wouldn't even let me get him into the shower when we made it to Amadeo's house. He was stretched out on the bedroom floor and was still there tossing and turning and mumbling in his sleep. There was blood all over him and I wanted to scoop him up and drop him into a damn bath. But for now, I had to let him sleep. What he'd just seen and done? It would stay with him for a long time.

Knock. Knock.

I glared at the doorway until Amadeo stepped through. He gazed at Calix before he nodded behind him. I didn't want to leave Calix, but I didn't want to wake him up either. Slowly, I followed Amadeo out into the hall after giving Calix one last glance. I closed the door slowly before we moved down the hall.

"He's asleep?" Amadeo asked.

"Yeah," I said. "I don't know how he can sleep after that."

"You know how it is. Some people's brains just shut down after something like that," he sighed. "The medicine didn't help."

"I told you not to do it," I hissed.

"He was hysterical," Amadeo pointed out. "A sedative was exactly what he needed before he ended up hurting himself."

I ran a hand down my face. Calix had been a mess by the time we arrived to Amadeo's. Amadeo had insisted on slipping a sedative into the drink he offered him and I had to admit Calix sleeping was better than him freaking out. I didn't want him to hurt himself either.

"There were people outside your place?"

I frowned at Ama. "Yeah. There's always a few men stashed over there to keep an eye on the place and they noticed them." I pushed my fingers through my hair and tugged until pinpricks of pain danced along my scalp. "This is my fuckin' fault."

"How?" Amadeo asked. "You didn't know this would happen."

"No, but someone must have followed me that night. I led them right back to Calix's place. He could have been killed."

"But he wasn't," Amadeo pointed out. "He's alive, you both are. Everything else we can handle."

Ric walked up the stairs and nodded at us. "Had a chat with Conor," he said as he pushed his hands into his pockets.

I balled up a fist and stepped toward him. "Where is that piece of shit?"

"He said he would have come, but he knew you were still too fired up. Conor didn't mean for any of this shit to happen when he recruited Calix. It was just-"

"If you say just business, I swear to god I will rip you to pieces with my bare fucking hands, Riccardo."

He nodded. "They're not having any easier of a time over there. He's got problems of his own. Or at least that's what he said. But in a day or two he wants to meet."

"Good," I said. "Because I plan on beating his ass."

"No," Amadeo said. "We both know that's a horrible idea. The peace we have is tentative at best and it looks like we're about to be in one war. No need to start two."

I scoffed. "If it were Six-"

"I'm well aware of my shortcomings," Ama bit back. "But I'm telling you this isn't going to happen. Conor will try to make up for it to keep us on his good side and you'll accept whatever the fuck he throws your way. He might have recruited Calix, but he didn't put a gun to his head, Gabe."

Amadeo held my gaze as I fought myself not to punch him instead. If Six was the one that had almost died, he would have lost his fucking mind. But I was expected to keep it together. *Double standard bullshit.*

"I'm not trying to fuck you over," Ama said. "I don't want you killed. Or Calix. If you're this messed up over a close call, imagine how you would feel if you made the situation worse and he ended up dead."

The pain that flared in my chest was enough to tell me he was right. I couldn't lose Calix or there would be no reason to keep doing this shit. My family meant the world to me, but I'd be damned if I went back to being lonely. If I returned to that place where the missing piece in me was even bigger than it was without Calix around.

"There's one more thing," Riccardo interrupted us. "Gonzalez and Son's gym was also burned down. We went over to protect it, but it was too late."

"Fuck!" I yelled and my fist connected with the wall. I pulled it back out of the hole I'd made and shook my hand out. "This is going to destroy him."

"So you need to keep him together," Amadeo said. He reached out and laid a hand on my shoulder. "That's your job now."

I looked at Amadeo and sighed. He was right. I had to be a rock for Calix or he was going to shatter to pieces. *This is my fault. I never should have brought him into my world.*

***

"Gabriele?"

I shushed him as I checked the cut on his knuckles. It wasn't as deep as I'd thought and it would heal quickly. But I wanted to make sure it didn't get infected. I laid his hand on my lap and glanced at him. I'd been by his side for hours, still caked in blood and soot. My skin crawled with the need to get clean, but I wouldn't move.

Not without Calix.

He looked up at me with big, sad eyes and I swiped hair off of his forehead. Calix looked half out of it.

"Are you okay?" I asked.

"Where are we?" His eyes darted around the room and he frowned.

"Amadeo's house. I would have taken you to my place, but we can't go there. Not right now." I frowned. "Are you okay?"

Calix gazed back at me and blinked. "I don't know."

Yeah, that was about what I'd expected. I couldn't blame him. Everything he'd worked so hard for was gone in one day and he was left with nothing. I couldn't even tell him about the gym. If he knew it was gone too, I knew he would go off the deep end.

"Can you stand?"

Calix shrugged. "I think so."

"I'm going to run us a bath and we'll get cleaned up. Together."

He nodded but laid his head back on the pillow. Calix stared straight ahead and my chest tightened. I didn't know how to fix people. I only knew how to take them apart.

I slipped away from Calix and padded to the bathroom. The garden tub was big enough for the both of us and I ran the water until it was steaming. When I returned to the bedroom Calix was still lying there and staring off into space.

"Come on," I said gently. "Let me get you into the tub."

Calix didn't move. My mouth went dry as I bent down and turned his face toward me. "You're scaring the shit out of me, *Tesoro*."

"Does my father know?" Calix asked. "That the house burnt down? I was going to ask when he would be coming back and then…" He waved a hand before he gazed up at me. "Does he know?"

I frowned and shook my head. "No."

Calix nodded and went back to staring straight ahead. I reached down, gripped him tightly and dragged him to his feet. He didn't protest, but he didn't help either. I shifted my weight and popped him over my shoulder before I stood up again.

"What are you doing?" Calix asked. "Put me down."

"We're having a bath," I answered. "And then you're going to eat and if you're still tired after that then we'll go to sleep in a bed. Not on the floor." I carried him into the bathroom and checked the water before I deposited him on the closed toilet seat. "You have to stop beating yourself up, Calix. What good is it going to do?"

He blinked at me as if he just noticed I was there. "What good is it going to do? Nothing." He laughed dryly. "I was an idiot. I got involved in shit I shouldn't have and look where it landed me. I'm a fucking killer. Everything I've worked for and sacrificed for is gone. What was the point of all those early nights? Not being around my friends because I was working hard? There's no good in anything."

I grabbed a fistful of Calix's hair and growled. "Stop fucking talking like that! If you want to be pissed at someone, be pissed off at me. I dragged you into this shit. And I'm the one that almost got us both killed."

Calix didn't deny what I'd said. Instead, he gazed away from me and my heart dropped. *He does blame all of this on me.* I released Calix's hair and took a step back. What had I expected? For him to say it wasn't my fault? The truth was that being a Bianchi meant the whole world wanted to watch you burn and I had dragged him into the fire.

I wanted to walk away and go in search of a stiff drink and a couple of smokes. Or better yet, I wanted to find the bastards who had broken the happiness that I'd finally found. *Yeah, that was a better idea. I want to make people crawl in pools of their own blood until they drown in it.*

But I couldn't leave Calix.

I started to take off his sweats and he smacked my hand away. "Leave me alone. I can do it myself."

Rage raced up my spine and I picked him up again. I ignored the yelling of his protests and walked him over to the tub before I dumped him inside. Calix sat up, water dripping off of his face as he spluttered and growled at me.

"What the fuck are you-"

I climbed into the tub fully dressed and cradled his cheeks in my palms. "You can hate me all you want!" I screamed as the dam broke and stupid tears poured down my face. "But I won't abandon you and I sure as fuck won't leave you alone right now." Calix stared up at me. "And I know I should tell you some shit like *if you want to leave me you can* but I can't do that, *Tesoro*. I can't. I'm a selfish asshole, but you're mine and I love you. Even if you hate me, I'll *still* love you."

Calix's eyes watered. "I'm so fucking lost."

I pulled his face against my chest and swallowed thickly as he sobbed. He clung to me as if I could save him, but the truth was that I would probably only drag him down. But I'd meant what I said. I wasn't capable of letting Calix go.

We stayed like that, holding onto each other desperately as his shoulders shook. I didn't move and I barely breathed. I ran my fingers through his hair and let him sob as tears continued to roll down my cheeks silently. He didn't need anymore on his plate from me.

The water cooled off and Calix finally sat back. He looked at me wearily. I reached out and wiped tears from his face leaving behind pink streaks of blood.

"Let's try this bath thing again," I said gently. I turned and pulled the stopper and drained the water. "Can you stand up for me?"

Calix moved this time and I helped him undress. I flipped the water on and plugged up the tub again before I helped him sit back down. I tossed my clothes over the edge and grabbed a bar of soap and a washcloth from the shelf beside the tub.

"Gabriele."

I gazed back at him with my heart in my throat. "Yeah?"

"I-I..." He shook his head. "I'm sorry. This shit isn't your fault. Not all of it. Like you said, everyone makes a choice and I made mine. It's not on you."

I scoffed. "My life is a heap of shit. Things like this will always be my fault but..." I sucked in a deep breath. "I don't want to lose you. So if I have to grovel. If I gotta bleed to make you forgive me for this, I will. I'll do anything for you, *il mio tesoro*."

"I know," Calix said as he reached up and held out his hand. "Can you just hold me for a while?"

"Anything for you," I said as I sank down into the tub with him. I pulled Calix into my arms and held him tightly.

Calix didn't move. He rested his head in the crook of my neck and his fingers drew patterns on my arm and side. But he didn't speak and I didn't try to make him.

All I could do was hold onto him and show him that I would never let him go.

Chapter Twenty-Eight

Gabriele

Calix sat by the window and stared down at the garden below. I'd tried to get him to walk around a little, but he'd spent three days out of it. At least he wasn't drugged anymore. I stood in the doorway and watched as he sighed, his shoulders slumping.

"Are you okay?" I asked and immediately regretted it. I walked over to him and laid a hand on his shoulder. "Nevermind."

"No, it's okay," he said as he gazed up at me. "I was just thinking." Cal picked up the cup of coffee I'd sat in front of him an hour ago and took a sip before he grimaced. "Gross."

"Yeah, it's been a while," I said as I pulled over a chair and sat beside him. "Want me to get you more?"

He shook his head. "I think I'd rather get dressed and go check on the gym today. Sam and Tal have been blowing me up, but I haven't been able to pick up the phone." He sighed. "Still need to call my dad and let him know about the house."

My throat tightened as my heart dropped to my stomach. *Right, he still doesn't know.* I'd given him a few days to breathe, but I couldn't hide it from him anymore. I reached out and grabbed his hand quickly. Cal raised a brow at me and my heart skipped a beat. I didn't want to hurt him any more than he already was.

"You can't go to the gym," I said.

He frowned. "What? Why not?"

"Because it's...it's gone," I spat out before I could stop myself from telling the truth. "I sent some guys to protect it, but by the time they got there..." I waved a hand. "There was nothing they could do."

Cal stared at me in silence. He didn't move for so long that I wasn't sure if he'd heard me. I opened my mouth and started to speak when he held up a hand.

"The gym is gone," he said.

I nodded. "Yes."

"It's gone." He turned to stare out the window. "Fuck."

"I'm sorry. I'm going to figure out who did this and-"

Cal stood up and walked over to the dresser without a word. He rifled through my clothes and pulled out a few pieces before he started tugging them on.

"What are you doing?" I asked.

Cal glanced at me before he went back to getting dressed. "I'm going to go find those sons of bitches and stab them to death. Never done that before, but I feel like it'll be satisfying," he said as he tugged a hoodie over his head.

I groaned. "You don't even know where they are."

"Do you?" he asked.

I did. Well, some of them. I still had to wait to find the big fish, but I had found more Russians and the seedy little joints they liked to hang out in. It was my intention to go pay them a little visit later. But Calix didn't need to know that.

"No," I lied.

He narrowed his eyes. "Are you lying?"

Goddamnit. The man could read me like a book now. He glared when I didn't answer and turned around before he found his cell and shoved it into his pocket.

"You don't know the first thing about killing someone," I said as I tried to sidestep him and cut off his path. "You'll get yourself killed."

"I don't care."

I grabbed his arm and yanked him back. "Calix, this is not the time to go running off. Besides, you don't know where they are and I'm not going to tell you."

He whirled around on me. "That's fine, Gabriele. I'll go have a chat with Conor Kelley's brother and I'm sure he'll have some information for me."

A growl rumbled up my throat. "No, he won't. They both know that if either one of them even speaks a *word* to you, it'll be the last straw that tips off a war. I will slaughter each and every one of them and they're not willing to take that risk."

He stopped and stared at me. "Tell me."

"No," I answered. "I'm not going to let you get killed."

Calix pulled out of my arms and headed for the door. *Damn it.* I didn't want to have to resort to drastic measures, but Calix wasn't going to listen. And I had to stop him before he got himself killed.

"Baby, don't walk out that door," I said slowly. "You won't like what I have to do."

"I'm not scared of you," Calix called. "You can either go with me and kill some assholes or I'll do it myself."

Sighing, I wiped a hand down my face. He clearly wasn't going to listen to reason. I walked over to my nightstand and pulled out a syringe. I bit the cap off, tapped out any bubbles, and went after him. He would be pissed when he woke up, but no one said being a Daddy was easy.

I marched after him. Calix was already halfway down the stairs, but the minute we reached the ground floor I struck. I held him against my body and stuck the needle in his neck.

"What the fu-" Calix swayed. "Gabriele, you asshole."

He slumped and I caught him in my arms. "Sorry, baby but you need to cool off for a little while." I looked up to see Six staring at me.

"Oh you are losing your fucking mind, man," Six groaned. "Really? Drugging your boyfriend?"

I shrugged. "I'm just doing my job?" I said slowly.

Six rolled his eyes. "I'll help you get him upstairs. You're lucky I like you."

I grinned. "We're back to being friends?"

"As long as you hide the fact that I slipped Ama's guards today? Sure."

"Shit. You're trying to get me murdered by two people in this house?" I sighed. It wasn't like I had a choice. "Fine."

We carried Calix back upstairs and tucked him into bed. He mumbled in his sleep, but he didn't wake up. I stroked the hair from his face and tucked it behind his ear.

"We'll talk about this later," I whispered. "I leaned down and brushed a soft kiss against his lips. When I straightened up, Six sat on the other side of the bed grinning at me. "Shut up. I need to go out."

"I'll keep an eye on him," Six said. "Pretty sure the guards are going to spill what I did anyway so I might as well have a safe place to hide out."

I shook my head. "Don't be a bad influence on my boy." I stood up and gathered my things. "Call me if anything happens. Shoot me a text every few hours just because."

Six smiled. "You really do love him, huh?"

I gazed down at Calix's sleeping face. "You have no idea." I let my fingers linger on his cheek before I gazed up at Six. "If anything happens to him-"

He waved a hand. "Yeah, yeah I know how you Bianchi's are. I'll lose a hand or get some bones broken or something else...creative," he said as he rolled his eyes. "Get out of here."

I grinned at Six. "Thanks."

He nodded and I turned around. The smile that had been on my face faded away as I grabbed my guns and headed for the door.

Someone had to pay for hurting my boy. And I had a feeling that his name was Andrei.

***

"Get him!"

The cry that came behind me made me move twice as fast. If they caught me, they were going to be all too happy to duplicate what I'd done to their fallen comrade and I had a thing about men being near my dick with knives. Sometimes double standards were a good thing.

Gunshots rang out and I panted as I slammed my back up against a stone wall. *These assholes really like to hide out in scuzzy areas.* First a crap hole bar and now a dank warehouse. The smell of mold and wetness was so thick I could choke on it, but I didn't have time to take in the surroundings. Gunfire picked up again and I slipped up a set of metal stairs.

There weren't many of them in the warehouse, but a few morons with guns was dangerous. But I was worse. The irritation I'd felt a few days ago had only grown. I was going to have to go back and deal with Calix after this too and he wasn't going to be happy with me.

Better make up for it the best I can.

I ducked down behind a file cabinet and waited. Patience was annoying, but I could have it on certain occasions. And this was one of the rare ones.

The sound of approaching footsteps made me tense. My muscles bunched as I gripped my gun tightly. The closer someone approached, the more the floor vibrated with his steps. I held in a breath.

The door creaked open and I counted, slowly before I jumped up and pointed my gun in a man's face. He jumped back and lifted his gun.

"Don't do it," I warned. "I'm here for information. Nothing more than that. But if you don't put that gun down I'll blow your brains out all over that fuckin' wall."

He looked around wildly. "I don't know anything."

I stared at him and knew he was full of shit. He was young, but he knew something. I stepped forward. "Put the gun on the ground and kick it this way. Do it."

The way his hands shook proved to me everything I needed to know. Young, dumb, naive. He'd just stepped into this world or at least he wasn't a killer like the rest of us. His eyes flickered toward the door and I clicked my tongue.

"Don't make me do it."

He jumped and sat the gun on the ground before he hesitantly kicked it toward me. *Big mistake.* I dragged the gun with my foot and kicked it into the corner behind me. The door creaked again and as soon as he turned to see who it was I was on him. I wrapped my arm around his throat and squeezed before I shoved my gun against his temple.

"Fuck, fuck," he whispered as he shook his head. "You said-"

"I lied," I answered. "If you're too stupid to understand that's all this life is then you're better off with me killing you now."

A man walked through the door and I shot beside his head. He jumped back. "Fuck! I told you not to leave my side," the man shouted at my hostage.

"I was going to get him."

"Shut up," I snapped. "How many more in here?"

"Three," the man spat. "Let him go."

I shoved the gun against his head harder and he hissed. "Oh, so he's important to you?" I grinned. "That's even better. Tell the other three to go outside and search. We'll have a chat."

He opened the door and shouted Russian. A storm of fleeing footsteps made my stomach ease a little. I had no idea if he'd really told them to leave, but as long as they were away from me now, I could deal with them later.

"Close the door."

He shut it behind him and glared at me. "If you shoot him-"

"Shut the fuck up. Tell me everything you know about Andrei."

He tensed. "What?"

"Don't stall," I warned. "I can see it all over your face. Where is he?"

"Nobody knows where he is."

"So you do know who I'm talking about," I said. "What *do* you know?"

"If I tell you..."

"Save me the whole if you tell me he'll kill you line because I can promise I'll do the same thing. Andrei runs things. That much I know. Why is he coming after my family? Why did he burn Calix's shit down?"

The man groaned. "Shit, I knew it was a bad idea."

I cracked the gun against the side of my captive's head and his knees buckled. A growl echoed from across the room and I shoved the muzzle against his head again.

"Why is he after us?"

"I don't know!" he snapped. "I take orders, that's it. All I know is your family did something to tick his off and he's coming for all of you. That guy, the fighter? He got in the way and got one of our men killed. We had to make it even."

"He had *nothing* to do with it."

"Bullshit. Him knowing you was enough to get him put on our hit list, but he stuck his nose where it didn't belong. There are consequences."

I stared at him and ground my teeth so hard my mouth hurt. "Where does he live?"

"I. Don't. Know."

"So that's it? You're all out of information?" I asked.

"Yeah."

I nodded. "You're right. There are consequences."

I stepped back and squeezed the trigger. My captive's brain decorated the man in front of me and flew back into my face. His eyes widened as he stared at me before realization kicked in and he scrambled for his gun.

But it was too late. I shot him in the chest and he stumbled back in shock. I squeezed off another round into his head and watched the light fade from his eyes as he collapsed onto the floor.

I wiped my arm over my face and gazed down at them. Whatever they were to each other, I hadn't been cruel. One wouldn't have to survive without the other. *Not like I did it to be nice. If I had more time and an empty room, I would have shredded them in front of each other until their brains broke.*

When it came to Calix, I had no limits.

Chapter Twenty-Nine

Calix

I stood in the mirror and stared at my reflection. Gabriele hadn't let me more than five feet away from him since we'd moved into Amadeo's. Even now I knew he was outside the bathroom, pacing back and forth and waiting for me to come out. I could see his shadow moving in front of the gap underneath the door.

Sighing, I straightened up and grabbed a brush. We had dinner to go to, something Gabriele insisted on. He wanted us to be "normal" but what was normal at this point? I dragged my fingers through my hair and pulled it up into a bun.

My phone rang and I picked it up. My coach. I'd forgotten all about Mel. The last few days had been a blur of eating whatever was shoved in front of me and going back to bed afterward. I hadn't even had the heart to call my dad and tell him what happened.

"Yeah?" I answered.

"Cal, I'm so sorry," he started. "I haven't heard from you but I figured it's because you're dealing with stuff. After your gym burned down I-"

I bristled. Ice worked its way down my spine and I had to grip the sink for support. "Can we not talk about that?"

"Yeah, yeah sure," he said, sadness in his voice. "I was worried about you that's all."

"What did you need?" I asked.

He paused as if he wasn't sure to tell me before he continued. "You have a match coming up soon and I wanted to know if you were going to participate or not? I know, you've been through some shit thought so-"

"I'll do it," I said as I straightened up and forced my emotions back down. "I need this."

"But if you need time..."

"No," I cut him off. "Time isn't going to help me. And if I miss this match I'll have to pay a damn fee and they'll start looking at me like I'm not serious about this and I am. When is it?"

"Three days from now, Saturday. Eight o'clock."

"I'll be there."

"Will you make weight?"

I frowned. That I wasn't so sure of. "I'll figure it out."

"Alright, call me back soon."

I hung up and let out a breath. No one was going to take away my dream. I'd lost everything else, but I could still do MMA. I could rise through the ranks and become the man I'd wanted to be from the start. Gabriele had cleaned up my mess, my friends still needed my support, and my father would need someone to look out for him too.

"Calix, are you okay in there?"

I shook my head and pulled on the clothes that Gabriele had picked out for me. A pair of dark slacks, a burgundy shirt, and a black jacket. Wherever we were going sounded fancy as hell, but that was Gabriele's style. And it wouldn't just be us, his whole family was coming along as well. I don't know how they fake normalcy the way they do.

Gabriele banged on the door and I jumped. My heart raced and I gripped my shirt for a moment before I walked over and ripped it open.

"I'm not deaf."

"You weren't responding," he growled. "Don't do that shit again."

"Fine," I mumbled as I brushed past him and picked up my locket off the dresser. It was one of the only things that had survived. "Let's go to dinner."

"Who was on the phone?"

I glanced over my shoulder at Gabriele. He looked good when he was all cleaned up. The dark suit was perfectly tailored to his body. His beard was neatly trimmed. And I could smell the cologne that clung to his skin when I walked past him.

"My coach," I said. "Mel. There's a match-up in a few days and he wanted to know if I was going."

He pushed his hands into his pockets. "How did he take the bad news?"

"The bad news?" I asked.

"Yeah, that you won't be fighting."

I scoffed and turned to him. "I am fighting."

Gabriele frowned. "No, you're not."

My nostrils flared. "We're not going to have this discussion. I've already told him I'll be going and I will."

He stepped toward me, his jaw ticking. "Let me try this again. You're not going anywhere, anytime soon."

"Yes, I am," I said as I clenched my fists. "If I miss a match I look like a flake and owe a fee. So, starting tonight I'll be working out, eating everything, and getting my ass in gear to make this weigh-in."

"No, you won't."

I stared at Gabriele. He wasn't backing down, but neither was I. He took a step toward me and I didn't move away.

"In case you've forgotten, there are Russians coming for your head. And mine. And everyone else's."

"Yeah and we're going to fucking dinner tonight."

"With the family and protection," he countered. "No one's stupid enough to make a move on us when we're together. If you haven't noticed, things have been quiet here and that's for a reason. There's safety in numbers."

"Then I guess everyone better join me for my match," I said as I turned back around. "Because I'm going."

"No, you're not," he growled.

"And who's going to stop me?" I snapped as I wheeled back around.

Gabriele moved so quickly that I barely saw him. He gripped the front of my shirt and shoved me backward. But I forced myself against him and growled right back.

"I'm doing it. Do you understand me? This is the last thing I have left!"

Gabriele swept my ankle and dropped me onto the bed. "And I'm sorry about that, I really am, baby, but I'm not willing to put you in any more danger. You're on lockdown."

I scoffed. "Lockdown? Things are bad enough and you think you can lock me up and throw away the key?"

"I'm taking you out tonight, right?" He pressed. "It's not like I'm shoving you into a closet or a basement or something."

"Not that you haven't thought about it."

Gabriele didn't flinch and I blinked up at him in shock. *He had thought about it. Not that it should surprise me. He's fucking batshit insane.*

"You've already drugged me," I growled. "And I forgave that."

"That was for your own good," he said. "If I hadn't you would have gotten yourself hurt or worse."

I growled. "That doesn't justify you drugging me!"

"Here we go with this shit again," he snapped. "You're not going to a damn fight and that's the end of the discussion."

No, the hell it isn't.

I listened to Gabriele when it made sense, but now it didn't. No matter what I did or where I went someone was always going to be after me. That was my life now.

"I'm not going to cower in a corner and not have a life, Gabriele. So if that's what you're asking of me, fuck it and fuck you. I'm going."

I shoved him off of me and grabbed my stuff. Gabriele could have a temper tantrum on his own. I wanted to live what little bit of a life I had left.

"You're gonna have to forgive me all over again."

"What?" I started to turn but I was shoved against the wall. Gabriele wrenched one of my arms behind my back and then the other. I heard the click and felt the cool steel of cuffs. "Shit," I snapped. "Are you kidding me!"

"I tried to warn you," Gabriele said as he turned us around and drove me toward the bed. "And I've been lenient, but you really like to push me." I hit the bed and grunted. Gabriele rolled up his sleeves. "But I've had enough."

"You? You've had enough?" I barked out a laugh.

"Yeah, I've had enough," he snapped. Gabriele ran a finger down my cheek. "So I'm going to-"

I turned and bit his hand. All of the rage I'd stuffed down inside of me came bubbling up. I tasted blood and Gabriele stared at me in shock before I unclamped and let him go.

He picked up his hand and examined it. "You shouldn't have done that."

I licked my lips of his blood and stayed quiet. Yeah, I'd just pissed him off, but that was his fault. He didn't understand that I was a ball of anxious energy and I had to get it out.

"You can't keep me cooped up in here forever or take me out for walks on some glorified leash. A restaurant? What's a restaurant going to do?" I asked. "I need to fight. I need blood and sweat and *something* to displace all of this rage," I snapped. "I need-"

"I know exactly what you need," he said as he gazed down at me.

I startled at the look he was giving me. Gabriele's eyes had gone dark and he looked like he was about to devour me. I shifted away from him subconsciously as he climbed off and disappeared into the closet.

"What are you doing?" I asked.

"This is my room here. Did you know that?" Gabriele asked as he rooted around in the closet. "I stay here a lot when I have to work late. Or if Ama and I get too drunk and I don't feel like going home." He turned around and carried over a box. "And of course, I had a few things shipped here before all the...unpleasantness," he said as he ran a hand over it. "Things I was sure I'd need in case we were ever here and I was feeling unsettled."

I blinked. "You're talking really fucking strange."

Gabriele grinned. "Don't worry, *cane*. I'm just going to put you back in your rightful place." He walked over and touched my cheek before he gripped my face hard. "I've been delicate lately. Trying to let you adjust to everything. But that was wrong of me. What you needed was an outlet and I can see that now."

I licked my lips where the taste of blood still lingered. "What kind of outlet?"

"The kind we both enjoy," he said as he pulled out a familiar sight. "I think we should start here."

I shook my head at the muzzle in his hands. "Fuck you! No!"

Gabriele looked calm as he clicked his tongue and shook his head at me. "I don't have a choice, baby. You decided to bite me, remember?" He held up his hand where blood still rolled down his skin. "Bad mutts need to be properly restrained or I'd be a horrible owner."

My breath caught in my chest. Gabriele loomed over me and I thrashed back and forth. I was *not* about to play his sick little games.

"Bad boy," he said as he showed me something shiny. It took my brain a moment to recognize what it was. A knife. "Hold still or I'll have to cut you. Even though I should do it now. Fair is fair after all, right?"

I shuddered. "I didn't cut you!"

"But you still broke the skin, baby," he growled as he placed the knife on my throat and it danced over my flesh. My cock stiffened as he gazed down at me. "So if I were to make a little nick.." I cried out as a sharp, stinging pain throbbed and he swiped his fingers over my throat. Gabriele licked his digits slowly as he smiled down at me. "Then it would be justified. Don't you think?"

Shit, he's terrifying.

I didn't know how to make my mouth work properly. After spending the past week wallowing in despair and self-loathing, my brain was not equipped to handle the insanity that was Gabriele Bianchi. He chuckled and warmth spread from my head to my toes.

"Excuse me?" He cut into my thoughts. "I asked you a question."

I stared up at him as my chest rose and fell rapidly. "I-I don't remember it." He stared at me and I licked my lips. "I don't remember any more, Daddy."

He laughed and gripped a handful of my hair as he slid the knife over my skin again. "Good. That just proves that this is exactly what I need to do to you. I'll make you forget everything but my cock and the constant, throbbing pain of being well fucked," he growled.

Tingles danced all over my damn body. I wanted to shake my head and deny what he said, but I didn't have a chance of that with a knife to my throat. And while I should have been freaked out by it, my dick was running the show. It seemed anything in Gabriele's hands became a toy and a source of excitement to me.

When did I get so fucked up?

Gabriele's hand gripping my hair and sending tingles over my spine grabbed my attention again. "Roll onto your belly. Now."

"How? My arms are-" The knife pressed against my throat harder and I let out a pathetic whimper.

"That's your problem, isn't it?"

I nodded hard. "Yes, Daddy."

"Do it, *cane.*"

The blade left my neck and I rolled over after struggling for a minute. As soon as I was on my stomach, the sound of ripping fabric reached my ears. Gabriele threw my suit jacket on the floor and the sound of tearing clothes continued. I felt air rush over my hole and I swallowed thickly as I struggled to glance over my shoulder.

"What are you doing?" I asked.

He smirked. "I figured it would be a shame to get you naked when you look so good in a suit," he mused. "So I've made it a lot easier for me to fuck your tight little hole."

I blinked at him. "You're such an asshole. All this because I refuse to give up fighting?"

"You're not going."

I glared not giving a damn about his knife or anything else. "I am. And you're not going to get in my way."

A knock rapped against the door and Six popped his head in. He froze and stared at us before Gabriele growled.

"What?"

"Amadeo, um, wanted me to, um," he stared up at the ceiling. "Oof he was asking about dinner and told me to come get you two, but you are clearly busy doing all of," he made a hand gesture, "all of that so, uh, I'll just go."

"No," I snapped. "Six, get me out of these fucking cuffs!"

Six shook his head. "No way in hell am I getting involved in this. I'm dumb, but I'm not that fucking dumb."

He slammed the door and the sound of his retreating footsteps took any chance of my release with him. I groaned and slammed my face against the bed. *I'm going to murder him.*

Gabriele walked over to the door and threw the lock before he walked back over. He rustled around before cool, wetness raced down my crack. *Lube.* I sucked in a breath before the muzzle was wrapped around my face and fixed into place.

"Gabriele."

"Shhh. I'm going to fuck the common sense back into you. Let me work," he said.

I shivered. I'd never known anyone to take sex as seriously as my boyfriend. My eyes widened. *Yeah, he was my boyfriend.* We were tied together at the hip and I knew there was no escaping Gabriele. And as much as he pissed me off, I didn't want to get away.

Gabriele dragged me down the bed until my feet touched the thickly carpeted floor. He hummed under his breath as he wrapped my collar back around my neck. That was one of the things that survived the fire as well. I hadn't even noticed it at the time, but he always put it around my neck before sex and I didn't take it off until it was time to shower the next day.

Part of me found comfort in it being back around my throat. It made me feel...safe. Gabriele might be rash and impulsive, but he looked out for me. He protected me.

"Ah, there's the leash," he said as he clipped it to my collar and tugged. My neck pulled back and he groaned. "Perfect. My *cagnolino* is all dressed up." He plunged a finger in my ass and I groaned. "We're just getting started and you're already hungry for more? You really did need this, didn't you?"

No, no, no. This was not what I needed!

I wanted to shout those words at him, but they would be a lie. He'd been soft with me since that horrible day. But I needed something more. I needed my Daddy the way that he was. Vicious, hot, cruel, selfish. He made my brain shut off and all the bad disappeared when he used me.

"Daddy," I groaned and it felt like gold on my tongue to say that again.

"I'm right here." He sank another finger inside of me and spread me open. "And I'll be here all night. Hell even if this takes us a good twenty-four hours I'll be fine." He kissed my shoulder blade before he bit it hard and I cried out. "Because we both need this right now."

I closed my eyes and nodded. Gabriele was right. But more than that I realized how little I had thought about him since the fire. He had saved my life and risked his in the process. And he'd murdered for me afterward and cleaned up my mess. Gabriele had held me every night, kissed me every morning, and told me he loved me as often as he possibly could. And I had let him sit with guilt and pain that it had been his fault. I'd only told him once that I had fault in it, but that wasn't fair. He needed to *know* that this shit wasn't all on him.

What if he's hurting as badly as I am?

I liked to think of the Bianchi's as the assholes, but I was no better.

"Fuck!" I cried out as his cock sank inside of me roughly. Tears sprang to my eyes. "Daddy, please."

"Shhh," he whispered. He placed the knife against my throat again. "Don't do anything but fuck yourself on my cock."

My body felt as if it was about to explode. I'd been so wrapped up in myself, but when Gabriele was buried inside of me and pushing and poking at the walls that I threw up, I couldn't resist. Heat raced over my skin as he fucked me like I would be ripped away from him.

I never want you to feel like that, Gabriele.

I moaned as he gripped my hip and thrust inside of me hard. The growl that echoed from his lips sent shivers down my spine. My knees went weak and it took everything in me to stay upright.

"I love you," I shouted. "Gabriele, I love you. I'll never make you feel like you could lose me again." He paused and I panted. "You still piss me the fuck off and sometimes I still goddamn hate you but," I glanced over my shoulder at him, "I love you. I love you so fucking much it hurts."

Gabriele stilled and the tip of the knife poked into the fleshy part of my chin. "Say it again," he demanded.

"I love you," I whispered. "I've never been in love before, but I know I love you."

The dark mask on his face disappeared and he looked at me curiously. "And you mean that?"

I swallowed hard. "Yes, Daddy." I relaxed against the bed and I was finally able to draw in a breath after days of holding it. "You've saved my life more than once. And you would do anything for me. What's not to love?"

Gabriele scoffed. "A lot."

I closed my eyes. "Say that shit again and I won't let you fuck me for a month."

The room fell silent before Gabriele burst out laughing. I opened my eyes and gazed back at him. He laughed so hard I was sure he was going to hyperventilate if he didn't stop. But it was infectious and I joined right in with him.

"I love you too," he said as he wiped his eyes. "Fuck, you're goddamn nuts."

"I learned it from my Daddy."

Gabriele rolled his hips. "I feel better hearing you say that," he said. "But it doesn't mean I won't fuck you like a whore off the street."

I pulled a face. "If you didn't, I would be offended." I shoved back against him. "Fuck me, Daddy. And do it right. But," I said and he paused, "just know that when you're done, we're still going to have our argument. I want to fight, Gabriele. It's all I've ever known. So, if I've gotta attend every event with a crew of guards and you by my side? That's what I'll do."

Gabriele sighed. "You can't just let me fuck you until you pass out and you forget?"

"Sorry, Daddy. I'm difficult. But let's be honest, that's why you love me."

He chuckled. "Yeah, it is, *Tesoro.*" He leaned over me and kissed my cheek before he sighed. "Alright, we'll talk about it afterward."

I gazed up at him. "Thank you. I know you're scared, but really. Thank you."

"You're lucky I would do anything for you." He jolted forward and I moaned. "But it's going to have to wait until I've fucked you a few times."

"I wouldn't have it any other way," I said as I grinned. Gabriele gripped my leash and tugged as he snapped his hips forward and my voice was stolen. I panted as I looked back at him and frowned. "Is that all you've got? Where's the knife?"

Gabriele smirked. "You filthy little slut. I'll show you exactly where it is."

FIGHT ME DADDY

The kiss of cold metal against my heated skin was a godsend. I bounced on his cock as he growled against my flesh.

"Take Daddy's cock. That's right. Fuck," he groaned. "You're tightening up like a little whore, you know that *cane*?"

"Yes," I moaned. "Yes, Daddy. Only for you."

Gabriele's heated words turned into smooth Italian. I couldn't understand a word he said, but every single syllable sounded like sex. My hole throbbed from his rough treatment and I only wanted more. I wanted this man to decimate me in every single way until I was nothing but a quivering, fucked up mess.

Sweat rolled down my skin as he panted on top of me like some wild beast. His hands grabbed, his teeth bit, his nails scratched and I was in ecstasy. I'd thought the last thing on my mind would be sex, but this was so much more than that. It was the connection between us and I craved it so deeply that I couldn't even comprehend how much I'd missed it.

My toes curled and I cried out. "Daddy, stroke my cock," I choked out. "I'm so close. So fucking close."

Gabriele wasted no time shifting me into just the right angle to open my slacks. His hot hand wrapped around my length and he stroked my cock with a slicked hand. Whether he used more lube or saliva, I had no idea. But it was enough beautiful friction to push me to the edge and shove me into the bottomless pit.

Sounds escaped my mouth that I'd never heard before. I came so hard my vision went dark, my knees went weak and I slumped. Gabriele held me up and still fucked me, his grunts and growls filling my ear before he roared through his orgasm.

My legs gave out as hot cum was pumped into my sore hole. Gabriele's strong arms heaved me back into the bed and I laid on my side, staring into space. I had no idea of how long I was there, but I felt something cool between my cheeks. When I gazed back, Gabriele was still panting as he cleaned me up. He disappeared and came back to walk to the door stark naked. For a moment, my stomach pitched.

"Where are you going?" I asked.

"I'm not leaving, *Tesoro.*"

I frowned. "That's not what I'm worried about. You're answering the door like that? Naked?"

He paused and blinked at me. "Are you jealous?"

I squirmed. "Maybe," I muttered.

My daddy chuckled. "It's okay, baby. No one's out there. I sent a text for them to drop off water and something to snack on, that's all." He opened the door slightly and then reached down and grabbed a tray. He set it down before he retrieved bottles of water. "See? We have a lot of privacy here."

I relaxed. "Okay."

"But," he said as he walked over, "I think it's beautiful, the way you wanted to keep me all to yourself just now. Keep that same energy forever, baby."

I groaned. "I am never showing you any side of me ever again."

"Lies, lies." He chuckled as he released me from the cuffs. I stood up shakily and he yanked me to the ground by the collar. "Did I say you could walk, mutt?"

My face flushed and I gazed up at him. "No, Daddy."

"Crawl to the table. I'm sure I can find a way to feed you on the floor," he mused. "Would you prefer a bowl? Or I can give you your meal piece by torn up piece."

I swallowed hard as my heart hammered in my chest. "Whatever you see fit, Daddy."

Gabriele's eyes glowed. "That's my boy." He led me to a chair and sat down in front of me before he bent over and cradled my cheek. "Say it one more time," he whispered. "Tell me you love me, Calix."

I gazed up at him as butterflies danced in my stomach. "I love you, Gabriele like I have never loved anyone else." I leaned into his palm. "We have our issues, but I don't care. I love you and no one else."

Gabriele sucked in a breath. "I love you too."

Our lips met and the sigh that left my lips turned into a moan. I kept my hands planted on the floor, like a good little doggy while we kissed.

Gabriele was my boyfriend. My owner. My Daddy.

I wouldn't have it any other way.

Chapter Thirty

Gabriele

The thundering of applause filled the room and people were up and on their feet as the fighters entered the ring. First, was a guy that was huge, a scar over his eye as he glared ahead. And then there was Calix.

My breath caught in my chest as my boy took his rightful place in the ring. He looked ahead, determination written on his face. Calix tilted his head left and right before he shook out his arms.

You've got this, baby.

Calix glanced over at me and I saw the corner of his mouth quirk up before the smile was gone as quickly as it had come. He turned back to his opponent and I was forgotten about entirely as he put all of his attention on the match.

"Can't believe you let him out of the house," Six said as he grinned and leaned back in his seat. "I was sure you would lock him up before tonight."

"I thought about it."

Six cackled. "Yeah, we could all see that. The way you were pacing back and forth every damn day was enough to drive all of us insane."

I groaned as he laughed at my expense. Yeah, I'd been an overbearing bastard the past few days, but I couldn't help it. When it came to Calix, I wanted to lock him away and keep him close, never letting anything hurt him. But I knew I couldn't keep him pinned down forever.

Fighting was everything to him. And I couldn't take away from my boy.

"Yeah," Amadeo said drawing my attention to him. "So you see what I was saying before?"

I glared at him. *Goddamn, that asshole.* The whole reason I'd gotten thrown into looking after Calix was because Amadeo wouldn't take the gym away from him. And now I knew I was as much of a sucker as my big brother was.

I flipped Amadeo off. "That love shit? It's fucking contagious."

He grinned. "I don't hear you complaining when Caslix is next to you."

"Yeah, but he ain't next to me right now," I answered.

"Don't pout," Amadeo cooed. "You'll have him back as soon as the match is over. Speaking of-"

He nodded toward the ring and I completely forgot about him. Calix shifted around. The man he was up against was bigger, but Calix was faster. He dodged a punch before his leg came up and he aimed for his opponent's stomach. At the last minute, however, the man grabbed his ankle and Calix went down hard.

I shot out of my seat. "Come the fuck on!" I shouted. "You seein' this shit?"

"He's got it!" Six called. "Come on, Cal!"

My heart squeezed in my chest and my fists tightened. As much as I supported him, I wanted to run into the ring and grab the other guy. How many times would I have to smash his face against the ground before he stopped moving?

"No," Amadeo said with a sigh. "Do not kill him."

A jab was thrown into Calix's face and blood spilled from his lip. Heat raced up my back and I moved forward before Ric grabbed me on the other side and shook his head.

"I wasn't going to-"

"You were," he said with a shrug. "I don't blame you, but this isn't the time or place. He'll be mad at you."

I bristled. I could already see Calix cursing me out for ruining his match. Knowing him, he'd ignore me until he wasn't pissed off anymore and I couldn't handle that. Nothing made him talk once he was mad. It was the worst kind of punishment.

He's turned me into a little bitch.

A growl slipped past my lips. When I got him home, cleaned up, and made sure he was okay, I would fuck him into the mattress for making me feel like this. Calix Gonzalez got to me in the worst kind of ways. He was so deeply embedded that I couldn't get him out of my head and I didn't want to.

Seth, Cal's opponent, landed an uppercut and Cal went down once more. My heart all but stopped. Watching my boy fight someone when I couldn't do anything? The hardest thing I ever had to do.

Every instinct screamed to go save him, but I stood back and waited.

Calix wasn't an idiot. He was good at what he did and after his stint of underground fights I knew he could hold his own. But that didn't mean I couldn't worry.

My boy raised a leg and it connected with his opponent's face. He dropped to the ground and Calix was on him in an instant. He wrapped his legs around the man and held him in a headlock. His rival tried hard to get free, but Calix didn't let up.

Seth tapped out and it was all over.

I yelled so hard my throat felt raw. Calix had won. His dream would continue and I knew he'd be happy as hell about that.

"I'm leaving," I called to my brothers.

"Be safe," Amadeo called. "We're still on high alert."

"I know!" I called back before I reigned in my excitement and cleared my throat. "I know," I said again, my voice calmer than before.

Once I turned around, I nodded my head and men moved from the sides of the rooms to follow me. The other guards stayed back, waiting for us to leave. On the way back to the locker room, I passed more of our men and even inside of the room itself, men were posted up watching and waiting. It was the only way that I felt comfortable allowing Calix out of my sight.

Calix stood talking to his coach and someone that looked like they were from the mania. I brushed past all of them and pulled Calix into my arms. My lips found his before he could protest and he kissed me as eagerly as I kissed him. Calix's tongue danced inside my mouth and he smiled when we finally pulled back.

"Hey," Calix panted. "Couldn't wait, huh?"

"Shut up," I muttered.

"What?" he teased. "Did you miss me?"

"I'll kick your ass."

Someone cleared their throat and I looked around. Mel raised a brow at us and I held up a finger. "He'll be back with you in a moment." I turned back to Calix and ignored everyone else. "You did a good job, *Tesoro*. I'm proud of you."

Calix beamed. "Yeah? Promise?"

"I promise," I answered. "Now get your ass showered and back to me in five minutes or I'm going to lose my patience."

"Think you can wait for ten?" Calix asked.

"No."

He shook his head, a smile on his lips. "Five minutes then. I'll be right back."

I watched him walk off. His coach glanced back at me and trailed him before the media guy did the same. But while they were trying to talk, Calix was getting his shit together to go.

Fuck. I really love that man.

***

"You didn't have to wear a tie," I told Calix as he fiddled with it in the car.

"This goddamn thing," he grumbled. "It's so stupid." His phone rang and he picked it up. "Hi! Yeah, I'm okay Mrs. Lopez. We're going to dinner. No, I haven't, um, left him."

I rolled my eyes. She called him every damn day and always asked if he had come to his senses about me. Thank God he hadn't. I couldn't even be pissed at the old woman the way I wanted to because she was right to caution him against someone like me.

But I still wanted to kill her. *She just has to put doubt in his head. What if he actually listens and pulls away from me?* My hands tightened on the wheel and I only gazed at Cal every once in a while as he fought his tie.

I pulled through the gates of my mother's house and climbed out before I rounded the car. Calix climbed out, his eyebrows knitted together. With a sigh, I knocked his hands away and started fixing it for him as his gaze bore into me.

"Everything's going to be fine," I said as I gazed back at him. "You've already met my insane brothers and cousins. The rest of my family isn't so bad."

"Says you," Calix muttered.

I smiled and pushed my fingers through his hair, gathering up the flyaways before I redid his bun. Once it was in place I kissed him and let my lips linger. Calix held onto me and I wanted to avoid the dinner altogether, go back, and fuck him until he begged me for more.

"Gabe, are you coming in?"

I sighed as a familiar voice called my name. My mother stood in the doorway, a smile on her face. No matter what was going on in the world, she was the beacon of light that made it all okay.

"Yes," I called as I smiled up at her. "Hey, Ma."

She waved a hand. "Come in, come in! Dinner's almost ready," she said as she wiped her hands on her apron. "You must be Calix."

Calix swallowed thickly. "Yes, ma'am."

She laughed and waved a hand. "Isabella is fine," she assured him before she looked at me, amused. "You found yourself a polite boyfriend I see."

I rolled my eyes. "Sometimes. Other times he's a pain in the a-"

Calix elbowed me hard. I grunted and rubbed the sore spot above my ribs as he continued to stare at my mother and smile without missing a beat.

"Well, come on in. You two can have a drink while you wait."

"Thanks, Mom." I waited until she was out of earshot before I bent over and whispered into Calix's ear. "You're going to pay for that."

"Yeah?" he shot back. "I'm not worried about you, asshole."

My cock throbbed and I swallowed the groan that threatened to come out. Calix gazed up at me and winked before he held out his hand. I took it and gave it a tight squeeze before I lifted it and kissed his skin.

"See, it's not that bad," I said as we walked down the entry hallway and into the dining room.

"There you go!" Six called. "Come on and help me bring all this food in. Thank fuck I have someone to help do this now."

Calix blinked up at me. "Why do I have to help?"

"You don't." I laughed. "But if you want to then you can. Besides, I'm pretty sure the drinks are in the kitchen."

"I'll be in there," Calix said as he walked away.

Six slipped his arm through Calix's and they disappeared into the kitchen together. I sighed, relieved that I had a moment to talk to the others. Six would keep Cal company. They might get into something, but I could sort that out later.

"Ay yo!" Nic called. "There's the simp of the fucking hour!" He grinned up at me and winked. "How does it feel to be whipped?"

I grabbed a handful of his hair as he bounded up to me and slammed him against the table. Nic grunted and squirmed in my grasp, but I ignored him.

"We all good?" I asked Amadeo as he sat at the head of the table with a cigarette dangling from his lips. "Did you find anything out about Andrei?"

Amado shook his head. "Not yet, but I'm working on it. Matter of fact I should have something soon."

I nodded. "Thanks. I appreciate it. As soon as you have the info-"

"Don't worry," Amadeo said. "I wouldn't move on this without you. Not after everything, that's happened."

"Yeah, thanks," I muttered again.

My chest tightened and I tried to rub the feeling away with my palm. Amadeo might have been acting like an ass before, but he gave a damn about not only me but Calix too.

And yet as much as I appreciated that, I didn't tell him that I already had every ear to the ground. If I found Andrei before he did, we would have a long, undisturbed conversation. Afterward, I would let Amadeo claim his prey. But not before I got in a hell of a lot of good and bloody hits.

No one fucked with my boy. I would devour them all if it meant he was happy and free.

Chapter Thirty One

Calix

I paced the airport back and forth nervously. Gabriele reached out and took my hand in his. After a tight squeeze, he offered me a smile that warmed my entire body.

"It's going to be okay," he said.

"Yeah." I couldn't pace anymore so I settled for rocking up on my toes and back down again.

"*Tesoro*," Gabriele said. "If you keep fidgeting I'm going to take you into the bathroom and fuck the nerves out of you."

I blinked at him. "Why would that be the first place you went? What is with you and sex to solve every problem?"

He stared back at me. "It works though."

I groaned trying to hide my laughter. The worst part was that he wasn't wrong. Whenever things were overwhelming I was starting to run to him for his cock to settle my mind. There was something about being able to completely mentally check out with him that made life a hell of a lot better than it had ever been before.

Gabriele shook my hand and nodded. "There he is."

I released Gabriele's hand and sucked in a deep breath. My father. I hadn't seen him in what felt like years. The closer he came, the more my throat tightened. I didn't know what to say to him.

"Son." As he got closer, I noticed how much weight he'd lost. Where he was usually clean-shaven, there was a scraggly beard and bags under his eyes. "I'm so glad you're safe."

He reached out and pulled me into a hug, his suitcase forgotten on the floor beside him. I let him hold onto me, my chest aching before I finally gave in. I hugged him back and all of the anger and disappointment that I had kept inside evaporated.

"I'm glad you're alive," I said. I stepped back and frowned. "You're an asshole."

"I know," he said with a nod. "Trust me, I know. But I didn't know what else to do. And once I ran I just-" He waved a hand. "I got in over my head. I'm so sorry, Calix. What I did was unforgivable."

My stomach tightened. "Yeah I know you are just…give me some time," I said. "I don't hate you. Not anymore. I experienced a lot of shit while you were gone and I can see some of what you did had reasons behind it. But leaving me like that…"

"I know," he sighed.

A hand rested on my shoulder and I glanced at Gabriele. "Are you okay?" he asked.

"Yeah, I'm good." I smiled at him. "Thank you." I glanced between the two of them. I didn't have to have an introduction stage because they were already well acquainted. "Mr. Gonzalez," Gabriele said.

"Hello, Mr. Bianchi." He looked between us. "Um, you're here with Calix, huh?"

Gabriele raised a brow at me. "You didn't tell him about us?"

"No, no, I did," I said quickly. I could see the danger in his eyes. "On the phone."

"He did tell me. I guess I'm just surprised to see you here, that's all." He cleared his throat. "So our business together is over, right?"

Gabriele nodded. "Yes, it is. But I want to let you know that if you do anything so goddamn stupid again and you put Calix in danger, you'll have to deal with me. And I believe we've gone over the ways in which I would have fun tearing you apart in the past."

My father shuddered. "Don't worry. I have no plans to screw up again." He pushed his fingers through his graying hair. "Trust me, no one can beat me up as much as I've beat myself up these past few weeks."

Gabriele grunted. "You say that, but-"

I groaned as my cheeks heated. "What have I told you about threatening people?" I asked as I glared at him. "And in public? Really?"

Gabriele shrugged. "Old habits. And I'm not sorry."

I rolled my eyes and turned back to my father. "Let me get your bag. Where are you staying?"

"There's a hotel not far from the house. I want to get some things together before I go back to New York." He waved me off. "I've got my bag, son."

As he started to walk, I followed him. "You're leaving again?"

He gazed over at me. "Well, yeah. There's nothing for me here. Not anymore. Once I found out about the fires, I just decided it was better to move on. I've let this place keep me prisoner for years. There's no reason to keep it going." He paused. "It's kept you a prisoner too. Maybe destruction was a good thing."

I nodded and walked in silence beside my father. There was still tension, but I wasn't naive enough to think that things would go back to normal overnight. And maybe he was right. We'd both damn near sold our souls to keep the gym in one piece and look how that had turned out.

"Over here, Dad," I nodded to the black car waiting by the sidewalk. "We can sit in the back." I opened his door and he smiled.

"Thank you."

Gabriele grunted. "So I have to sit in the front by myself?"

"Yes," I said through gritted teeth. "Don't start acting crazy or I'll cut you off."

He raised a brow. "Is that what you think is going to happen?"

"It's what I *know* will happen."

"We're talking about this when we get home," he said as he walked over to the open passenger-side door where the driver waited patiently. "A lot."

"I look forward to it."

The glare he gave me made me want to chuckle, but I didn't want to die when we got home. I slipped into the backseat and closed the door. My father was staring at me and I shrugged.

"Don't ask."

"I don't have to." He chuckled. "I have to say when I found out about the two of you I wasn't all that surprised."

I stared at him in disbelief. "What? How? Because I was shocked and I've been here to live through it."

He laughed. "Back when he and Niccolo used to come to the gym, he always stared at you. He would pretend he wasn't, but I could see him out of the corner of my eye."

I looked up at the rearview mirror. "Excuse me?"

"Yeah. He used to just stare for the longest time. Whenever you looked at him, which was rare, he'd go back to doing his job. But other than that?" He shrugged. "I always figured he had a thing for you and it used to scare the hell out of me. But I can see you're okay."

"I'm great," I said, my gaze not leaving Gabriele's now narrowed eyes. "Especially now."

"Gonzalez," he growled. "Unless you want to walk the rest of the way to your hotel, I suggest you keep your mouth shut."

"No, no, no," I said as I leaned forward. "You were staring at me so much that my father noticed? Do you know how out of it he usually is at work, but he noticed *that*?" I whistled. "You were obsessed with me even back then."

"I will kill you, Calix."

"You won't," I said fully confident that he would throw himself into a burning building head first if he ever lost me. "But it's cute that you were practically a puppy for me."

Gabriele nodded and I watched a nerve tick in his jaw. He didn't say anything more to me. *Oh, he's fuming. Can't wait to deal with that later.* I chuckled as I turned back to my father.

"Thanks for telling me that. I needed to hear it."

He grinned. "Don't make fun of him too much. That's how I was with your mother. She thought I was a weirdo."

I tried to imagine my mom being weirded out by my dad and I couldn't. They'd been so in love I thought it had always been that way.

"I never knew that."

My dad nodded. "That's my fault. I haven't been able to talk about her for so long and that's not fair to you. We should do that more often, talk about her. And everything we miss."

"I'd like that." My heart squeezed.

It felt like I was getting my father back. Finally. I'd missed him more than I admitted to myself. Even after all the shit, we went through I just wanted things to go back to normal. I saw the remorse in his eyes and maybe I was a little soft but if it wasn't for him...

I never would have fallen for Gabriele.

At the end of the day, I could forgive everything because of that fact. I would have turned my nose up at Gabriele forever and I would still be lonely.

"Calix?"

I shook my head. "I'm still here," I said as my gaze flickered up to the rearview mirror again where Gabriele held my gaze. "I was just thinking about something."

The smile Gabriele gave me made butterflies zip around my damn stomach. one look from him and I was a mess. It was ridiculous how twisted he got me.

"I need to grab something to eat. Mrs. Lopez said she made some food for me. Do you mind if we stop by there first? I'm craving her food," Dad said.

I laughed. "Actually that sounds great. Let's go give her a visit. She'll have gossip and questions about how Amadeo is doing."

Gabriele groaned. "She loves him."

"She really does." I sighed as I gazed at my father. "You're really not coming back to Georgia?"

"Nah," he said and I saw the exhaustion on his face. "I mean it when I say it's time to move on. Of course, I'll come back often, watch your fights, and spend the holidays with you. But I think I need this." He frowned. "Unless you want me to come back and then I'll get right on it. I owe you my life at this point."

I shook my head and a shudder worked its way down my spine. "No, you don't. And don't say that shit again," I sighed. "And it's fine. It's about time you started living your own life. I'm an adult now and I can look after myself."

"And I'll be looking after you all the time," Gabriele added.

I jerked a thumb toward the front seat. "That one wouldn't let anything happen to me."

My father smiled and relaxed against the seat. "Good. I feel like I can go get a job and start working on myself."

I smiled at my father. Just like I'd told Gabriele, he wasn't a perfect man. But then again, who was? At the end of the day, we were alive and after tangling with the Bianchi's that was a miracle.

Epilogue

Gabriele

I glanced over at Calix as he walked out of the bathroom. Damp hair clung to his back and I resisted the urge to walk over and sweep it off of his skin. He sat his phone on the dresser before he glanced up and met my gaze.

"Seriously, I'm alright," he said.

"I didn't say anything."

Calix chuckled. "You didn't have to. All night you've been staring at me like I'm going to fall apart, but really. I'm okay." He walked over and pushed my legs apart. Calix stood between them as his fingers pushed into my hair. "Thank you for being concerned. I know it was hard for you to keep your temper in check today. Thank you for that too, Daddy."

My body responded immediately. I grabbed him and yanked him forward trying to press him as close to me as possible. He chuckled and leaned down. Calix's lips brushed against mine and my grip on his back tightened.

I'd been worried all night that he wouldn't be okay. Or that he would say he forgave his father but it would send him into a tailspin. But from what I could tell, he wasn't bothered. That still made me crazy though. I thought his father at least needed to be punched a few times but he begged me not to do that and I was trying to get better at giving him what he wanted.

"So you were stalking me all along?" Calix asked as he pulled back and grinned down at me.

I groaned and tried to pull out of his grasp. "Don't start that shit again."

"It's the truth though." He laughed as I pushed him away, but he came right back. "You were stalking me, Gabriele."

"So what?" I growled.

"That's so sweet," he cooed as he leaned down and kissed me hard. His mouth lingered and I groaned as his tongue swiped over my lips until they parted. He pushed me back hard and climbed on top of me. "You wanted me all that time. And yet you acted like a fucking jackass in the beginning."

I rolled my eyes. "You annoyed the fuck out of me, that's why." I grabbed the collar around his neck and yanked him forward. "Knock it off."

"Or what?" he mused. "You'll love me harder?"

"That's it." I flipped us over and he let me, a laugh bubbling out of his lips as he hit the bed. "You're in trouble, boy."

He batted his lashes. "Little old me? Soy un ángel, Papi."

"Lies," I hissed at him. I kissed him so hard it hurt. "Move to the floor and get on your hands and knees. It's time to put my sexy little cane in his place."

Calix groaned. "When you say things like that, it drives me crazy."

I smirked. "You used to hate it."

"I've given up on trying to majorly train you. Stopping you from threatening old folks and killing people who look at me wrong? On my list of things to work on you with. You calling me a mutt and making me feel like a whore?" He raised and dropped a shoulder. "What can I say? I accept it. And love it."

I beamed at him and felt every bit of the love-drunk moron that I was. Calix had turned me into a softie, something I was sure would never happen. And yet he did it with ease. Just by being himself.

"Then move your ass and get on the floor, mutt."

"Yes, Daddy." He smiled and moved as soon as I was out of his way. He shifted down to the floor and positioned himself as he gazed at me. "What are you going to do to me?"

I shuddered at the image of him presenting himself for me. Every muscle in his arms bunched and his round ass begged to be turned a beautiful, deep red. I traced my fingers over his backside and my cock jumped in my boxers.

"Amazing things," I said as I pushed my fingers through his quickly drying hair and gave his locks a sharp tug. A gasp tumbled from his lips and I glared down at him. "But dogs don't talk. Do they?"

Calix closed his mouth and shook his head. I grinned. "There's a good boy. Stay just like that."

I stood in front of Calix and slipped the dark underwear down my thighs. He watched every moment, transfixed. "Watch me like that forever. Don't ever stop, baby." It was as if he couldn't get enough of me and the feeling went straight to my head.

Regretfully, I walked away from him and into the closet. I carried out the familiar black box that held all of our toys. Once I set it on the bed I went over to the door and made sure that the lock was thrown. Six had a habit of bursting in at the wrong damn time and I would strangle him if it happened again.

I went over to the box without sparing Calix a glance. We were in the best headspace, the one where he wanted to be my slutty little mutt and I loved him for it. Afterward, I would treat him the way a Daddy should. Hug him, hold him, kiss him. And we'd fall asleep together just like that, all tangled up in each other.

As I gathered up my supplies I smiled. "Do you know why I like calling you my mutt?" I asked Calix. "You can bark."

A tentative noise greeted me. "W-woof!"

My cock begged for me to slip it inside of Calix as he gave in. I turned to him and his cheeks were dusted a hot shade of pink. So fucking cute. I could eat him up right now, but he wasn't ready.

"I know you think it's because I think you're beneath me. That you think it's because of my enjoyment of turning you into my dog." I crouched down and situated the muzzle before I secured the leather straps behind his head. "But that's not it."

He gave me a confused look, but I turned and picked up the chocolate brown dog ears. They were expensive, but they looked so much better than the cheap crap I'd found online. A woman, who was apparently into something called cosplay, had made them especially for Calix and I'd tripled her payment in response. They were perfect. So was the fluffy, dark tail plug that went with it.

"So, do you know why?" I asked again knowing he couldn't give me an answer.

"Woof!" He shook his head and his ass wiggled right along with the motion.

I chuckled. "You really are a cute dog," I mused as I grabbed the bottle of lube and lathered the plug with it. I walked back and rubbed it against his hole. Calix jumped before he came back and held still. "Good boy."

I pushed the plug into his ass slowly and watched the way his hole opened up, stretched around the silicone, and then swallowed it. My fingers pressed against it, pushing it in deeper and he let out a moan.

"Wiggle your hips," I demanded.

Calix shook them for me and his tail wagged like a dog happy to see its master return home after a long day of work. I leaned down and bit his right ass cheek. He let out a whimper and I soothed the bite with my tongue.

"I couldn't help myself," I said as I breathed against his flesh and growled. "Every time I'm this close to you and you do something adorable, it makes me lose my fucking mind." I palmed his left ass cheek and slapped it. When he whined, I did it again. And again. "Hold still, baby. I'm not done."

The way his skin shivered under my palm made me feel high. Slowly, his skin went from creamy brown, to blush pink, and then into a beautiful shade of red. I switched to the other cheek and gave it the same treatment. Every hit became harder, faster, stronger until he was moaning and humming and rocking his hips back against me.

I panted as I pulled back and rubbed his sore skin. "I like calling you my mutt because they're playful, show attitudes but don't mean it." I kissed one heated cheek after the other as he moaned. "And because they're loyal to the ones they love. That's you, Calix. It's everything that you are and that I fucking love. You make my heart feel like it's going to explode and I hate and love it all at once." I laughed as my voice caught in my throat. "You've changed me in ways that you will never see or understand. But know that you have, baby."

Calix glanced back at me and I saw the wetness that decorated his lower lids. It felt stupid, but I was just as bad as he was. Calix made me fucking feel. Not the surface, bullshit good mood that I usually displayed, but something deeper and more meaningful than I had ever felt with a stranger. My family had always been my reason for everything, but now here he was making me insane and stealing my heart.

I stood up and grabbed the cage of his muzzle, yanking him toward me sharply. "On the bed," I growled. "Present your ass to me."

Calix barked and moved quickly up to the bed. He pressed his chest to the bed and offered up his ass to me. I groaned. My fingers moved down my chest and to my aching cock as I took up my place behind him. I made short work of lubing myself up before I pulled the plug out and he moaned in response.

"Good boy," I said as he reached back with a hand and pulled his hole open wider for me. "Fuck. That is going to be burned into my memory forever," I said as I watched Calix spread himself for me.

I couldn't hold back anymore if I wanted to. Shifting forward, I pressed my cock against his ass and he sucked in a breath. I let him have a moment before I thrust in and his head shot up. He didn't let go of his cheek, however, determined to be a good boy for me.

"You're perfect," I groaned as I leaned down and nipped at his upper back. "Fucking perfection."

Calix rolled his hips. "Woof!"

I chuckled. "You can talk now. I can't resist the things that come out of your mouth when I'm fucking you."

"Daddy," he moaned. "Don't hold back, okay? After today I need it."

I paused and squeezed his hips. "You said you were okay."

He glanced over his shoulder. "I am, but... I just need this right now, okay?" His voice was quieter now and I saw the desperation in his eyes. "I'm not in a bad place, but I need to feel your love. Please, Daddy."

My chest tightened and I nodded. "Fine. But after this, you will talk to me until I'm satisfied. Do you understand me?"

"Yes, Daddy," he breathed. "Whatever you want."

I nodded and snapped my hips forward. My cock slammed inside of him and Calix made a sound that was a mix between a moan and a scream. I gripped a handful of his hair and rocked into him hard.

Seriously, what have I become? I used to hope no one would want to talk to me after sex and now?

Well, not it was all I wanted to do. Calix had been hiding his true feelings after his meeting with his father and I wouldn't rest until I had talked him through everything. Until I was sure that my boy was happy.

My cock slid inside of Calix and he let out a long, low moan that made every nerve in my body light up. I drove forward and he pushed back, his hands gripping the blanket tightly. He panted and wound his hips, pressing back against me as his eyes rolled back.

"Fuck. I hope you never showed that expression to anyone else," I growled.

Calix shook his head. "Never, Daddy," he panted. "Only you get this part of me."

I searched his face and determined that I believed him. Sure, I was still going to figure out who his exes were and get the truth out of every last damn person that had touched him. But for now, I believed him.

"Daddy, let me ride you," he moaned. "Please!"

I didn't hesitate. Right away I pulled out and picked up the leash from its box. I attached it to Calix's collar and he moved quickly. As soon as I was on my back, he hovered over me, his hand around my cock as he lowered himself down.

"Fuck!" he cried out. "I could do this forever."

I tugged his leash and he shot forward, his hands resting on my chest as he took in more of my length than he'd bargained for. His eyes stayed huge, his mouth parted. I chuckled and tweaked one of his nipples.

"Let's see how long forever is to you." I grinned. "We've got all night."

Calix shivered. "Shit. I talked too much, didn't I?"

"Oh yes."

I thrust upward and Calix cried out before he collapsed onto my chest. I wrapped my arm around my boy and held him close as I fucked into him wildly. Maybe after I got off, he could ride me on his own, have a little bit of control. But I wasn't ready to give that up to him. Not yet.

I wanted to possess Calix and for that? I needed to be in control.

He bucked as he sat up and began to match me thrust for thrust. Long curtains of his dark hair obscured his vision as it covered one eye and I admired how animalistic he looked. I gripped his ass cheeks and slammed him down on my dick as he opened his mouth and screamed.

"Gabriele! Fuck!"

I unraveled. Hot cum pumped inside of Calix and he fisted his length. It only took a few pumps before his seed decorated my stomach and chest. He slouched and I held him up as he worked through the after-effects of his orgasm. Finally, he planted his hands on my chest and gazed down at me.

"I love you," he moaned. "So much, Gabriele."

My lips turned up into a smile. I admired the dog ears and the big, bushy tail that swayed behind him every time I moved. And his eyes. They were huge and warm. He looked like an adorable puppy and my heart squeezed.

"I love you more, Tesoro. You have no idea how special you are to me." I grabbed him and tackled him down to the bed before I left a trail of kisses all over his cheeks and forehead. "But I'm going to show you. Every single day."

My fingers worked quickly to get rid of the muzzle. As soon as it was gone, our lips crashed together. I rolled us over until I was on top of Calix and our kisses deepened.

I still had shit to figure out and problems to solve. But for a little while when I had Calix in my arms I didn't give a damn about the Russians, fires, or bullshit. I could be a normal man in love.

But I would find the bastards who had hurt my boy. And there would be hell to pay. No one who crossed Calix deserved to live.

I'll make sure they pay, Tesoro. Every last one of them.

Thank you for reading Fight Me Daddy. Gabriele and Calix were pure chaos and I was here for it all. One moment they were up and the next moment they were at each others throats like cats and dogs. I had a lot of fun writing out their dynamics and seeing what kind of daddy boy relationship they'd have. Gabriele was for sure into darker things then his brother Ama but it only made him that much better in my opinion. I do hope you enjoyed their story as much as I loved writing it.

I hope you're looking forward to the next book which will be Watch me Daddy. I bet you're wondering who from the Bianchi family is next? Well I'm keeping it a secret for now so make sure to keep your eyes peeled on my Facebook group (Snow's Angels) or newsletter. It's going to be Life changing, wild, and steamy.

If you wouldn't mind leaving a review informing other readers your thoughts on Fight Me Daddy, it would be greatly appreciated.

Skyler Snow

MAFIA DADDIES SERIES
(Contemporary Daddy Romance)
Break Me Daddy
Fight Me Daddy
Watch Me Daddy
Obey Me Daddy

About the Author

Skyler Snow is the author of kinky, steamy MM books. Whether contemporary or paranormal you'll always find angst, kink and a love that conquers all.

Skyler started off writing from a young age. When faced with the choice chef or author, author won hands down. They're big into musicals, true crime shows, reality TV madness and good books whether light and fluffy or dark and twisted. When they're not writing you can find them playing roleplaying games and hanging out with their kids.

— Skyler Snow